A Dark Victory

A Dark Victory

The Tenabran Trilogy Book Three

Dave Luckett

Omnibus Books

Omnibus Books
A.C.N. 000 614 577
52 Fullarton Road, Norwood, South Australia 5067
part of the SCHOLASTIC GROUP
Sydney · Auckland · New York · Toronto · London
www.scholastic.com.au

First published 1999

Typeset by Clinton Ellicott, Adelaide
Made and printed in Australia by McPherson's Printing Group, Maryborough, Victoria

National Library of Australia Cataloguing-in-Publication entry
Luckett, Dave, 1951– .
A dark victory.
ISBN 1 86291 406 0.
1. Title. (Series: Luckett, Dave, 1951– . Tenabran trilogy: bk 3).

A823.3

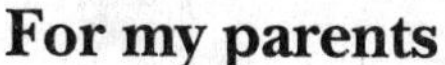
For my parents

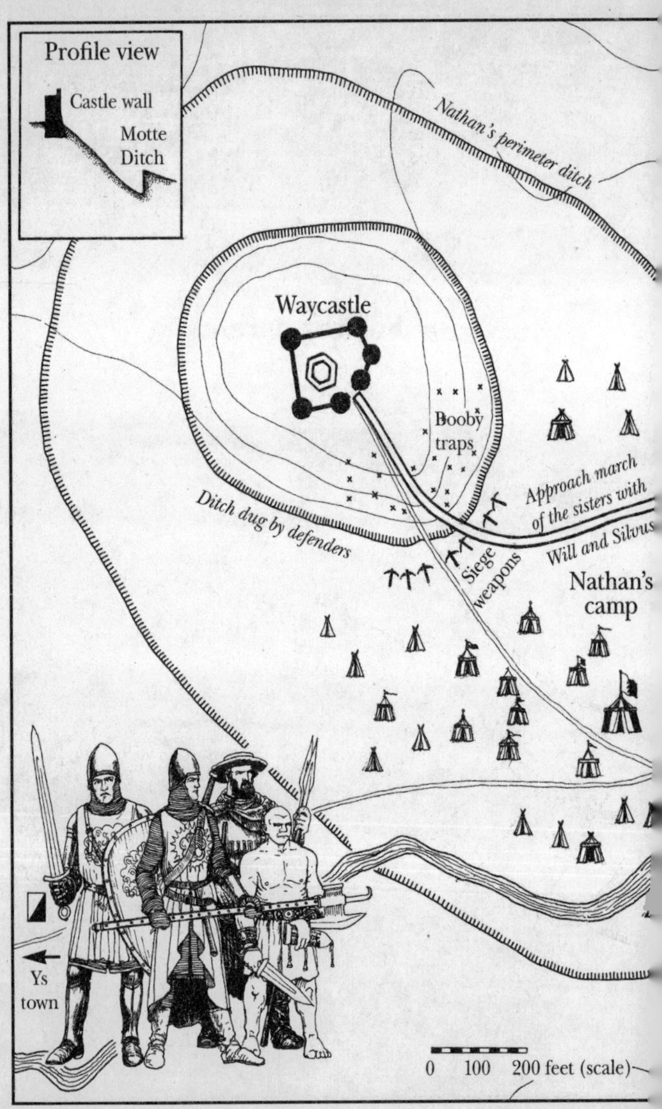

Profile view
Castle wall
Motte
Ditch
Nathan's perimeter ditch
Waycastle
Booby traps
Approach march of the sisters with Will and Silvus
Ditch dug by defenders
Siege weapons
Nathan's camp
Ys town
0 100 200 feet (scale)

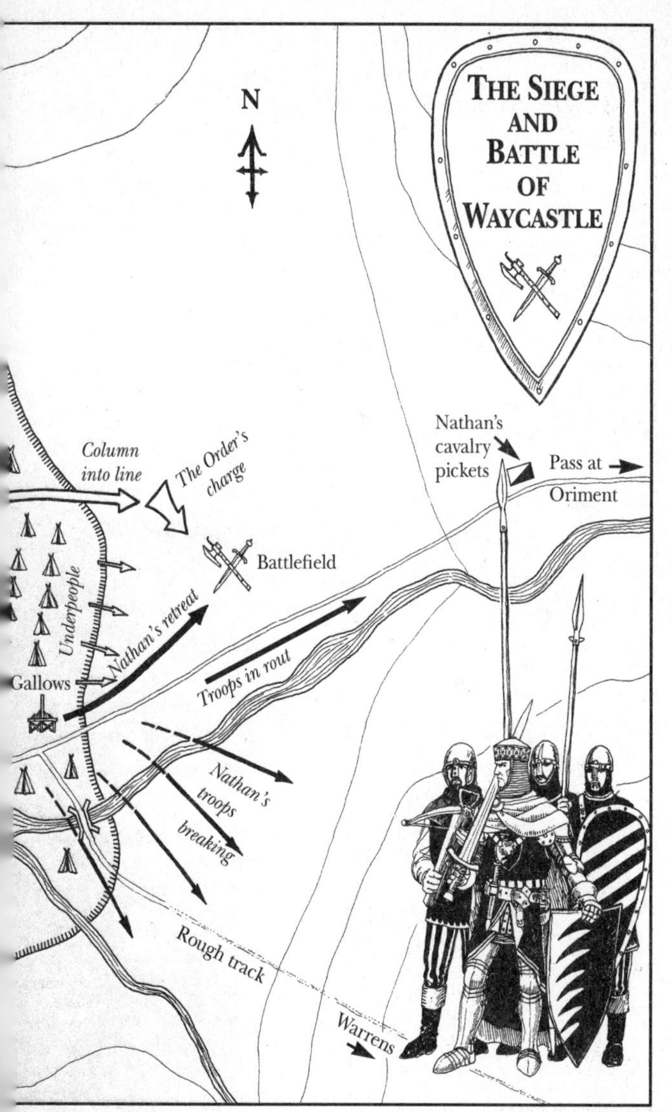

N
THE SIEGE AND BATTLE OF WAYCASTLE
Nathan's cavalry pickets
Pass at Oriment
Column into line
The Order's charge
Battlefield
Underpeople
Nathan's retreat
Gallows
Troops in rout
Nathan's troops breaking
Rough track
Warrens

Sister of the Order of the Lady of Victories

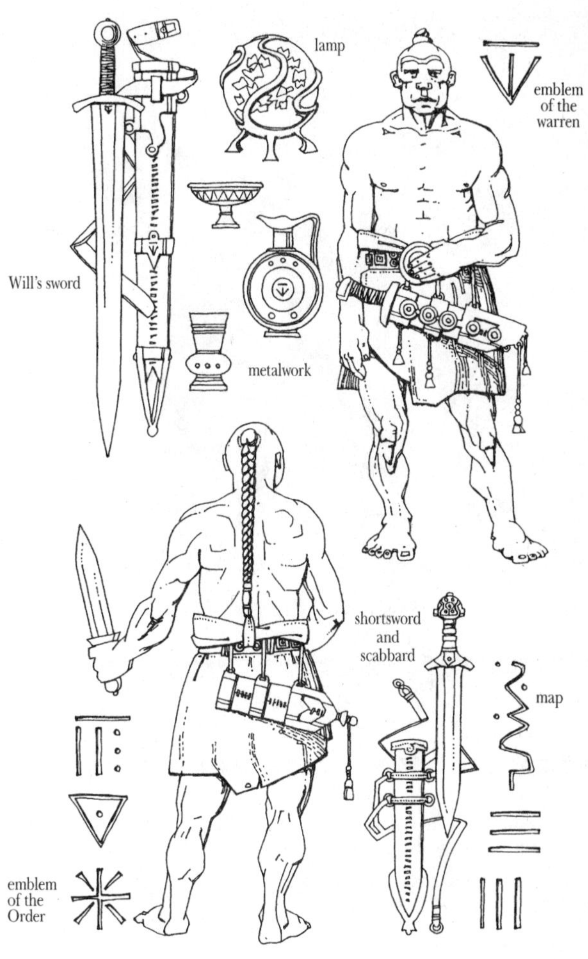

Goblin warrior

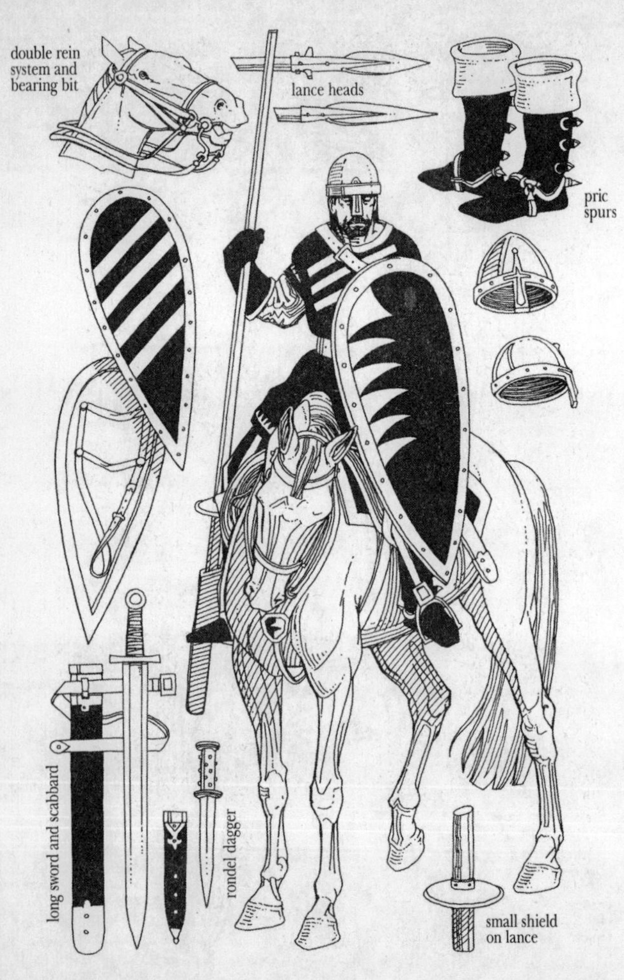

Nathan's Horseguard

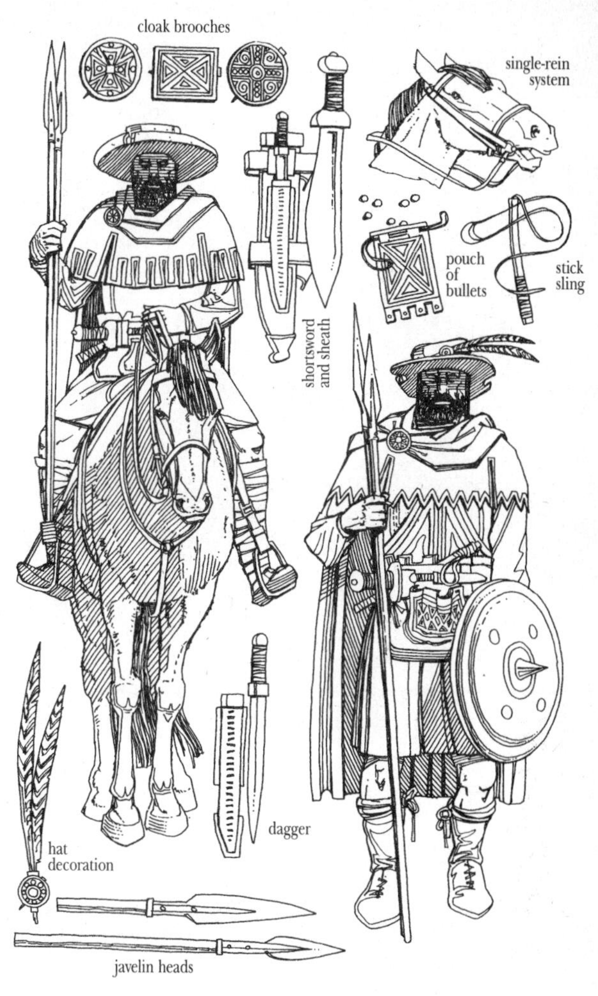

The Order's Auxilia

CHAPTER

ASTA

p Servinghill Street and round the corner into Basin. Past the Blue Man, running as hard as I could, dodging a drunk come staggering out into the weak sunshine. Behind me, one corner back, the *whang-whang-whang* of the City Watch, beating their billy clubs on walls and door-posts as they came.

And the cry, 'Stop, thief!'

They weren't dropping any further behind. Usually I could outrun them, but it was market day and the streets were crowded. People got out of their way, but not out of mine. And I had to keep changing direction, or they'd sight me. That slowed me down.

Nothing for it. Have to take to the alleys.

Hard jink into Cooper's Yard. Risk here. Some careless clod might have dropped a nail. I'd pick it up, nothing surer, in my bare foot. I made it, though. Then right, scrabbling on the slippery cobbles, and into the alley between the yard and the back end of Cabbage Row.

Another risk. There was usually a pair of rumblies staked out there, waiting for trade, and if they thought fast and moved faster, they might snag me and come the honest cit to the Watch for the reward. I hoped I could dodge them, if they tried it, but they weren't there at all. It might have been a slow day, or a fast one and they'd already scored, or they didn't really want to talk to the Watch after all, but anyway they'd legged it. So I slammed into Cabbage Row, up three doors, swung into Mama Purd's laundry before the first of the hue and cry came out of the alley, shot straight through and out the back into her yard. Fred, Mama's mastiff, who knew me, accepted the end of the sausage I threw him as a toll, and didn't make a fuss.

I was over the low place in her back wall, dropping on to a stack of firewood for the bakery on the other side, before the chase reached the row behind. That meant I'd lost them. Mama is a large woman, and she came to her front door as the Watch started shouting questions about which way I'd gone. She doesn't hold with being rousted around by the Watch. She launched into her usual speech, the one that starts, 'I'm a respectable

widow trying to make an honest living ...' Fred added a snarl or two, and I was away down the delivery lane for the bakery, then a left turn into Flesher Street, making for the Backs. I was nearly home.

Nearly. One of them had a horse. Not a watchman. This was one of the party I'd rolled, the old man's son, maybe. He must have known the streets, or he got lucky. And he could ride, I'll give him that. He'd gone around, and caught me as I was crossing Flesher Street. He shouted, and I broke into a run for a few steps. No good. I still had a hundred paces to go before the turn. He'd catch me, sure.

Flesher Street used to be a market street, but the butchers moved east years ago, so it wasn't crowded. People who weren't at the market three streets away leaned on walls and stood in doorways. Women watched their washing, looking out of top floor windows. Little kids played, rolling around in the gutter. A lot he cared about them.

He yelled again, but happily this time, dug his heels into his horse, and came for me, pulling out a sword. And I still had a hundred paces before the alley mouth that led towards home.

No time. I had to use what I had.

The horse was a quiet cob, not used to such wild shenanigans. It obeyed the urgent spurs, though, and stretched itself into a puzzled gallop, people jumping out of the way in all directions. Nevertheless, it didn't like this, all the yelling and the sudden movements, the spurs, the way its rider was flapping around on its back, and it grew more and more frightened and uneasy as it came. I could feel that. I worked on it, but it wasn't enough.

And then a petticoat, hung out to dry, flared suddenly in a stray gust of wind, and in the horse's alarmed mind it was a tiger, leaping …

That beezer could ride, all right. A real gent. When the horse shied and reared, he leaned, held on, and then drove the beast forward again, roaring abuse at it and at me.

I told him what I thought of him, using the gestures that called him a capon and a cuckold and a smocksniffer, and at the same time the horse suddenly thought a brown rat in the gutter was a snake. It reared again, this time less daintily, whinnying like somebody had hocked it.

He was so busy waving that sword at me – I was still a good twenty paces away – that he had no attention to devote to just hanging on. This time he lost the reins, slid backwards over the beast's rump, and hit the ground on his own behind. In the gutter.

I paused a moment to watch, and then took it on the toes again. Maybe I could have taken his sword off him, and then I'd have had his purse as well, but there was no time. I ducked into the alley, ran down the slope, and took three corners more or less at random. This was the Backs, the old river quarter. I was safe from the Watch here. I was not safe from anything else, but that was the sort of danger I was used to. I caught my breath.

The alley I was standing in had no name. The houses on both sides leaned towards one another as if for support, a patchwork of used lumber, paintless and grey, and ill-smelling thatch and tar. It began to rain, as it had been threatening to do all day. Good; the streets in the Backs sloped steeply – the port was at the bottom of that slope. The water ran strongly in the gutters when it rained, and that washed the garbage away and kept the rats down. Some said it kept the plague away, too. Maybe so.

This was no place to open the purse I'd taken, though. The alley looked empty, but there were sure to be eyes watching me from behind the shuttered windows. People in the Backs learn to notice what's happening outside their doors. I stowed the telltale bulge a little further down by my side under my tatty old shirt, cursed the rain, and dodged drips down three streets and across one, heading back home.

Home was a room. Well, sort of. In weather like this it leaked, but it was over a shop that sold eel pies, and there was a shanty two doors up, so Sart had everything he needed in life, right close to hand. And it was fairly near the docks, as well. On those days when Sart woke up sober enough to work, he could walk down to the port and quite often get a few hours in. Sometimes he'd even bring some of the money back.

He was awake when I got back. Bleary, grumbling, and with a bad head, but awake. He'd worked, two days before; in fact the straw boss had come looking for him – three big cogs had come in from Khiree, and they needed every man. What with the special rate and the usual perks, he'd made three days' pay in one, and even though he'd spent yesterday in the shanty he'd still not drunk it all. At this rate he'd have to stop working soon. It wasn't good for him.

He usually looked pretty grim in the mornings anyway, but this time he was actually yellow under the grey. His hair was getting thin, and so was he. Oh, he was still a big man and gnarly, but the way he was going …

I'd give him a year or so. Depended. But he'd stopped looking after me a long time ago, and now I was looking after him, more or less. I owed him that much, I reckoned. Even though he wasn't my da, he'd kept me from starving or freezing when I was little, out of liking, I guess, for my ma. Ma was dead – died when I was small. I never saw my own da at all. Sart was the nearest thing I had to a relative. He'd taken up with Ma after my own da got lost. Sometimes he'd tell me stories about Ma, and he smiled then. If he was maudlin-drunk, he'd cry, too.

I got the purse out while I was climbing the stairs, which were outside, down the side of the building, on the alley. Petey, the son of the eel-pie shop, was in his usual place watching the street, and he saw me when I darted into the alley-mouth and started up. I didn't think he glommed the purse – it was well hidden under my arm – but Petey's cold eyes didn't miss much. If he figured it

for what it was, he'd want a share. A big one. Sart I could get around. Petey wasn't the sort to be flannelled.

And this was no common purse. The party had been three men – what looked like a big-time farmer, his son and a serving man – come to Tenabra for the market. They'd been down in Fuller Street, looking at silk and velvet. Probably for a wedding. Maybe the son's. And they had the money for it.

I'd picked them up and watched them through three stalls. They were out of my usual range – they all wore blades, and the serving man looked hard and compact, an ex-soldier for sure – but I'd felt lucky. And I knew that I had to start scoring bigger, if I was going to get ahead. Or change to something else entirely.

Mother Lessing had already made me an offer – some of her customers liked their girls young. Well, it was a possibility. Not one I cared for. Sure, some managed to buy themselves out of the house, or even got married. Most didn't, though, and they got old fast. Faster even than Sart had. And my talent was no use to me in that job. You can't use it to change a human mind.

So I followed this party of rubes, considering. They were watching the toughs hanging around, and not me. I was maybe fourteen, but I looked twelve, and what did three big men have to worry about from a ragged little girl?

The answer was *plenty*. I'd spent nearly a full day down on the river, mudlarking, only yesterday.

Sometimes the river throws up stuff that you can sell, though it usually runs more to dead cats – and people. I was working the banks, and I'd have picked up anything that was going, but that wasn't the reason I was there. It was for the power. The river brings power down, power that I can store up and use when I use the talent. And the river was in late winter spate, when it had more than it did at any other time. So I had power, and I could fuel my talent.

I didn't know then what my talent is. All I knew then was that I could … make things do things. Animals loved me, if I wanted them to. Given time, I could make them see things my way. I could make them change, too, I mean, change their bodies. Fred, now: I'd healed his mange, and I was one of the few he allowed to come near him. Fred was crazy, as dogs go.

So when these three marks had made their purchases, and were loading up their packhorse, what should happen but that the horse suddenly felt like he'd been stung on the hock by the biggest horsefly in Tenabra – and he kicked? The old man took it fair in his ample stomach, and he sat down abruptly on the cobbles, too winded to cry out. The other two were on the other side. The only person to see was a small girl, who ran forward to help the poor old geezer, got him to his feet, and helped him walk it off. She disappeared into the crowd, just as he started to grope for his purse for a copper to reward her. The rest is history.

So there we were. I checked the purse over as I

pulled at the door. It was worth something in itself – good soft leather with solid brass fittings, in spite of its cut strap. But what was inside concerned me more.

I let myself in. Sart was, as I said, red-eyed, grey under his tan, and yellow under that. His skin was starting to look waxy. In a year he'd look like a corpse. Maybe – probably – he'd actually be one. His head turned to watch me. The rest stayed still. He'd learned three years ago that he couldn't catch me any more.

I pulled the purse open and spilled it out on the plank over sawhorses we were using as a table.

'Thieving again!' snarled Sart. But then he saw the gleam of gold, and he shut up. I said nothing. I was counting. Three … four … five yellowboys! Five Tenabran five-crown gold pieces! And about another three or four crowns in silver. Gods! Four months' pay for a longshoreman winked up at me from the table. I stared at it in dismay.

I'd thought I'd solved our problems for a while. What I'd actually done was to make us a much bigger one. I'd only ever seen two gold pieces before, and not together. They're not a sight you see very often, in the Backs. Five of them together was … very unusual, very unusual indeed. In fact, fatally so.

For what would happen if I bowled up to the local fence, who was Petey's dad, and asked him to change a gold piece or two? Or five?

I'd be lucky to come away without a parting in my throat, that's what. I'd lose the money, that went without saying. And worse, somebody would be sure to shop me, if they didn't knock me off themselves. I could get my neck stretched for this, for all that the gold was useless to me.

I stood there and stared at the pile of money. I'd overreached myself, and I was suddenly aware of it. This was enough to call down a lot of trouble. Sart stared at it, too.

'Who saw you?' he asked, after a moment. There's a practical streak to Sart, under the drink. I was thinking the same thing. People who could finger me, he meant. I shrugged.

Sart glared at me. 'Anyone and everyone, you mean. Gods, girl. One of these' – he picked up a five-piece – 'posted as a reward, and half the city would turn in their own mothers.'

I knew it. I kept staring at them, trying to think. I needed to do it aloud. 'No one saw me for sure who knows me. The Watch were never in sight. The old man and the other mark saw only a girl-child they never saw before. But Mama Purd's the weak link. She didn't see me either – her back was turned when I came through – but she knows there's very few people could get past Fred, and I'm one of them.' I shrugged again. 'She might keep her mouth shut. She likes me, for curing Fred.' Sart looked disbelieving.

So he should. But there was worse. I'd been fingered in Flesher Street by the younger mark, and even the Watch would be able to work that one out. In that much time, I could only have got there over the back fence of one of the houses fronting

Cabbage Row. They'd grab anyone in the row whose front door was open at the time, which included Mama, and sweat them, and eventually she'd remember my name, just to make them lay off.

That was that. Time to get out – now – or they'd be fitting me for a hemp collar this time next week.

'You notice anything about these pieces?' asked Sart, suddenly.

'They're yellowboys,' I said. I was ratting my shelf for my stuff and bundling it up in an old shawl.

'I know that. But they're all new. Haven't even been clipped. Fresh from the Mint.'

I shrugged again. So what? The bundle went over my shoulder, no bigger than a melon and half the weight. Half the silver I tied into a piece of cloth so it wouldn't jingle, and after a frozen second I took the yellowboys too. If I was grabbed, it was no use coming the innocent, and I might be able to fence them in another town. Or maybe melt them down and sell them a bit at a time. They went into an old purse I had, and that went under my blouse. I'd made a cloak from a piece of frieze by sewing a drawstring in it, and that went over the top, hiding what I was carrying, mostly.

'Yeah,' said Sart, watching me. 'You gotta go. I'll just tell them I ain't seen you in days.'

'No good,' I told him. 'Petey saw me come in, just now. He'd shop his old man for half a crown, let alone me. You'll have to shift, too.'

It was Sart's turn to shrug. 'Nah. I'll tell them I turned you out for thieving, I never saw no gold, and I don't know nothing about where you are now. Which I won't. So go. I ... guess anyway I wouldn't be much good any more, on the road. Probably just slow you down.'

He looked ashamed at that, but it was true. The drink had him too tight now, and he'd never shake it, and he knew it. Mostly it didn't hurt him any more. But sometimes it did, and then he'd think of Ma, and it hurt more. That was what he was doing now.

'I'll be back when the weather's better,' I said.

'Sure, sure. Take care of yourself, kid.'

And that was all our goodbyes. I never saw him again.

Getting out of Tenabra was a problem in layers. First I had to get out of the room without Petey seeing me. He'd notice the bundle and the cloak, figure something was up, and shake me down. So it was out the back by the only window, on to the skillion roof, down the slippery thatch in the rain, and hang from the eaves, bundle in teeth, before dropping to the back yard. There was a gap in the wattles of the fence.

Ten minutes later I was heading for the western city wall, after I circled around the streets where people knew me. There were only two gates I could use – the West Gate and the Rivergate. Crossing the bridge over the river to get to the east side would add risks and cost – there was a toll, with the

Watch guarding the tollbooth. The question was, which gate to use?

I'd try the West Gate first. It led to the Great Western Road, and the road led anywhere I wanted to go. It went west at first, but then it divided and followed the border. South to Wydemouth or north to Wele and the other Riverland towns. Ma had come from there, from the north. I had a notion to go that way, but first I had to get out of Tenabra.

I figured it wouldn't be all that hard. After all, it was still less than an hour since I'd rolled the old geezer. The Watch would still be listening to outraged complaints. Probably they wouldn't even have got around to rousting Mama yet, and she'd hold out for a while, at least. All they'd know was a small dark girl did it. They couldn't shake down every small dark girl in Tenabra.

But when I got to the West Gate it was guarded, all the same, and not by the City Watch. I knew the difference. Those three goons looked harder, their uniforms had gold braid across the front, and they were looking at every face that went out. Noble Guard. Prince Nathan's own men. I held back, to chew it over.

We'd had our own City Guard until last year. Then the old Count, Ruane, got killed out in the west, somewhere, and Prince Nathan took over. He outfitted the old City Guard with his own colours of black and yellow, and called it the Watch. Nobody mentioned Ruane any more, as if he'd annoyed the Prince about something. But these were more than just City Watch.

What *was* this? Sure, the city was busy, and there were lots of soldiers about – Prince Nathan was going to have a war with somebody pretty soon now, and there were parades and recruiting sergeants and all that. But what were his soldiers doing guarding a city gate? What was it to him if some farmer got rolled, no matter for how much?

Because that was the reason they were there, all right. While I was watching, a family group tried to go out, and the soldiers stopped them, pulled a girl maybe a year or so younger than me from the cart, and shook her down. Then they commenced to searching the cart, and when the beezer driving it sounded off, they shoved a blade under his nose and told him that if he wanted to flap his face they'd give him another hole to do it through.

Well, that meant they didn't know me by name, just by description. But it also meant that there was a really big hunt up, and the Prince was in on it. That wasn't good. That was, in fact, very bad. It meant that even if I got away clean, I'd have trouble wherever I went in the Prince's lands. And that didn't leave much. Seemed like he owned most of the world. I wondered, briefly, who he was going to fight. Maybe *they'd* be worth a try.

First things first. I faded back up the alley I was in. The gates had been ruled out. In darkness, I could maybe get over the city wall – there were places where you could climb it. But only in darkness, and night was a long way away. Time to go to ground.

I risked a fourpenny piece on a double loaf of

bread, a piece of cheese and a bag of dried apples at three different shops, not going to places I knew, because they'd know *me.* And then it was off to the burying-ground, the old end of it that wasn't being used any more.

Graveyards are quiet. Nobody comes around much, and if they do you can either hide or else make like you're there for the same reason they are. There was even shelter from the misty rain, though I avoided the tombs used by the people who actually lived in the graveyard.

Oh, yes. There were people who lived there. People who had nowhere else to go. Some of them were crazy, and some of them weren't. Mostly, they avoided other people, which suited me fine. They might be dangerous after dark, but I'd be gone by then. And the dead – well, they don't care.

I settled down in a dry spot, just inside the recessed opening to some family's last building investment, with the wind on the other side of it. There was a door at my back, locked, but sagging. I could have found a way in, I guess, if I'd wanted, but there was no need, and anyway it's not a good idea to hide yourself in a place where there's only one way in – or out. It wasn't because I was frightened of bones, or spooks. Dead people are just that, dead. They can't hurt you.

It's true there's something about them, though. You get them floating down the river, sometimes, and there's a feeling about them. As if the talent could make them do things, too. Creepy.

I thought about the talent, as I sat there out of

the wind and gradually got warmer, eating some of my bread and apples. I'd had that sausage earlier, so I wasn't hungry. What the talent amounted to was that you could make things do things, that was all. Most things took time, though, and time was what I didn't have. And though you could change an animal's mind – well, at least the way it felt about something – you couldn't do that to a human. Human minds are like the marble balls on gate-posts. Hard, shiny, heavy. There's no way in.

But the dead, now. I sat and listened to the wind, and it seemed like I heard their voices on it, coming from all around me. And yet I wasn't scared. It was just … wrong, somehow. Like Mother Lessing's offer. I'd sooner have thieved than that, and that was plain silly, because she was a decent enough sort, and her girls were fed and housed and clothed, whenever they were wearing clothes. Here I was, sitting in a dead man's doorway just out of the rain, with Prince Nathan after me. Even so, thieving seemed more … honest.

I shook my head. What was honesty to me? I was a thief.

It would be a good idea to get some rest, as much as I could. It'd be a long night. I was fairly dry by now, fairly warm, and fed. I'd slept a lot rougher than this. So I slept.

The day warmed a little more in the afternoon. Spring would be here soon, and that was good. There'd be work on the farms, in a little while, for anyone who'd work for keep. But the darkness still fell early enough. Late in the afternoon I stretched stiff legs and arms, and waited for it to come.

When I could see the lights being lit down in the houses, I moved out. It wasn't quite full dark yet, but it would be by the time I got to the wall, and I wanted to be out and down with as much of the night to travel in as possible. There were farms and villages a day's journey out, and I was carrying silver, enough silver to eat on for a month or more. I couldn't believe that even Prince Nathan would scour the whole countryside for one small thief. For one thing, he'd need to use an army to do it, and it seemed that he'd be needing his army fairly soon.

As I moved, I wondered why he was having a war. Things seemed to be looking up, generally. Even Sart could make a living on the docks, and the city was getting busier. Sure, prices were high, but there was money around. Witness my haul of the morning.

And witness also the buildings near the wall. It actually got more crowded and the streets got narrower as you got near to the edge of the city, as new people tried to squeeze in. Which gave me a way.

There was a warehouse on the north wall, not far west of the Rivergate. I checked the Rivergate, and found it was closed for the night, and what's more, the log boom across the river had been put in place. That was unusual. There was a boat, smack in midstream. More guardsmen, I'd bet.

And torches, all around the wall. I could see movement on the guard walk, too. I counted, in mounting dismay. Holy gods, they'd doubled the Watch!

This started to smell. The fuss they were making would cost as much as the money I'd lifted. Could it be that the old geezer had so much pull that Prince Nathan would put every man he had on the job of finding me? Maybe the old coot was a visiting prince, or a whatyoucallit, envoy. From another country.

Just my luck. I had to get out, quick. I headed for the warehouse. It backed up on to the wall, and you could climb to its roof, if you were careful, and from there to the guard walk itself. Then it was a long drop down the outer face, but I had a rope.

I got to the roof, moving carefully in the shadows, but it was a bad job from the start. They were watching it, and I'd guess they were watching every place a person might get over the wall. I could see one of them as soon as my head poked up over the eaves, and he was standing not ten paces from where I'd have to cross. Full mail and helmet and sword. He couldn't miss me if I climbed up, and I couldn't possibly take him. I eased down the half-timber wall of the warehouse again, clinging to the toe and finger holds.

Back in the alley, I took stock. I had enough food for a couple of days, if I stretched it. If I could find a place for that long. They couldn't watch the wall like this all the time, and guard

the gates as well. But I was on my own. Anyone else'd turn me in.

There was a place by the river. Ando the waterman had had it, but Ando had died three days back, of the blackwater fever. It was just a hut under the old river docks, but nobody would be in there, yet. Probably. Blackwater fever brought bad luck. I couldn't think of anywhere else, anyway.

So I moved towards the river, keeping to the alleys. But I had to cross the Bridgegate, the main street that leads from the West Gate to the bridge, and that's where my luck ran out.

A patrol, for the gods' sake. The streets were quiet after honest cits had gone home, and I stood out. I should have seen them. They picked me up as soon as I tried to cross.

A shout. I turned, saw the soldiers a hundred yards away, put my head down and ran for my life.

Three of them. I could lose them. Maybe. North, then a jink. *Whang-whang-whang* on the cobbles behind me, calling in other patrols. Answering shouts from ahead. Gods, how many of them were there?

Left, right. Then up an alley. More of them, east of me. I recognised the wall ahead, little red-brown bricks, topped with spikes. The burying-ground. Over, and there was a moment to breathe in the cool dark among the tombstones.

Torches on the other side of the wall. Two parties met. Male voices. 'She didn't come past me, sarge.'

'Better not have. You two, down that way. It's a blind alley, but check the doors …'

I crept away. They'd work it out soon enough. I had to move.

There were little fragments of power in the stones. The marble and granite, hard slabs of hard rock that they chip out of the deep hills. Tombstones are made of that sort of stone. Only tiny amounts of power in them, but I picked up all I could as I moved, putting a hand on each big stone as I came to it. I'd need every bit I had.

And the dead were calling to me again. It felt wrong, terribly wrong, but not half so wrong as standing on a gibbet at the break of day, waiting for them to kick the ladder away. Still, I'd get out over the opposite wall if I could and circle south again. The chase must have sucked them away from the Bridgegate, and I could …

Torches by the entrance. The rumble of the gates opening. Keep going, head for the east wall.

But I stumbled over somebody, a drunk asleep among the tombstones, and he ran wailing and wobbling away in the dark. Shouts, coming my way. I sprinted for the wall, but there were more voices ahead.

They were coming for me. But they wouldn't take me easy. The fear and the fury were taking hold of me now, and the dead were whispering in my ear again, low murmurs, caressing me like a mother. I was frightened, but not of them. The fear was for myself, for me, and I told them of that, and they came to help me.

Light from a torch lapped over me. A shout: 'There!' And I snarled, and called.

A slab moved aside, grating. The dead man was bones bursting from his gravecloth in knobbly yellow sticks, but he stood up, and climbed out of his hole and moved towards the soldier. He was asking me what he should do, and I told him, and he reached for the man, grinning emptily, dropping pieces of earth as he came. The soldier shrieked and dropped his torch and bolted into the darkness.

Well he might. Triumph surged through me. That, and the thrill of raw power. Grinning, I strolled towards the east wall as shouts and yells gathered in the shadows behind me, and I came to it, and set myself to climb. I let the dead man go, and he sank to the earth again.

There were more soldiers creeping up on me, and I called again, harder this time, and a grave burst open like a cut boil and the dead marched towards them, stiffly, munching jaws, reaching for them, and they fled, screaming.

I laughed, power running through my veins like fire. I laughed in delight and wonder at what I could do, and I pulled myself up on the wall. The soldiers were fleeing from me like leaves from the wind, and it didn't matter any more.

I reached for the spike, and as I did the leaves of the bush beside me parted, and a narrow, clever little face looked out at me. The man shook his head.

'Power is a fine thing,' he said. 'But don't let it

go to your head.' In a rush of sudden fear I called again, and a grave opened, but all he did was shake his head again, almost regretfully. 'Too late, I'm afraid.' There was a movement of his arm. I tried to fling my own arm up, but my bundle and cloak entangled it, and next moment the night exploded into stars and darkness.

CHAPTER

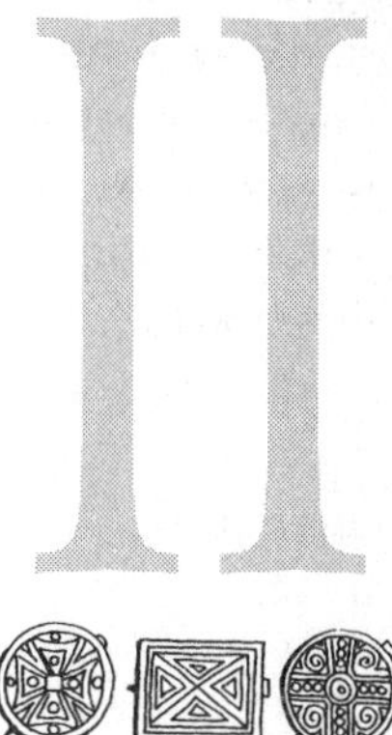

WILL

'... *and bring him to Your peace and the light of Your garden at last. Hear me, O Lady of Mercy, Lady of Victories.*'

I picked up my steel cap and stood. Nobody in the work gang had so much as blinked when the noon bell rang from the keep at Waycastle and I had laid my shovel and knelt down. I said the short prayers to the Lady, asking Her mercy for the soul of a man I'd murdered. That was part of my penance. Many of the others, being sisters of the Order, had knelt too, but their prayers were their own.

Ser Silvus de Castro, to whom I had been squire before the Order claimed my service, nodded approvingly. He was now the supervisor of my

penance, which meant our relations had hardly changed. I picked up my shovel again.

We were digging a ditch. Rather a specialised one, a deep wide trench in a ring surrounding the mound of the fort at Waycastle, in the Brokenbacks. We had dug it with the outer side a straight drop of eight feet, but its inner side sloped at the same angle as the mound itself, so nobody could find cover in it from missiles shot from the fort. It was there to slow an attack down and break it up, and to impede the approach of siege engines. Later we'd set sharpened stakes along its bottom.

The stony soil was hard to work, but the Order was determined and as enduring as any stone. Picks could break rock, given muscle and sweat, and the sisters of the Order had as much of both as the Lady required. They were supremely sure that it would be enough. I wished I felt as certain.

I wiped my brow and struck in again. No point standing around getting chilled. There was a cold wind up the pass, but it was from the west. Spring was nearly here. The thaw had started two weeks before, and the river, just down the slope, was loud and brawling with the meltwater. Higher up the pass – the pass at Oriment – the snowfields were shrinking rapidly. They'd be gone soon, and soon after that Prince Nathan of the Riverland would arrive with his army to grab another piece of the world for himself. And to express his annoyance. He was annoyed with the Order, and with me.

A wagon passed by on the road, double-teamed, grinding up the slope to the castle. It was loaded with little barrels, and the barrels were marked with the flameburst symbol of the Order's liquid fire. However annoyed he was, Nathan was going to get a warm reception at Waycastle. The supply wagons had been coming in all week, from the first day that the roads could take the heavy traffic, bringing stores. The castellan – the Sister Castellan, to give her her proper title – was in the cellars all day, every day, stowing it all away.

For a moment I wished that Waycastle were as massive and as powerful as Ys had been. But that mighty fortress, the Order's main base and Motherhouse, had been demolished by the Order itself. Its stones had been so huge that they retained mana, the mana that flows from the earth, the Power that fuels magic. The temptation to misuse that Power had been too strong for their last prioress, Merceda. She had the talent, and the mana had called to her. Called her to her own destruction.

Magic does that. It calls people to destruction. So the Order had pulled Ys down, for all that it was the strongest place on earth. The Order does nothing by halves. And Prioress Winterridge was a true daughter of the Order. She was in charge now.

I watched her, in between shoves with the spade. She was not above swinging a pick herself, but at that moment her business was to drill a couple of sections of her sisters. They were moving very quietly and cautiously in columns of three, down the mound and towards the only flat ground anywhere near, the meadow across the other side of the river, which was the only place where Nathan could set up a camp. They had to move cautiously. Every one of them was blindfolded.

I grunted and threw another spadeful of broken stone on the rampart. When the dust started flying, the garrison might want to sally out to raid the besiegers' camp. If so, they'd have to do it under cover of night. They'd need to know every inch of the ground blind, not to get lost and to outpace the pursuit and get back in the dark. If Prioress Winterridge had her way, they'd be able to recognise every rock on that hillside by feel, smell and, if necessary, taste. I bent again to my work. Another half-hour to the midday meal, and my digging shift ended then. But there was no need to repine. After I ate, I'd get to do some foot drill myself. Oh, joy.

Other teams were clearing the spindly trees and brush, denuding the ground of all cover a ballista shot out from the walls. The ballistas themselves, engines like giant crossbows on frames, had been set up on the battlements and the range tried with the six-foot iron javelins they threw, missiles that would go through three men at a range of four hundred paces. I only hoped that it would be merely men that they were shot at. I'd had monsters enough to cure me of curiosity forever, last bout.

The bell rang again. We changed shifts. I handed my spade to my relief, a silent farmer from down the valley somewhere, who was still wiping

his mouth after his meal – we ate in sittings. Work went on all the daylight hours. The castle was being strengthened in every way a committee of experienced, resourceful and devious minds could think of.

We stumped up the hill together, Silvus and I. The gates stood open, the portcullis up. The gatehouse was massive, glowering, with flanking towers on either side. We moved briskly enough – we were hungry. Nothing like six hours of hard labour in the keen cold air to give you an appetite, and in my case there was the added incentive of seeing Arienne.

She was on light duties by then. Everyone worked, and she did her stint in the kitchen. But Arienne had to study, too, for that was her penance, or part of it. She had to because she might be our best chance. Our only chance. Arienne had the talent, too, and it must not go awry.

She had a smile for me as well as a platter of boiled salt cod and bread and cabbage, served up from pots on a trestle table outside the kitchen, as we filed past. The kitchen was a separate building in the bailey, and we took our platters into the hall of the keep to eat at the trestle tables there. Silvus set about his meal with a gusto that was at odds with his spare frame. In spite of his gentleman's table manners, which he'd come by honestly, the food disappeared at a rapid rate. He was almost halfway through by the time I'd filled two jacks with beer from the butt and returned. He nodded thanks, and took a long pull at his. I dug in.

'We'll be finished with the ditch tomorrow,' he said, setting to his food again. 'Start on the stingers and the lilies then.'

I grunted, breaking bread, thinking how much better he looked now than only a year before, when he'd been eating his heart out as an ensign in the City Guard at Tenabra. He'd always be lean, but he'd put on some weight, and his colour was healthier. The grey of his hair was the same, but it had stopped thinning. You'd have taken him for five years younger than his forty-six. Good, and better than good. We'd need him. I needed him.

The stingers and the lilies were booby traps on the approaches, lightly covered little pits with an old spearhead or a sharpened stake fixed at the bottom. After that there were earthworks to go in front of the gatehouse, to stop a ram from getting close. That would finish the digging, and the unskilled labour force – that was us – could then be set to weapons drill. The masons were building massive new buttresses for the outer wall, smiths were turning out pikeheads, carpenters frantically worked on spear shafts and crossbow butts, bowyers were smoothing bows, fletchers feathered arrows. Even the tinkers were busy, making spouts and conduits for the liquid fire. When May and Nathan arrived, Waycastle would be fit to receive him, and the reception would cost him dear.

Nathan was still at least a hundred leagues away, across the moors in Tenabra. He'd be pleased to see the sort of violent activity his name had stirred

up. Still, I began to wonder whether it had been worth annoying him quite this much. For he was coming for us, nothing surer.

Communications across the moors were chancy at the best of times, and in winter especially. But fishermen ranged this far west, and Ys town, twenty leagues down the road from us, was the only port on the west coast. News had seeped through. Nathan was recruiting. He would march west as soon as the snow was off the high moors. His engineers were already improving the ancient ruined road that ran from the valley of the Wydem to the pass at Oriment, the only gateway to the western country.

Come to think of it, I'd get off doing foot drill this afternoon. Silvus, too. There was a staff meeting. He cleaned his wooden platter with a piece of bread, sat back and sighed.

'Maybe we shouldn't have run off,' I said.

I was continuing a conversation that had started shortly before dawn that morning. There'd been precious little time or breath for words since then. Silvus looked across at me.

'And the alternative?' he asked, as if curious.

'Play along. Set up Nathan's college of magic for him. Have all sorts of technical difficulties. Achieve very little. He'd get tired of it sooner or later.'

'I doubt it. Nathan is both persistent and impatient of failure. He also has a nose that can detect flannel at a hundred paces.' Silvus folded his hands over his narrow belly. 'He'd be a superb

ruler, you know, if it were not for his megalomania and tyranny. And ruthlessness. And lack of any tincture of morality or honour.'

Silvus didn't like Nathan. You could tell, if you listened carefully to the nuances of his speech.

I tried to lift one eyebrow in the way he could, failed, and ended up feeling silly. 'You think open warfare with him is better?'

'I think open warfare now is better than desperate rebellion later, when he's likely to have a college of magic, a Dark mage as a subject, and a collection of monsters as weapons.'

'Hmph. He hasn't got a Dark mage yet.'

'He'll get one. There's a few with the talent born in every generation. He'll find one and groom him. Or her. It's only a matter of time. We have to deny him the time.'

Time. Time to do what, I wondered.

The staff meeting was set for an hour after the meal. I could go down to work on the ditch again, but I'd be there no sooner than I'd have to come back up. So I volunteered for kitchen duty. Well, I had to be doing something useful. I really feel better if I'm doing something useful. Actually, I quite enjoy scraping pots and raking out fires.

Actually, I rationalise a lot. Arienne was working in the kitchen. A tallish, slim, dusty-blonde girl with grey-green eyes that looked right through you. We'd run away together, in a manner of speaking. Run away from Nathan. With Silvus. And, also in a manner of speaking, with Master Grames, who wanted to be head of Nathan's

college of magic, and whom we'd murdered. It was for his soul we prayed daily, as we were required to do, both of us. After our year of service to the Order was finished, I rather hoped that Arienne would do me the honour of marrying me. If we were both alive by then.

I picked up the first three pots in the pile and took them out. There was a sluice and a sand pile outside, by the pump. Scouring out pots is relaxing work, not requiring thought. The same does not apply to conversation with Arienne, thank the gods.

'How's that side of yours?' I asked. She was scrubbing vigorously at a carving board, hands red, not showing any pain. But then again, she wouldn't.

'It's fine. Not a twinge.' Remarkable. Five months before, she'd taken a crossbow bolt in the ribs. I slapped sand down and ground it in with a leather pad.

'Good. Talked to any underfolk lately?' She grinned. It was a sort of standing joke. Arienne not only had the gift, but she also knew how to talk to goblins, which is our impolite name for the underfolk. They, for their part, call us 'the sun-people' if they're being polite, and have an expression that means 'termites' if they aren't.

'Yes,' she replied. 'They'll supply the lamp oil on credit.' Their lamp oil was an ingredient in liquid fire, the complete recipe for which was the Order's most closely guarded secret. 'And they didn't reject outright the idea of allowing us to use their tunnels. Just didn't want to tell us where their entrances were. I can't blame them for that.'

'Can't have the one without the other.'

'No.'

'So will they come around, or not?'

She bit her lip. 'I can't tell. They're slowly beginning to trust me, but the Order, well …'

'We could really use their mining skills.'

'I know. But they will either offer them freely, or we will do without.' Steel was under the words.

'Amen to that,' I said.

A dreadful irony. Arienne had the talent. She could make the underpeople do as she wished, and they had no defence. Their minds were not like ours. They could read each other's thoughts, to some extent, and because the gates of their minds were open, their emotions could be manipulated by someone with the talent. That was why they appeared in every Dark mage's army, and it was also why the Order had persecuted them.

But forcing compliance was the essence of the Dark. Arienne had tasted the thrill of using the Dark, once. And I had been the one who had pushed her into it, to my shame and the peril of my soul. Never again. Not for her, not for me. We'd die first. We'd even let each other die first.

I looked across at her. She had finished with the carving board and was pumping up more water to deal with a bucketful of ladles and spoons and carving knives. Her plain grey gown and overdress were simple and severe, and unladylike muscles worked in arms and shoulders and back.

Her hair had been trimmed to fall only to the nape of her neck, the waves of it shading from nutmeg to wheat. I wondered how she'd look in a sea-green silk gown, hair just so, with jewels winking from throat and arms and fingers. One day, I promised myself, I'd find out.

My own working clothes weren't exactly court dress, either. Over my quilted arming doublet I was wearing an old mail shirt and steel cap, because you have to keep accustomed to the weight of armour, but the rest was leather breeches, a pair of the Order's soft brown boots, and wool hose, much darned. And an apron.

'Staff meeting in a little while,' said Arienne, drying a knife with a cloth and oiling it.

'Yes. Sister Informer is in a taking about something.' I thought about that, and didn't care for the implications.

'Sister Informer doesn't get in a taking easily,' Arienne remarked, echoing my own thoughts.

'No.' There'd been a dispatch rider in from Ys town that morning. I'd seen her clatter up the hill, and the foam on her horse's neck was telltale. The summons to the meeting had gone out shortly afterwards. Silvus and I were bidden, too, because we knew something about Nathan's army. 'You've been called in as well?' I asked.

'Yes.' That would be because Arienne knew the most about the talent, partly because she had it and partly because she had been studying it ever since she had been able to sit up in bed.

'So …'

'Whatever it is involves both Nathan's army and the talent. Yes.' She had worked through the same process I had, only faster.

'Uh-huh.' Ominous. I dried the pot and put it aside. When I had finished the stack, it was time to go.

The staff met in a chamber on the second floor of the keep of the castle. It would have been a lady's solar, if the Order ran to such things. Now it was furnished with a table that had chairs at its head and foot and two benches along its sides. In peacetime, those present would be the College of the Order, its senior sisters who held office. This wasn't time of peace. Now they were the staff of an army.

We stood a few moments, until Prioress Winterridge walked in, and then we sat when she did in the chair at the head. She removed her helmet, parking it on the floor. Her plaited hair, light and dark brown together, fell to her shoulder-blades. There were tiny flecks of silver scattered through it like the first touch of frost, but her face was as it had been, square, taut over high cheek-bones and long nose, though it was as tired as it had been the first time I had seen her. Smudges showed under the clear green eyes, but they were still alert.

'Old business first,' she said, crisply. She nodded down the table. 'Sister Castellan.'

'All food stores complete for six months save pickled cabbage, Sister Prioress. Of that, only one hundred days. Of fire …' She read through the

list, ending with: 'Water. The bailey well is drawing over a hundred gallons per day. But if we lose the bailey …'

'Yes. We really need a well in the sub-basement of the keep. We have discussed this before, and agreed that it's beyond our resources. It would have to be driven through rock, and we have neither the time nor the labour.' She did not so much as glance at Arienne. If the underfolk could be brought to our aid without invoking the Dark, Arienne would bring them. There was no point in asking more. 'Sister Bursar.'

'The treasury is bare, Sister Prioress, until the summer taxes come in.' The bursar made a helpless gesture. 'All I can do now is keep track of our debts.'

'If we are here to pay them, the debts will be paid.' Prioress Winterridge had a face that you had to search very hard to find expression of any sort, and the words had sounded austere. But her eye twinkled, just a little. 'If not, I doubt that the duns will reach us, care of the Lady. Sister Infirmarian.'

'In sick bay, three, all from accidents, Sister Prioress. Light duties, five, including one who thinks light duties include chopping wood and carrying water, which they don't.' Sister Infirmarian glared at Arienne, who looked unrepentant. 'No fevers. No flux.'

'For which let us all be grateful to the Lady, and then to you and your people. Any more?' The Infirmarian shook her head. 'Sister Castellan.'

'The buttresses will be finished in a week, so

the master mason tells me, Sister Prioress,' said the Castellan. 'We can clear the scaffolding by next Threeday and start timing drills on turnout to the walls.'

The Prioress nodded. 'Fighting garrison only in a fortnight, then. I want everyone else gone, scattered into the hills or back to their homes by then.' Silvus made a motion. 'Yes, Ser de Castro?'

'The commander of the armsmen asks if he may call for volunteers among his men to form part of the garrison.' Silvus shrugged, slightly. 'I believe that he and all his men intend to volunteer.'

The sisters looked dubious. The Order, always short on recruits, had for some time past allowed some men to bear arms as auxiliaries. That didn't mean that they were considered the equals of the sisters of the Order in battle.

'No.' The Prioress was as firm as she was always. 'We cannot find places on the walls for every sister who would be here. Full garrison is no more than two hundred; any more would simply be so many extra mouths to feed. And his men are not trained in full battle drills, nor are they used to armour – most of them, anyway.' She shot a glance at me. 'But I appreciate the request. If the commander will attend me after this, we will concert plans for his men to carry on a harassing operation, raiding the enemy camps, and so forth. And' – she looked around the table – 'if he and his men are to fight beside sisters of the Order, it would be well to have him attend command briefings with the other unit leaders.'

There were pursed lips and lowered eyes around the table. Nobody said anything, though. 'Note that, Sister Bursar. Is there anything further? No? To new business. Sister Informer.'

Sister Informer was atypical, for the Order. She was short and wiry, with her dark hair cut in a soft cap, and she was possessed of an evil sense of humour and the ability to put two apparently unrelated pieces of information together to produce a startling new one. She proceeded to demonstrate that.

'Sister Prioress, fifteen days back, Nathan turned out the entire City Watch of Tenabra and the Noble Guard and sealed the city off completely for a day. We know some of their orders – soldiers talk in taverns – and those orders were to prevent a small dark female of about thirteen years of age from getting out of the city. Every girl who came near to that description was held and searched and subjected to inspection at the gate. Then Nathan declared a curfew, put large numbers of troops on the streets, and started a house-by-house search of the city, looking for the same person. To do all that required every man he could get his hands on, including troops that were needed for other tasks.'

'Why?'

'The troops were told that it was because she was a thief who had stolen something very valuable, with no specification as to what it was.' Sister Informer said that straight-faced, but it was clear that she didn't believe it. 'But there is

more.' She turned to another report. 'I have my ears in Tenabra very alert for anything that might be a manifestation of the gift. As a result, I get a lot of false positives – I hear of every three-legged calf in the Riverland. But this is interesting. The same evening there was a tumult or a riot of some kind in the old cemetery on the west side of the city, not far from the north wall. Witnesses speak of many torches, soldiers, and then terrified yells and cries. All I have apart from that is second- and third-hand. Wild tales of soldiers crying that the graves opened and the dead rose from their rest. My informant can't find any soldier who was there, which is significant in itself; but Baron Langland's pike regiment is now confined to barracks under guard. Nobody goes in or out.'

Sister Informer put the report aside. 'The last piece of information is negative, Sister Prioress. The curfew was lifted the following morning, and all troops save that one regiment returned to normal duties. The Watch was stood down. No trace exists of this thief.'

'So Nathan failed to find her. If he had, he'd have had a trial and an execution.'

'So he would, Sister Prioress. If she were only a thief. But if he failed to catch so important a thief that he'd turn his whole army out for her, he wouldn't just stop there. Nathan is thorough. There'd be rewards posted and a hue and cry throughout the countryside. A rigorous search of the city. Doubled guards on all the gates. But all

of that was called off after this … disturbance. In the cemetery.'

'And you think the two are related.'

Sister Informer nodded, slowly. 'Sister Prioress, I think that the best reason for ending a hunt is because the quarry is taken. But I wonder who might be important enough to Nathan to justify such effort. Not a common adolescent thief, surely, no matter how lucky. And then I wondered, in a spirit of idle curiosity, what actually happened in the old cemetery that night. It was in that spirit that I asked Mistress Brooke' – she shot a glance at Arienne – 'at what time of life the talent came to its full strength in her.'

'Ah. And it was …?' The Prioress looked at Arienne.

Arienne's eyes narrowed. She nodded. 'As the body changes, Sister Prioress. About the time a boy becomes a youth, or a girl a maiden.'

'I see.' Prioress Winterridge pushed her chair back and braced her arms straight, palms flat on the table. She included Silvus and me in her gaze. 'It wouldn't be the first time that Nathan's potential mage has attempted escape.'

'It wouldn't be the first time he's used his army to try to drag one back, either,' remarked Sister Informer, drily. 'There is one thing more, Sister Prioress.'

'I had the feeling there might be, sister. Let's hear the worst.'

'This is a mage just come into her strength, and Tenabra, as Ser de Castro will confirm, is not rich

in mana. Nor is there a rich source within a week's travel or so.' Silvus, watching, nodded, and so did Arienne. 'Yet she led Nathan's army a merry dance, and if I'm right, she seems to have had enough power for some major necromancy – raising the dead.'

'So she's talented.'

Sister Informer nodded again. 'More, I suspect, than she herself knows, Sister Prioress.'

CHAPTER

ASTA

I was first aware of the eyes, I think. They were looking straight into mine, and I was aware of them for a long while before I could think what they were. They were slightly bloodshot, like somebody who'd been up for a long time, but not with that bruised look around them which says their owner is used to sleeplessness. They were set deep, of a greeny hazel colour, with pale lashes around them.

The space around the eyes gradually built up into a face, narrow, foxy-haired, freckled, the nose a smudge, the mouth a thin bloodless line, but a face under a philosopher's forehead, high, balding.

Slowly, the space around the face became the walls of a room.

Long before that happened, I knew that my head hurt. That was almost the first thing I knew, in fact. And that I couldn't move my arms or legs.

'Good,' said the face. 'You're awake.' He sat back. The last mists cleared from my sight.

I was sitting in a chair in a small square room that had one door and one window. The floor was wood – closely fitted, rich dark wood, and polished, once. Now it was dusty and unswept. The walls were plastered, but there was that dead coldness in the air that tells you that they're thick stone under that. The window was high. Through it I could catch a glimpse of the corner of an eave, tiled, with painted roof beams, and a patch of lowering sky. Morning sky.

The chair I sat in was padded and comfortable, and very solid. It had arms, also padded, which was just as well. My own arms were tied down to them, and my ankles to the legs of it. I couldn't move much, except for my head.

I moved that around, to see what would happen. More of the room came into sight. It was bare, except for me and him and the two chairs. Bare and tidy only in the sense that there was no mess on the floor, no marks on the walls. It was grimy and the window was dirty, with cobwebs and undisturbed dust. Nobody cleaned up in here, and nobody lived here, either.

The man in the seat facing me put his hands on the arms of his chair, as if mimicking me. He

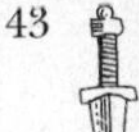

nodded, satisfied. 'And now you're awake, we can begin.'

Begin? Begin what? I spent a moment looking around the bare little room, and then it struck me that there were terrible answers to that question, and I panicked, pulling on the bonds, which didn't give at all. I hauled on them, and the skin started to peel off my arms, and I still hauled on them, and they still didn't give. I knew, you see, that sometimes the law didn't just take you out into the marketplace and hang you. I'd seen what they did, sometimes.

I was babbling, too. 'No, please, I …' I couldn't think what to say. *I didn't mean it?* Of course I did. *I knew it was wrong* … So why'd I do it then? *I'm sorry*. Fat lot of good that was. 'I'm only thirteen,' I gasped, instead. 'You wouldn't …'

Of course I knew he would, if he'd been told to. It was just something to say, while my heart raced and a sick cold fear started in my belly. But he just looked at me. 'I won't hurt you,' he said.

He said it in a funny way. Clipped. Like saying 'Good day', a thing to be said to get it out of the way. Like saying something you didn't necessarily believe, but it was only words, and it was neither here nor there whether it was true or not. He leaned back and went on. 'My name is Teska. Vinker Teska. I have been waiting for you to come along for some time. We will be working together.'

What? *What* did he say?

I stopped squirming, and sat and blinked instead. Then, 'Working together? What d'you mean, working together?' I tasted the words, and they tasted strange. 'Don't I get a trial or something first?' And then my brain caught up with my mouth. 'Working how? On what?'

He just stared at me, and then sighed, but very faintly, as if somebody had told a lame joke. 'Which question do you want me to answer first? A trial will not be necessary. Indeed, it has already been held, in a sense. When I say we will be working together, I mean just that, and we will be working as and how His Highness the Prince directs.'

He looked at me as though that was all the explaining he needed to do. I looked right back at him.

I have to say that it wasn't often that I felt right out of my depth. I knew the city, and that meant knowing its people. But he wasn't like anyone I could get a handle on straight off. He looked like a tradesman on Highday – wore a sober darkish suit, somewhat ill-fitting, of worn good cloth but not rich – but his hands were soft and white as no tradesman's are. Then he groped at the side of his chair and pulled out some papers, and that told me something else about him. It was the way he did it, as if it was the papers that were real, and everything else around, the room, the window, the city and me as well, weren't.

Suddenly I knew his type. He was the Prince's man. Not the City's, like the Watch. He was like the customs inspectors they had down at the docks, eyes on every bale, a paint marker in one hand and

a tally stick in the other. The City goons looked the other way if you paid them, or simply because it was a hot day and they didn't feel in the mood to chase you. Or maybe other times they'd kick you around, just to say hello. But the excisemen – they were different. They'd screw the eyes out of your head if there was a duty on them, but not for the fun of it. They'd do it because it said on some paper somewhere that they *could* do it.

He looked at the papers, then at me. 'Now. Your name is Asta Harrower. You were born in Tenabra, or you came here as an infant. People remember you that far back. You live – you lived – with your stepfather in a room over Hook Street, in the Backs. Mother dead. No other family known. You're a street urchin and a thief.' He frowned down at the page. 'A rather poor one.'

I bristled, before I could stop myself. He noticed it. 'You're a poor thief because you don't observe very well, and when you're in a hurry, you don't think things through. Like how that young fellow you threw off his horse knew you. He didn't, of course – he'd hardly seen you. But you were about the right size and age, and in about the right place. He shouted, and you were the one who ran. You panicked. Panic is something to be avoided.'

He said that in a dead flat voice, calm as a mill pond. Mill ponds feed mill races. People drown in millraces. He went on, unblinking.

'But you compounded that error with another, more serious. You used your talent on his horse, just as you had used it earlier to make the original

grab. You gave yourself away, and then you gave your talent away.'

He took up another paper – or rather a set of them, bound together at a corner. 'We have been aware for some time that a thief with the talent was operating in the city. Actually, it's a logical occupation for someone like that. So we were on the look-out for odd events – previously well-schooled horses that shied or kicked without cause, dogs that didn't bark, secure doors that opened without being forced, strange animals – wherever they helped a robbery. You provided them.'

I had been getting steadily angrier during this recital. Mad at him, and, I suppose, at myself. There's only one thing worse than being called a fool, and that's being proved one. So I showed it. 'It took your whole army to run me down, though. How many soldiers to catch one girl? And a lot of them were running away from *me*, at the end. Proud of yourselves, are you?'

He looked at me and shook his head mildly, sorrowfully. 'Ah. But that was because you did something truly extraordinary. You raised the dead. Necromancy.'

'Necro-what?'

'Bringing the dead back.' His eyebrows lifted. 'The worst kind of Dark magic.'

I knew what the Dark was. It was armies of monsters and walking dead led by a Dark mage in a black robe, rocking with evil laughter. I wasn't a … was I?

He was nodding. 'Dark magic. Yes, indeed.

Necromancy. Do you know what the penalty is for necromancy?'

I attempted defiance. 'You can only hang me once.'

'Hanging? Oh dear me, no. Nothing like that. We don't hang necromancers. Necromancers are burned alive. The statute calls for a small flame, too, so that you char slowly. It can take a surprisingly long time.' He stared at me right in the face, and his expressionless eyes were saying that they had seen the thing done, and that it had in fact taken a surprisingly long time.

'You said you wouldn't hurt me,' I whispered, while my belly cramped and cold sickness rippled up my spine. To say that was useless, I knew, but I had to keep him going.

'I won't hurt you,' he said again. 'That would be up to the officers of the law. His Highness has a settled policy on necromancy. People hate it, and so does he. No doubt there would be a good turn-out for your execution.'

He had said 'would be', not 'will be'. I ran a dry tongue around my lips. 'But they're not going to burn me.' Even as I said the words, I shook.

He shut his eyes slowly and opened them again. 'That depends on you.'

He had also said that people hated the Dark, before he said the Prince did. Maybe the Prince hated it because they did. I had an idea then what my life would really depend on. But I asked him anyway. You always want to know the asking price straight out. It might be less than you think.

'How does it depend on me?'

'You might show remorse and contrition. You could do that by putting your talent to work serving His Highness, and serve him, his heirs and successors faithfully for as long as you live. For this you will be well rewarded. Or you might decide not to serve him, or to serve falsely. In that case you will burn in Temple Square on the morning following. And possibly during much of the afternoon as well.'

I think that last bit was Vinker Teska's idea of a joke. At any rate he smiled – well, at least his mouth stretched. Then he went on, 'The choice is up to you.'

'Some choice,' I said, because you always bargain. But he only shrugged.

'It's the one you have. And if you think that you'll be allowed to make the bargain and then betray it, think again. You'll be rewarded, your life enriched and made secure and even luxurious far beyond the best you could ever manage on the streets. But you will never, never be trusted; there will be soldiers an arm's length away every moment. And if you ever do turn traitor, if you try to lie or to cheat us, then you go to the fire.'

I had nothing I could say for a moment. He nodded as if I had asked a question, though. 'Yes,' he said. 'And that will be how matters stand for the rest of your life.'

I sat there staring at him. He stared back, and his little eyes were frightening.

'We know about the talent, you see. It's very

powerful in some ways. You can change animals, not just their minds, but their bodies, given time – and animals includes goblins. You can enter an animal's mind and see through its eyes, feel with its senses. You can alter things – like metal, making it harder or more brittle, or air, to make the weather different. You can raise the dead, if you want to. All very, very useful things. Valuable things. Things that His Highness would be prepared to pay well for.'

I blinked. I never knew all that was possible. But he was shaking his head, as if he was sorry for me.

'But all those come with weaknesses. It takes time to do any of them. You can't create a dragon by snapping your fingers. And you have to be able to see the animal you use, either through your own eyes or another's, at least at first, and the talent rapidly degrades with distance. You have to be close to what you change – and before you start thinking that you can rot those cords, I remind you that I am watching you every moment. A shout from me, and there will be a dozen men in here, and the stake awaits. Which brings me to the most important limits of all. You can't fool a human mind. We don't know why not, but it is so. You can't make me serve you, and you can't make any other human do it either. And to do anything at all, you need mana.'

Mana? My face must have betrayed the question. His stare became dry, his manner lecturing.

'The talent is fuelled by mana, as wood fuels a

fire. Mana flows from the deep bones of the earth. It is stored in rocks and ores, though it may be found in streams fed by springs. There is little of it here in Tenabra even with what the river brings down, but you managed to create the effects you did on that little. Your talent is strong, then. It therefore cannot be ignored.

'So you must choose. There is no bargaining, no to-and-fro. Serve the Prince, and accept his bounty, and your life as it will be. Or choose death by slow fire.' He leaned close, and his rat-trap mouth and little eyes filled my vision. 'Choose now.'

When we went to find the Prince, it turned out he was in a tent in the field among his soldiers. His camp was on the river flats south of the city, on land that was fallow that year. We rode there in a tight little group, me on a mule that Teska was leading as he rode on another, and around us a dozen soldiers. They were Noble Guard, Prince Nathan's own, and they rode with their swords level across their saddlebows. Their horses were bloodstock, and my mule was elderly. We rode sedately out of the South Gate, past the parks and gardens that rich people had outside the walls, and crossed a ditch. Spread across the fields in front was Prince Nathan's army.

I knew that the taxes had been bothering people who paid them, but now I could see where the money was going. I lost count of the regiments that were there, let alone the soldiers. There were horse-soldiers, with armour and without, trotting

and wheeling in groups; there were archers bending bows, and columns of footmen with long pikes, stepping all together in squares and lines and files, all turning and wheeling and changing the pattern to bawled orders, moving stiffly like puppets. There were women washing clothes and carrying babies and cooking, and strings of mules and wagons loaded with supplies. There was a hubbub of noise, like a market day.

It was like a city in itself, all made out of canvas and rope. The tents had lanes marked in between them, like streets, and as you came closer to the centre of it, the lanes got broader and the tents got better – larger, with flags on the poles and with coloured panels. Then we came into the central square of the canvas city, and there before us was the biggest and prettiest tent of all.

I thought of a spider's web. All around, all up and down the streets that spread out from this one brilliant point, were other tents, dotted along them like the wrapped bodies of flies. And here I was, being taken to see the spider.

Somebody took the beasts away as soon as we got off them, in front of the tent. The thing was canvas, striped black and yellow like a bumblebee, and it had poles inside to hold up the roof and outside to extend the walls, and it was the size of a house. Several houses. Banners flew from the poles, all brightly coloured. I craned my neck like a farm girl come to the city, and saw that the one that flew from the tallest pole of all was made of silk. The guards at the tent flap had golden lace

on their puffed sleeves, and uniforms even more gorgeous than the Noble Guard's.

'Gentlemen of the Presence,' murmured Teska. 'His Highness's personal bodyguard. They do not leave his side.'

I looked them over, carefully. Gentlemen, yeah, right. They had faces that looked like they cracked walnuts with their eyelids. The City Watch was watched by the Noble Guard, and the Noble Guard was watched by these prizes. Prince Nathan must think there was a point in having them all watch each other, as well as watch out for him. I wondered who he was so afraid of. Me? I doubted it.

We were searched, all of us, with a quick impersonal efficiency that was almost gentle. The whole time four soldiers stood just out of my reach with drawn swords. Two more stood further off. They had cocked crossbows, which were pointed up, but all six of them never took their eyes off me; and they all closed in around me when we got the nod from the head ugly, so for twenty paces I didn't see anything but armour all round. They were so close I'd have had to peer up to see their faces. I didn't, of course. What was interesting about their faces? They were blank as a guard dog's. I just followed in their footsteps, with somebody almost treading on my heels. Was it really going to be like this for the next fifty years? I shuddered.

We ducked through another flap, like a wall of cloth, heavy silk. Ten steps beyond it we stopped, and the steel fence in front of me moved aside. I was face to face with Prince Nathan.

I looked about at first, to see if there was anyone else in the room that was likely to be more important. I didn't pick him at first. He and Teska were the most soberly dressed men there. He wasn't tall or broad, either, and he wasn't wearing a crown. How was I to know he was a prince?

And yet … I did know. Maybe it was because everyone was looking at him, and inside their eyes was a faint worry, a concern that asked *Have I pleased him? Am I safe for now?* Or maybe it was because he was the only one there who was doing anything else. He was reading a paper. When he finished, he reached out without looking and somebody put a seal into his hand and somebody else dropped melted yellow wax on the paper, and he set the seal to it. Then he held the paper out without looking, and somebody took it and bowed away, walking backwards. Prince Nathan didn't look at that, either.

He was looking at me.

Teska bowed from the waist. The Prince's eyes flicked to him, and then came back to me. I ducked my head. Nathan nodded without smiling, but to himself, not to me. When he waved a hand, a chair was placed behind him and he sat, without checking that it was there. Perfect assurance. I had the idea that if it hadn't been right where he wanted it, somebody would have been flayed alive. The chair was gilded wood, and the floor was carpeted. It was as if we occupied a room in the Palace, except the walls billowed slightly and glowed with the day's light.

We remained standing, three strides away. If you stand over a man, you're supposed to feel more confident, and he's supposed to feel less so. But it wasn't that way at all. Prince Nathan just stared, and it was me who began to feel uneasy. More uneasy, that is.

Then he leaned back and crossed his ankles. '*This* is your mage?' he said, to Teska. His voice was a rich dark baritone without a hint of gravel.

Teska nodded, as if confirming that he thought the sun would rise tomorrow. 'Yes, Your Highness.' The voice was eager. Seeking to please. If a dog could talk, he'd talk to his master like that.

The slow inspection again. 'She's very young. Ragged, too.'

Teska's eyes closed and opened slowly, the same gesture he'd used on me. 'And no doubt verminous as well. Yes, sire, she is. But she put the fear of several of the gods into a company of your best troops, and she has been a sore trial to find, and more of one to catch. What she will do when she has access to mana is something I wonder at.'

'So do I. Perhaps it would be as well not to find out.'

Teska wagged his tail again. 'Your Highness understands the … difficulties better than I. Nevertheless, the advantages …'

'May be greater still. Indeed.' He inspected me again. 'How old is she?'

I was getting tired of this. Uneasy or not, I refused to be talked about as though I was a heifer

at a sale. Teska glanced down at his papers, but I forestalled him. 'I'm fourteen,' I said.

Prince Nathan raised his brows. Teska opened his mouth, but the Prince waved him off.

'Well. Fourteen,' he said. 'And your name?'

'Asta Harrower,' I answered.

Teska intervened. 'His Highness the Prince is addressed as *Your Highness*,' he snapped. I flinched, and looked down and then back up into the Prince's eyes. They were dark brown, with little amber flecks.

He tilted his head. 'Softly, Teska. She's frightened of you, and I've no doubt you've given her good reason to be. But there are limits to what can be achieved by that.'

I noticed he didn't actually tell Teska not to frighten me. He watched me for a moment more. Then, 'Asta. Teska will be in charge of you, because I've found him to be very efficient. But neither he nor anyone else will be permitted to hurt you in any way, unless you misbehave. I think he's already told you what would come of that.' I shivered. He nodded. 'Yes. I see he has. Tell me, have you ever lived outside Tenabra?'

'N-no.' I hesitated, because the question was unexpected. He arched an eyebrow. 'Your Highness.'

'Well. You will now, for a while. The nearest reasonable source of mana is …'

'A week's journey east, Your Highness,' supplied Teska. 'The old workings at Etterden.'

The Prince nodded. 'A week there, a week back.

She won't be able to ride, of course. Have you thought of that?'

They were talking over my head again. I tried to keep small.

'I had arranged a coach, sire. The roads are still miry, though.'

'Yes. The roads are the only thing keeping me here. But I must be gone in three weeks. How long will you need at Etterden?'

'A few days only, I should think, sire. Asta strikes me as being very quick. We should be able to prove the first talents by then.'

'Well, if I've left, you can catch me up. Perland will see to your warrant for supplies and horses. Be as quick as you can. I want to see a mage in the making, not a bedraggled street-rat, before I'm a day on the moors. There's another source there, I'm told.'

'Yes, sire. The witch Arienne used it. I'm sure Asta is at least as strong as she.'

'Very well, then. Get her cleaned up and fed and clothed. Hear that, Asta? No more pickings in the streets for you.' But his eyes flicked back to Teska. 'And find a woman to watch her. A matron. A reliable one. No charming the guards; change them every week. Have that added to the warrant, Perland. Teska is to be accorded full cooperation and be assigned escort at his request by local commanders.'

A flunkey nodded, scribbling furiously. 'Yes, Your Highness.'

'No, wait,' said the Prince, and the scribbling

stopped. 'Add two short words to that warrant. That's *Squire de* Teska.'

Teska drew his breath in. 'Sire ...'

The Prince smiled, easily, generously. 'We'll take the squire's oath of fealty as read, de Teska. If you deliver a full-fledged mage to me, it's likely to be overtaken anyway, by another oath, more senior. But do not fail me in this.'

Teska bowed. 'My life on it, sire.' The horrible thing was, he meant it.

'I don't want your life. I want a way to beat the Order. Give it to me, and you can be Duke of Ys.' He nodded. It was a dismissal. 'About those siege machines, Perland ...'

Teska bowed and backed away. I watched him, and copied what he did. It seemed I'd be doing a lot of that from now on.

CHAPTER

WILL

'So. He's coming for us.'

'Yes, Sister Prioress. His siege equipment had to wait for dry roads, but he broke camp a week ago and moved by river up to Conflans. From there his engineers should have finished work on the first part of the old way leading across the moors to the pass at Oriment by now. Already his cavalry patrols are ranging ten leagues out into the moorland, sweeping for my watchers.'

'Have you lost any?'

'Sister Halmasdotter should have reported by now, by pigeon, Sister Prioress. But she …'

'… always took too many risks.' Prioress Winterridge's lips thinned. 'We were novices

together. She may have wanted to get too close to Nathan's camp. Nords!' Pause. 'How overdue is she?'

Sister Informer looked down at her hands. 'A week, Sister Prioress,' she said, in a small voice.

Prioress Winterridge nodded. 'She will be in my prayers, and has always been in the Lady's hands. Are there any others, close in?'

'I have a groom actually in Nathan's camp, Sister Prioress. The problem is getting his information out. His messages tend to tell me where they were two days ago.'

'If they moved as soon and as fast as they could, where would they be now?'

Sister Informer turned to the strip-map we had made of the old road we had travelled, Arienne and I, last autumn. It had been cobbled together from our memories, some information from sisters operating as scouts, and old books in the library. Nobody quite knew how accurate it was.

There was the thread of the old road. Hardly a road at all when we travelled on it, a vague thinning of the scrub that appeared and disappeared and reappeared as you looked at it, like a trick of the light. It ran from the valley of the Wydem near Conflans to the pass at Oriment, and it had been built by the underfolk, ages ago, when they lived in the sunlight, before the Dark – or something – drove them to hide under the hills.

Sister Informer bent over the map, tracing the road with her finger. 'They might have marched from Conflans Seconday last week. The siege engines will slow them down, and no army this size can move as fast as a single regiment. It takes up too much road. Say six leagues a day on the good road and four on the old one. That would put them ... there.'

She pointed to a place where the old road climbed into the high moors, not far from where we had joined it. I remembered how it had been; you could see the road only as a vague streak of lower scrub and different soil, pointing to the horizon in long straight drives. The bulwarks of the moorland hills shouldered up around it, and it ignored them where it could, cutting its scar across their weathered faces, a seam like a scratch-mark in old rust. Always climbing, as you headed west, out of the valley of the Wydem up to the moors, which rose inexorably to the ragged fangs of the Brokenbacks. Patient, endless leagues of heather and gorse, swept by the eternal wind out of the limitless sky. Gusts passing over the great swales would expose for a moment the silver-grey undersides of the leaves, so that the land rippled like a stream bed seen by moonlight. Beautiful, and empty, and desolate as the sea.

Prioress Winterridge was staring at the spot. 'Well. Cavalry sweeping ahead of Nathan's army, you say, is making life difficult for you. We have – let me see – about a hundred sisters who are familiar with the moors to one degree or another. At least they crossed them to join the Order. It would surprise me if we could not in turn make life difficult for Nathan's cavalry.'

Sister Informer grinned. 'There is also the auxilia, Sister Prioress.'

'Well thought. This is just the job for them. If they can ride.'

She looked at me. I looked at Silvus. 'About half ride passably, Sister Prioress,' he supplied.

She nodded. 'Good. Ask Master Rookwood in. This concerns him.'

A messenger sped for the auxilia commander. The sisters settled into that curious stillness they have when waiting, without small talk or movement as if neither the delay nor its outcome chafed them at all; they had done what they could, and the rest was no concern of theirs. I fidgeted. Silvus watched the map for a bit, then nodded, as if he'd come to a decision. He smoothed his grey hair and tucked his helmet under his arm in a formal sort of way. 'Sister Prioress?'

'Yes, Ser de Castro?'

'I would like to offer my services with this detachment.'

'And I,' I put in.

'We'll see what the auxilia commander has to say. Ah. Master Rookwood.'

Rookwood was at the door. Not having a helmet to tuck under his arm, he had removed his broad-brimmed hat and was holding it in front of him with both hands, which gave him an anxious look. But he was wearing his leather war-coat, home-made but strengthened with slips of steel between its layers, and the hat had a steel crown. He carried a shortsword, but like his men, his main

weapons were a sling and a pair of javelins. The sling hung at his belt with its pouch of leaden slugs; the javelins stayed outside in the hall.

'You sent for me, Sister Prioress.'

She waved him in. 'Come in, Master Rookwood. Look at this map with me.'

Within ten minutes he was nodding. 'Aye. I know the ground, from here back.' He indicated a sweep of road out to ten leagues or so from the pass. 'Hunters range out that far. Beyond that, no. But it can't be that different.'

'It isn't,' Silvus put in. 'Gets a little lower, and maybe more boggy, towards the east.'

'Well then. We'll slow them down for you, Sister Prioress. Send a few of them home the long way, too.' He sounded eager to go.

'I'll be sending a company of sisters, as well,' she said, thoughtfully, watching his face. It fell. 'You'll need them, if it comes to a cavalry action. They can cover your retreats. This will be a hit-and-run business.'

The sense of this was so obvious that even Rookwood nodded. 'Aye,' he sighed. 'I'll tell the lads to get ready.' Then, fidgeting. 'If you'll tell me who commands the sisters, I'll go pay my respects and get my orders, Lady.'

'Wait.' Sister Winterridge turned to Silvus. 'Ser de Castro. You have more experience of the land beyond the Brokenbacks than any here save me. We have both crossed it both ways. Further, you are an officer of great experience, with knowledge of Nathan's methods and army. Sister Informer,

here, will command the sisters, so as to observe Nathan at close range, and Master Rookwood his armsmen. Will you command the whole?'

'Lady, you do me too great an honour. I would have been happy to serve under Master Rookwood.'

Now, that tells you something about Silvus. He was a de Castro by right of birth, no matter what Nathan might say, and the de Castros were an ancient family to whom Nathan was an upstart. Nathan's father had started out as a twopenny upland baron – *His Highness,* indeed! But here was Silvus, for all his proud lineage, saying that he would have been happy to serve under a commoner. He would have been, too. Silvus doesn't lie.

The Prioress smiled. 'I think your appointment in command would be more suitable.' She nodded to Rookwood, who had ceased to look resigned and disappointed, and was smiling again. 'I'm sure Master Rookwood agrees.' He nodded enthusiastically. 'More suitable for all parties.'

And that tells you something about Prioress Winterridge.

ASTA

Ladies rode in these things, it seemed, to preserve them from the public gaze. A closed coach. A box made out of wood and leather, on four wheels, pulled by two horses. Or more than two horses, on bad stretches. It swayed and jolted on the potholed road, and I spent most of the first two days in it as

green as an old chop and heaving fit to die. Teska took no notice of that at all. This was on one of Prince Nathan's post-roads, and Nathan's post-roads were better than most. Pity the poor ladies.

He didn't take notice of much, did Teska. Except to watch me, every time I moved or spoke or made a sound. However much he seemed to be asleep or absorbed, the slime-green eyes would sharpen, and he'd be flicking little glances at my hands and the leather of the seat under me, looking for anything that changed. Widow Pila was even worse. She watched me the same way, going with me to the privy. Privy! Now I knew in my soul that nothing I did would ever be private again.

He'd actually anticipated Prince Nathan's instruction to hire a woman to watch me. Widow Pila was small and as gaunt as a gallows, but not nearly so cheerful. She said little, and that little in the fewest words, as if it hurt to open her rat-trap of a mouth. Her cuffs and collar and wimple were painfully white, threadbare with scrubbing; her gown was sad-coloured and heavy. I've known brown-haired women who shine like new pennies – why, I'm nut-brown myself – but the widow's hair had the colour and sheen of mouse droppings. I bet her husband had been happy to go, poor sod.

I had been looking out of the little window, but the rain started again, and I tied the leather flap across to keep it out. Now there was nothing to look at but the inside of the coach, which included the seat opposite, on which sat Teska and Widow Pila. There was nothing outside but dripping

hedgerows and sodden fields and the wet horse of the nearest damp trooper of the soaked escort, but that was better than this. I sighed, and shifted a little. Teska watched me, and Widow Pila watched a point an inch above my left shoulder. She never looked directly at anything.

'Etterden tomorrow,' I remarked, cheerfully.

'Yes,' said Teska, and no more. He didn't stop watching me. I looked him dead in the face, which makes most people slide their gaze away, but he just continued to stare me out, those pale-lashed eyes expressionless. There was something inhuman about Teska. Dog-like in front of Nathan, inhuman for me. It figured. I leaned forward, but he didn't react, except to watch more closely.

'For the gods' sake, Teska, talk to me,' I said. 'If we are going to spend the rest of our lives staring at each other, at least let's talk.'

'What about?' he asked. He sounded as if he'd never before thought of such a thing, talking to someone else just for company. Or heard of anyone who'd want to.

'Etterden,' I said in desperation. 'Or anything. Anything. The rain. The state of the roads. The crops. What we're having for supper. Anything.'

Widow Pila gave the smallest of snorts, and sat a little further back on her seat.

A roar on the roof announced that the main squall had arrived, and for a moment conversation was even more impossible than usual. As it receded, Teska was shrugging in the gloom. 'Etterden's just a village. No different from many others, except for the old copper workings, the mines that are in the hill hard by there. There's a spring rises from them, and I suspect it must bring mana down. It comes from deep underground.'

I nodded, and cast around for something to keep him going. 'Who, or what, was Etter, or Etta?'

'What?'

I sighed. 'Etterden must mean Etta's wood. *Den* or *dene* means a wood.'

His eyes narrowed again. 'How did you know that?' he asked, as if accusing me of something. 'That's the old speech.'

I shrugged. 'Sart came from west a way, and they speak funny there. We'd go berrying in autumn, sometimes, out as far as the sheepwalks, a day's journey, sleeping in a haystack. He used to say *den* for wood, but with an accent that lengthened the middle out; and *coom* for a valley. He used to call the dip on Stuckey Street a coom. And he had some other odd words. Like *hlong* for a ship, but he only said that for an old-fashioned narrow one, with a sternpost and a steering-oar, not a modern cog. So I guessed the words must be old ones.'

Teska sat and stared at me some more. 'You're quick. Quite wrong, in this case, but quick. There is no Etta, nor ever was.'

'But …'

'You didn't know the other old words. *Tor* is a hill. Etterden was once *e-tor dene*, the wood on the hill. The hill always was the most important part of the place. It's a rocky outcrop. Among the rocks is

a vein of copper ore, which has been worked time out of mind. The mine is now very deep. Water is pumped out continuously. It must contain mana.'

Widow Pila snorted again and pulled a piece of hookwork out of her bag. She only worked on it when she was sure I was safely out of the way for a bit.

'*Tor* is hill, in the old speech? Do you know any more of the old words?' I asked.

'A few. It was one of the first areas I investigated. But what I also know about them is that they have nothing to do with working magic, so you can put that out of your mind straightaway.'

I tried not to look disappointed, and he knew it right off. He smiled the only sort of smile he ever could, the slow closing and opening of his eyes that meant he was pleased with himself.

'I know that the old speech is associated with magic in the popular mind. But it's a rumour, no more. There may be some connection, somewhere, but the words have no power in themselves. You won't be able to say a magic word and vanish, thus to break your bond. The restrictions on your talent remain as I have listed them, no matter what you learn.'

'You seem to know a lot about the talent,' I replied, sourly.

He nodded, as if I had congratulated him. 'Yes. I have made it my study these last five years, at the behest of the Prince. I have learned much.'

'What, for instance?'

He gave a funny little grunt. A moment later I

had realised it was meant to be a laugh. 'Am I to give you freely what I have spent much effort to acquire? No. As you return good service, I will teach you more. That service will itself bind you to the Prince, and by doing so, bring your power more under control. In time you will need the Prince even more than he needs you. But until that time, I would not trust you with the power to call a rabbit.'

I sat back and watched him, just as he was watching me. After a moment I nodded. 'Fair enough,' I said. He didn't even blink at that.

The rain had stopped, or at least eased to drizzle. I opened the little flap of a window again and looked out of it. But I wasn't watching the greens and browns of the passing plough land. I was thinking about what Teska had just let slip.

Service will bind you to the Prince, he had said. I knew my man Teska by that time. 'Bind' he had said and bind he meant, and not with ties of love and loyalty. No. Teska would mean something more compelling than that. *You will need the Prince more than he needs you*, he had said. What for? Why would I need Prince Nathan?

I knew what I'd need him for. I'd be bound to the Prince because I'd have no other choice. I'd have to serve him, because once I'd done a few of the things he wanted me to, I'd need his protection.

Say it again. Once I'd served Prince Nathan for a while I'd need protection, and the people I'd need it from would be my own folk. People don't

like the Dark, and I'd be a Dark mage right enough, if Teska had anything to do with it, and he'd make sure people knew. The fields and belts of woodland passed, unreeling like thread from the spool, and I watched them and didn't see them at all.

We came into Etterden village on the tail of a long stage, splashing through puddles as the clouds massed and another night's rain began. It had been dark for hours. We climbed stiffly from the coach and hobbled fast through the rain to the covered entry of the only inn. Teska had sent a man ahead on a fast horse to bespeak rooms in the Prince's name. I hoped the place wasn't full up. If it was, someone had just been turned out to make room for us, and I couldn't face the idea of making new enemies quite so soon.

The village boasted only one inn, but that was new, and larger than you'd expect from the number of houses. Somebody was doing well enough out of the new post-road. There was traffic passing even now, even in the dark. As we passed the second door into the front parlour I was alert for raucous shouts from the taproom. It was late, as farmers count time, but still I expected a drunk or three. Drunks start trouble and what they do is unpredictable. If somebody did something very unpredictable indeed, it might have taken Teska's attention off me for a few moments.

No such luck. It was all prim and proper, all drunks safely stowed. Genteel as a temple picnic and quiet as falling snow. The rooms were ready. I shared mine with the widow. Naturally. She clamped the window shut and parked her bed underneath it. I took a good look at the lock on the door, and it was about what you'd expect – I'd have been able to pick it with one of her knitting needles. Only it wasn't locked. Instead, there was a large, hairy soldier outside in the hallway, and there would be one there all night. Just as there would be one outside every room I ever slept in, every night for the rest of my life. I was already getting used to the idea. A little. Maybe. I went to sleep with Widow Pila still watching me, as somebody would all the time now. The candle would burn all night, too. If she slept at all, it wasn't while I was awake.

If there's nothing you can do about what's happening to you, you should suffer it with good grace. Whoever's doing it might get careless. And there was nothing I could do about it until that happened. Meanwhile, I was being herded like a sheep in the shambles towards a gate, and behind the gate was a man with a knife. Behind me, urging me on, was fire. Fire was in my dreams. Fire at my feet and at my back.

In the morning it had stopped raining, and the air smelled washed and grassy, the first spring warmth touching the fields. There were flowers in the woods, and people looked out of their doors, wondering if it was time yet to unstitch their winter flannels. They'd look at the weak sun, clear but

pale, and think *Perhaps not yet. But we could maybe sow the peas this week.*

Widow Pila brought breakfast in on a tray that had been left at the door by the serving-maid. She opened the door wide, so that the guard could watch me for the two heartbeats that it took her to pick up the tray, and I sat still as a post on my bed while he did that. We ate, her eyes never off me. When Teska walked in ten minutes later, he didn't bother to knock.

'Ready?' he asked, and it wasn't me he was talking to. Widow Pila nodded, a sharp dip of her head. She didn't bother to check with me.

We went downstairs, two soldiers before, then Teska, then me, then Widow Pila, then two more soldiers, one of them carrying a satchel. Where there was space, Teska and the woman walked beside me, and the soldiers spread out to give themselves more space to react. I walked quietly with my head up, like a robber I once saw on his way to the gallows. He'd made a good impression on me. There wasn't any reason for it, but it made me feel better to walk that way.

And there was something else, too. We walked away from the road, out of the village by a path that led over fields, over a stile in a hedge, and on up the hill through stands of plum trees that were bare but beginning to bud. There was power in the air, and it was increasing as we went. Further up the slope, somewhere, there was a source of power.

How can I describe it? It's like a quiver in your stomach, and like a clear fountain in the air, and

like a hum that's so low you can't hear it with your ears. All of those and other things beside. And I wanted to go to it.

People had called me 'mudlark' because I went so often to the river in Tenabra, especially when it was swollen with the rains. I pretended I did it for the pickings that the current brought down, but that wasn't so. The river also brought power down, pale and faint, but there, and I felt it the way that Sart felt strong ale. There were tiny chips of power like fragments of crushed gems in the big hard stones of the city streets, sometimes, too. But I never thought that there might be more power than that around, in the world. After all, what did I know but the streets of the city?

But that was what was ahead of me, a little way up the slope. Power. Wisps and tendrils of it seeped down, caressing me like a mother. It was like heading home on a sleety night, warmth and safety calling to me across the hard cobbles. I found myself starting to hurry, and then Teska glanced back at me. His eyes opened and shut, his only smile.

I slowed my step and ignored the call to rush. Ignored the surge of need and desire that was making my heart pound and my palms sweat. No need to make Teska glad about something. If he ever felt glad about anything.

Now I knew how it was for Sart, going to the grog shop with a day's wages in his hand. All the promise in the world was waiting ahead of me. All the promise …

And then it washed over me, as if I'd plunged into an icy pool. Like Sart going to the grog shop. It was just the same. I felt my face forming itself the same way his face did when he clutched his coins and calculated how much oblivion they'd buy him, worried and happy and guilty at the same time. Going to a lover, and hating himself. In him, it was a sickness, a thing that fed on the sorrow of his soul. What was it in me?

I had to keep up with them, but suddenly my feet were dragging, in spite of themselves. I knew what that sickness was. I'd seen it eating away at what had once been a fine man, and I'd thought myself free of it. And here it was, leering and laughing at me. And Teska smiling.

Up the slope, on a path, and suddenly we were walking beside a rill, a tiny stream that leapt down among the rocks that broke through the thin soil. Trees stood around, pines now, the air whispering and moaning in their needles, droning under the silvery tinkle of the water. And here …

I couldn't help myself. I went to the water, scrambling down among the stones to reach it, and I put my hand under a spray where it fell, a miniature cataract, over a step. The power tingled and prickled in it, and my hand felt cold and hot both at once. My mind relaxed and expanded like a flower after rain, and the power flowed in.

The river at Tenabra sometimes brought power like a quivering in the water. As if you were holding down a piece of wood that someone was sawing. But this was different. This was stronger, fresher,

like putting your hand on the shaft of a mill. The power built up, and as it did, the world changed. Suddenly I could see the way that the trees were built, the lines of the strain of their branches, the dots and whirls of their inner selves. I was aware of a wash of minds around me. Some, like those of my escort, were hard, white and impenetrable, but there were also small animal minds everywhere, open to me. There was a bird in the pines, and I felt his happy lust in the spring sunshine and his wariness and his knowledge of the wind. I listened to his world and saw it through his eyes, shadow and shape and well-known flight ways, danger and food and mating …

There was a pricking sensation low, next to my spine. A voice said, 'All right. Enough for now. Stand up.'

That was Teska, a pace away behind me. The sharpness was a dagger-point, and the dagger was in the hand of a soldier. I looked over my shoulder to see him, and for a fleeting instant there was a temptation to reach for the steel and show him how weak a thing it really was. A fleeting instant only. Weak it might become, but not before it had let my life out on the grass.

Teska's eyes were fixed on me. Apart from the soldier with the dagger, the others stood in a circle five paces off, crossbows unslung, bent. They pointed them over my head, but not far over, and their fingers were on the releases. Any quick move, and the bolts would cross each other in me.

'Move away from the water,' said Teska, and the

air crackled. Power ran along my limbs and sang in my blood. I stood and backed away from the power, and the steel point in the small of my back moved with me. 'Now,' said Teska.

The satchel that the soldier had been carrying was on the grass. From it Teska produced a small wickerwork cage, and in the cage was a forlorn bundle of feathers. It was a starling, one of the birds that stays on through winter. Usually they cheer me, with their bright eyes and yellow legs, but this one had been rubbing her head hopelessly against the sharp bast of the wicker, and the down was roughened around her neck. She was blinking in the sudden light, confused and frightened. I could feel and taste her fear.

'Now,' said Teska again. 'Let us see some magic. Change it.'

I looked at the bird in the cage. 'Change her? How? By doing what? I've never …'

Teska shot a glance at me, suspicious, jealous. Then he sighed. He groped in an inner pocket, and pulled out a notebook. Flicking over pages, he remarked, 'No. I don't suppose you have. And there's nobody to show you what to do, now. But … let me see … ah yes. Here. You can't read, I suppose.'

I shook my head. Actually I could, a little, but I wasn't about to give Teska the information for free, any more than he'd give it to me.

He nodded, and read aloud from the book:

It's a matter of persuasion. You convince the creature, body and mind, that this is the way it should be. That it should be bigger, or that its bones would be better if they were made from stone, or that it should have fangs or tusks or wings, or breathe fire. Whatever. Anything you want. And it will conform to your will, if your will is strong enough, and the power sufficient.

He looked up and blinked. 'Is that of assistance?'

I was watching his face, which as usual gave nothing away. 'Who said that?' I asked.

'A man who knew what he was talking about.'

'Who?'

He closed the book with a snap. 'The name would mean nothing to you. But if the words help at all, use them. Or do it some other way. But try. Try now.'

I stared at the starling, feeling confused. She was watching every movement, probing the shadows around her in helpless fear, and I felt sorry for her. I knew how she felt. I tried to say that to her, the way I used to work on Fred the mastiff, to tell her that it was all right and nobody would try to hurt her. Slowly she calmed. I watched her, and saw a dusty grey-brown bird, thin, with greedy eyes. She gave a thin squawk like a creaking door.

I thought how plain she was, like everything that stays over winter. Winter is grey and colourless, with its close skies and mists and mud. When spring came, as it was coming now, everything should be different. Sart used to have what he called a spring clean, in the years we had before he was really taken by the drink. We'd sweep and brush and scrub whatever we were living in, and

clean our clothes. Even take a bath, if there was something to take a bath in. When we were finished, the place would shine, and the rats and the fleas would be gone for a while. In spring the birds should sing and shine like jewels for the honour of the sun and the new earth. Everything should be clean and burnished bright, remade and reborn clear and sharp and glistening like the rain on the fresh grass. There should be …

It was one of the soldiers who hissed, and I noticed it in the back of my mind, the piece that wasn't speaking to the starling.

Her feathers were shiny, now, and her beak a bright new-minted gold. As I watched, half with my eyes, half with something else, and told her how the spring should be, her plumage lengthened, and grew coppery lights along its tips, and then the dull muds and greys flushed a deep green, green as moss, but glinting like the sun on the river. Two plumes grew from her tail, bright feathery silver. That beak opened, and a rich liquid trill sounded, full of spring sunshine and joy. The feathers of her neck ruffled up, stippled brilliant gold.

She glowed and glittered in the soft sunlight, and hopped in the cage and trilled again, a sound of pure beauty.

Teska's face had hardly changed. He picked the cage up and inspected the bird, and then pushed it into the clumsy hands of the soldier standing by. That man looked from the bird to me and back again, and his mouth was open. The bird preened. I suppose I did too, a little.

'Very good,' said Teska. His voice was dry. 'It was useful to do that. Who wants a bird with scales, or two pairs of wings, or a poisonous bite? This, on the other hand, is something that will sell. There are people who'll pay for an exotic and unknown species of cage bird.' He nodded to himself, and his eyes closed and opened again. 'Well done,' he added, like a man throwing a crust to a beggar.

He had looked at the cage bird and then at me, but now he continued to watch me. Widow Pila had never taken her eyes off me, wonders or no wonders. She knew what she'd been hired for, and it wasn't so she could lollygag about and gawk at things.

The cage and its occupant were packed away, and we descended the hill again, the bird in one cage, I in another, and both of us bought and sold.

CHAPTER

WILL

The snow was wet now, melting from the sun side of the stones as we passed. It would cling to the shade side for a while yet, but it was time to be going. The pass at Oriment was open for business, and so were we.

We moved out at a purposeful march, two hundred strong. Ahead was a fringe of scouts, and they would fan out to screen us once we were through the pinch of the pass. Then the auxilia, mounted on sturdy ponies. They'd been practising skirmishing drills for mounted infantry, taking up position, forming line, horse-holders to the rear, advance, engage, fall back by files, mount and away. They were getting good at it, too. Silvus was happy with them. Which was odd. Silvus had been born an aristocrat, which should have made him happier to be behind a shield and a couched lance in a heavy cavalry charge, all plate armour and plumes and no brains to speak of at all. Then he'd been a captain in a mercenary pike regiment, where close-order drill and movement by the numbers are everything, because any hole in the wall of pikeheads is disastrous. With that background, he should have been a drill master, a noble pinhead with a liking for showy horseflesh and brightly polished everything.

Instead, he'd been the one to insist that the auxilia wore dull green and brown, and that the sisters browned their armour with vinegar. Not so much as a polished button among the lot of them. And here he was, mounted on a workaday cob, wearing dulled mail and grey-green leather, like mine. Even the banner that I carried to justify my position as ensign was muted. He had approved – no, required – that his own pennon, his family arms of a silver tower on a scarlet ground, be toned down to grey on dull maroon. Most knights would be studying ways of making themselves more conspicuous.

I twisted myself in the saddle and looked back at the column of sisters of the Order that was following us, and not a gleam reflected, for all that the morning sun was in their eyes. They looked grim and businesslike enough, well mounted, with cavalry blades if they needed them, but they, too, would fight on their feet for preference. And they

would fight awfully well, using the weapon that was the Order's own, the two-handed poleaxe-cum-halberd they called a *rhamfia.* Sister Informer, who commanded them, brought up the rear under the banner of the Order, the rose in glory. That, too, would disappear once we breasted the slope. Sister Informer and Silvus were as one on the subject of hitting the enemy when he wasn't looking, preferably before he knew we were anywhere near. Then the pack train, then the rearguard. I looked further back, to the battlements of the castle, and I thought I could still see a tiny flicker of white. Arienne was still waving her kerchief.

'If you ride much further with your chin on your shoulder, your horse will start wondering which way to go. Kindly give him some indication of your wishes, if you please. He can't read your mind. Not yet, anyway.'

I turned myself about, checking with one hand that Arienne's favour, a ragged strip of dull blue cloth, was still securely tied around my upper arm. Silvus glanced at me. 'Your seat is improving,' he allowed. 'A year or so ago you'd have fallen off if you'd tried that.'

'I was thinking …'

'Commendable, in an ensign. Can be overdone, though.'

I ignored that. 'You once told me that a gentleman wore plate armour and the best of everything.' I indicated his equipment, and mine. I was wearing auxiliary kit – browned mail, javelins, sling. He looked just as subdued as I did. 'You've

changed your tune. A little.' His eyebrow lifted. 'Ser,' I added, hurriedly.

'Indeed.' He shifted his weight forward, to give his horse more purchase on the slope, which was steepening. The peak of the pass lay just past this turn in the track, and the castle was already hidden by the mountainside. 'Recall the circumstances then, though. We were a contingent sent to Ys to fulfil a vow, so we were supposed to be obvious. And also very knightly and chivalrous, and there were other knights with us. I had just been given the accolade – again – and I was for a while touchy about the fact. Touchy for your sake, too.'

'And now?'

He shrugged. 'Things change. Our job on this jaunt isn't to make a show of keeping a knightly vow. It's to sneak up on the enemy, hit him hard while he's looking in the other direction, and then run away and hide. Running is easier if you ride light. Hide-and-sneak is easier if you don't catch the eye.'

'As a method, it's less than honourable,' I remarked. I didn't disapprove: quite the reverse. I was just exploring what Silvus thought about it.

He was as sure as I was. 'More useful, though. And it is also our job, having hurt Nathan and slowed him up as much as we can, to bring this command safely back. Quite apart from the auxilia all having wives and children, a fifth of the fighting strength of the Order is riding with us. We can't lose them, however willing they might be to fall in battle for the Lady. They'll be needed on the walls.'

I nodded. I'd thought as much, but it was pleasing to be thus reassured. I was, I realised, becoming more reluctant to die, not less. I had more to live for these days, and most of it was back in that castle, watching me ride away.

But I'd still rather die than live in a world ruled by Nathan and populated with his creatures.

'Long stage today, shorter one tomorrow,' said Silvus, breaking into what were becoming gloomy thoughts. 'Once we're out of the mountains, we'll do daily drills working the units together. The auxilia to sting the enemy and then run away, the sisters to hit the pursuers once the latter have blown their horses. Or we could trap them in between us.'

I shook myself. It was my job to find ways of making Silvus's wishes into reality. 'They'll need to cooperate at a distance …'

'Yes. So we need signals. I thought flags or mirrors. We'll mostly be attacking at dawn or dusk, if it's a camp. That would mean …'

ASTA

'A hand taller, Squire de Teska. And just look at the condition he's put on!' The groom was trying to sound enthusiastic and pleased; maybe he really was, but it was because he liked horses and money, not because he liked what we were doing. He never spoke directly to me, and I knew he disliked me. When things weren't going well and I got testy, I could sense his fear, as well. Folk don't like the Dark.

Teska grunted, and spared the pony a glance. Widow Pila did neither. I tried to watch all of them, the pony, the groom and my minders.

'Too slow,' said Teska. 'Three days, and all we've got is a slightly larger and much showier pony. The colour is all very well, but I was looking for a warhorse by now.'

'I'm doing my best,' I said, and cringed at the whine in my speech.

'I hope so.' Teska's own voice was bleak. 'I have to show His Highness something, very shortly now.' He said *His Highness* as some men say *the gods.*

'Getting something to grow is … much harder. Everything has to work together, bones, muscles, blood … everything. It's not like changing his colour, or curing him of the croup.'

'Mm.' Teska was still staring at me. That was bad. I could hear the faint crackle of the faggots at my feet.

'But I've a surprise.' I hoped I could distract him.

'What?' Teska sounded like a person who didn't like surprises.

'You said you wanted a steed suitable for a prince. Tall, milk-white, golden mane and tail, beautiful paces, fast.'

'I know what I said.'

I grinned, trying to sound confident. 'But every

prince has one of those.' I nodded at the groom. 'Lead him round.'

The mane had been the easiest part, and I had grown it long, curling on the animal's forehead. Now I parted the silky golden hair so they could see.

Teska's eyebrows climbed for a moment. 'Interesting,' he allowed. 'It will have to be longer than that. But interesting.'

Widow Pila sniffed. I didn't spare her a glance. 'How many princes can say that their personal mount is a unicorn?' I asked.

'None, and not our Prince, either. That beast's barely fourteen hands, even now, and that will never do. I said a tall horse. The Prince needs to be seen.' Teska was returning to his complaint like a dog to vomit. 'We've three more days, no more, and then we'll have to return.'

'I can do it, but I'll have to take up some more *mana.*' The word came more easily to me now.

'If you say so. We'll go now.'

'It's dark. Been dark for hours.'

'There are such things as lanterns. There's nothing about the dark that prevents you taking up mana. Then you can do another hour in here before you go to bed. We'll start again in the morning.'

I wondered, as I squelched off in the cold rain with my escort, whether this wasn't proper, after all. Off I go in the dark to work myself further into the Dark. It was appropriate. As right as it was wrong.

As wrong as it was right. As I let the power flow

into me I almost giggled, and realised that I was getting a little light-headed. Drunk, almost. Drunk on the power.

I was trembling again when I came back from the stream, like Sart when he had the shakes bad. The power was more than October ale, more than wine. It was like the *sandast* they sold at Petey's place, to those who wanted it and had money. Ale is all right, wine can be fun, though it'll rot your brain in time. *Sandast* gets you so you don't care about anything else.

It was just so … wonderful. To see it in my mind, and then watch it happen. The power quivered in my blood and bones, and I hardly noticed the cold and the rain on the way back. The stable was warm, and the pony was peacefully asleep standing up. Fine. I could work with him in his dreams. Dreams about size and power, about mighty limbs and effortless running on the wide plains, of the herd he would control, the mares he would own. I had in truth been dragging my feet because I didn't really want to do this. Teska had reminded me of the rules by which I now lived, and would live by forever. I settled down on a hay bale to work, and the groom watched me for a time, with two bored soldiers. After a while I forgot they were there.

By the time we moved out, he was … satisfactory. Somewhere in the back of my mind I knew that I'd shortened his life, for all that he was lovely to look at. Tall, dainty head with its delicate spiral horn held regally high, beautifully conformed,

coat a glossy ivory, mane and tail sparkling gold. He glowed like moonlight, and moved as lightly as the breeze in the new grass. I'd kept the temperament and easy paces of the pony he'd once been. He was … nice. Unfortunately, he was false, and the falsehood would kill him. It wasn't that I'd made any errors, so far as I knew, even though I was working very much in the dark. (In the dark. Now that was a thought.) No, it was just that he wasn't meant to be this way, and he … well, we'd make it up to him. No more pit work for him. He'd be pampered all his days.

And I'd learned a great deal. The next job would be swifter and more sure. I was getting better at this. But it was a shame to have done this to him, all the same.

He didn't even have to move on his own feet. To preserve his condition, Teska had him carried in a cart of his own. He'd been interested in an apple, and was quiet enough to stand peacefully while the fields passed slowly by to the plod of other hooves and the creak of the harness that he was so used to. I said that I needed to continue to work on him, and so I sat with him in the open as the miles unreeled, staring at my craft. At what I'd done.

Oh, I did work on him, too, some. I strengthened him where I could, bone and heart and everything else, but I knew much of it was too subtle for me. Soon, in a year, maybe, something would break down. But what was the life of a pit pony to me? I was a mage. A Dark mage.

So mostly I just sat, watching him as the guards watched me. They watched all the more carefully now that they knew what I was. The worst of it was that he was used to me now, and he liked having me there. He trusted me. Trusted *me*! Yes. That was the worst part.

By the time we reached Tenabra again, the Prince and his army had left. They'd moved on up the river, and the Prince had left orders that we were to follow as quickly as possible. So Teska merely picked up fresh guards, bundled us aboard a barge, and set off in the gathering dusk of the same day that we arrived. That night I slept properly for the first time since Etterden, and still my dreams were full of sorrow and pain.

When the old guards were paid off, they were tipped. I saw the coin passing, and I wondered why Teska had done it; he wasn't the man to put out a groat more than the amount contracted. He would only do such a thing if he felt it was absolutely necessary.

And that was the reason, of course. It was necessary, from where Teska stood. A few extra pennies to drink ale in a tavern and tell their adventures. And to wash away the taste that comes of breathing the same air as a Dark mage. A few extra quarts of ale, a few more people to hear the tale. The word would be spreading, soon enough. Teska looked at me, and his eyes closed and opened slowly again.

The river was high in spring spate. There was no trouble with sandbanks or bars, but the current

was strong against us. We plodded north, past the city walls and then on into country I had never seen, bare brown fields from the autumn ploughing just beginning to show a fringe of green, sheep, cattle on the common and the fallow. Overhead flew the wildfowl, heading for the mountain lakes in the north, which would be melting now, their ice water feeding the river. The bargee was unsmiling and silent, though he ducked his head in an embarrassed way whenever he met my eye. Probably thought I'd blast or curse him as soon as look at him.

There were times when I wished I could.

WILL

'Smell it?'

I sniffed, and so did Silvus. Yes. It was smoke on the night breeze. The sergeant of scouts held up a wetted finger.

'Fluky, but from the east and a little north. They're camped off the track, I reckon, trying to be clever.' He sniffed again. 'And that's bacon frying, or I'm a Nord. A couple thousand paces off, maybe.'

Silvus nodded. A camp, for sure.

The conversation had been conducted in mutters. Now it ceased to be carried on by voice at all. Silvus pointed his shuttered lantern rearwards and opened the shutter once, twice. A minute later Sister Informer and Master Rookwood slid up.

Silvus made hand signals. The scout and his section disappeared over the next rise, and we settled down to wait.

The last light faded and stars appeared, while I counted heartbeats. Five hundred. A thousand. Two. Silence all around, except for the wind in the leaves, the creak and shrill of crickets. Our own bivouac was still and fireless, and it stayed that way, downwind from us where we crouched amid the scrub on our hillock. Word had passed back, and the silence settled even more firmly. We were alert, and expecting him, but I still didn't pick the scout who'd been sent back until he arose from the bushes in the hollow before us, not skylining himself.

More hand signals. The enemy was cavalry. Four fires, tents and horse lines for forty. Silvus replied. Search for a detached party. They might be smart enough to set up an ambush of their own, or at least leave a picket out.

A longer delay. The scouts were being careful. No doubt they'd get quicker as they got more practice. Just at the moment, I was happy to be slow and sure.

Finally. Another muttered conversation. Silvus nodded, turned, and gave orders. This business would be on foot – they'd be sure to hear horses coming up, and after all they were only a squadron or so in strength. I wondered where their regiment was. Not in touch, at any rate, or we'd have found them by now. Or they'd have found us. Careless of them. It would cost them dearly.

The arrangements were working well. The auxiliaries moved out in small groups, each one guided by a scout. They'd surround the camp. The sisters split into two companies, and worked around to the right and left. They'd cut off any break-outs. We, the command group, moved off after them.

The last two hundred paces were very slow and silent. We could see their fires, and shapes moving around them, when we halted. They'd camped in a hollow out of the wind, a natural thing to do, but stupid. Hadn't they heard they were in a war?

The orders were that the auxilia section that had the furthest to travel – the one that had to get right around to the other side – was to shoot first. I wasn't aware that they had begun, until I saw one of the guards fall. He'd been leaning on his spear, closer to the campfire than he should have been. Bivouac guards should be outside the camp perimeter and in cover themselves. Nathan's cavalry had not done well, on the whole, so far. No doubt they'd learn better, in due course.

This group wouldn't get the chance, though. The nasty thing about slings is that they're almost silent – you can only hear the evil little buzz if a slug passes close to your ear – and so it took the cavalry some time before they realised they were under attack. Even then, they thought that there were only a few peasants out there in the dark, and anyway their first reaction was straight out of cavalryman's instinct. They made for their horses and tried to mount and ride the attackers down.

That only made larger targets out of them. By the time Silvus blew his whistle – two short and one long – and the sisters stormed into the camp, there were only a dozen or so of them still standing. Only four had the wit to bolt before the attack closed to sword's length, and they were dragged down on the perimeter. It was all over in three minutes, and I hadn't done a thing except sit and watch in perfect safety and comfort. Arienne would have been pleased. She had been very eloquent on the subject of not sticking my fool neck out.

Silvus was certainly pleased, too, although you'd have had trouble seeing it unless you knew him well. He and Sister Informer made an excellent team. He strolled into the circle of firelight to question the prisoners, a languid aristocrat to the life, while she all but foamed at the mouth and twitched with holy rage. For my part, I had pulled a knife from my belt, and now I started heating the blade in the fire, flicking glances at them from time to time.

There were ten or so of them. Mostly young, including the only officer, an ensign about my own age. There was also a hard-bitten sergeant with a hatchet face, only lightly wounded. Best to separate him straightaway.

Silvus clearly agreed. He nodded in polite fashion towards the veteran, and two sisters pounced on the latter and hauled him to his feet. I turned the blade over in the fire and stared broodingly at him.

'Lord Corwell's regiment, I see,' drawled Silvus,

flicking a finger at the man's badge, scarlet helmet-plume and breeches. 'A fine body of men. Did very well in the Wend uprising. Burned down more temples and raped more women than any two others. This one would have been there – he's old enough.'

Sister Informer's eyes were showing white. 'Then the Lady's vengeance is on him,' she said, relishing it.

Silvus shrugged. 'If you must,' he allowed. 'There's an officer here, anyway.'

She smiled in unhealthy glee, and gestured. They hauled him away into the darkness while the prisoners glanced at each other and the auxilia stood around, sombre, unsmiling. They had been absolutely forbidden to smile. Within moments, shrieks followed from the same direction, steadily rising, each one followed by a chorus of catcalls and mocking female laughter.

Silvus smiled, in urbane and apologetic fashion. 'I do beg your pardon,' he said to the young ensign. 'When one is forced to work with fanatics, what can one do? I am Silvus de Castro. May I know whom I have the honour of addressing?'

'Alphan de Pesquales, traitor.' The young man did not lack spirit. Brains, yes. That he lacked. Silvus's eyebrow cocked.

'De Pesquales? Indeed. The cadet branch of the de Corwells themselves. And from the annulet on your badge you must be the second son. I knew your uncle Maurice well. We served together at Hoppelin Moor, and elsewhere.'

Another blood-curdling scream split the night, followed by a series of high-pitched yelps – 'Don't ... don't ... don't' – and more laughter.

Silvus ignored it, as a well-bred man ignores all unfortunate noises. 'I trust your honoured uncle is well?' he asked, solicitously.

The young man spluttered. 'You will find out, you swine, if you take your scraggy collection of ill-matched assassins but a league down the road. He will avenge me.'

'I doubt that he will have occasion.' The airy insouciance dropped away from Silvus's voice. 'All right. Take him away. We'll question the rest separately.'

They didn't know much. We already knew all we needed to. By midnight we had all we were going to get, terrified as they were. A decently proffered bribe had done the rest.

They were reassembled, the veteran sergeant included. He was gagged but otherwise undamaged. One of the auxilia guards was hoarse, though.

Silvus gave orders. 'After they've buried their comrades, we can send them west.' He counted heads. 'Ten of them. Keep the ensign and sergeant separated, and they can walk. Tie them together. Five for an escort.'

I watched them go. 'We can't afford too many of those detachments,' I said, stating the obvious. 'Providing escorts will bleed us dry. Even when they get to the castle, they'll only be more mouths to feed. Nathan will never exchange, not when one behind our walls is worth ten of his outside.'

Silvus was watching them. He didn't turn. 'Yes. But I won't be the one to cry 'no quarter', all the same. And once we're in contact with their main body, we'll not have to bother. We can just leave their wounded where they lie – they'll slow Nathan up.'

'And we are in contact now.'

'Not quite. In fact, we're a little closer than I'd like. A stray patrol might find us – will find us, if Maurice de Corwell thinks to enquire what's become of his nephew. Fortunately, he's as thick as purser's paint, is Maurice. A league away east-wards. Imagine. And de Corwell's Horse are heavy cavalry. Using them on picket duty must mean that Nathan's short of lights. They won't be far from the main body.'

'And the nephew said they were on the road, too.'

'Good point. That was kind of him. Gives us a bearing. So we should be able to pull back north a way, let them go past, and then hit them from an unexpected direction.'

'And Nathan can't chase us too far that way. Takes him off his line.'

'Yes. Let's do it.'

ASTA

We passed Conflans in the night. Teska was wasting no time, and the letter and authority over the Prince's seal got us through rapidly. I began to

think that Prince Nathan must know what he was about, the way people jumped to do his bidding. Even his name and seal at the bottom of a paper made guard sergeants stiffen and watch-commanders turn all courteous and helpful.

So all I remember of Conflans is the lights on the water, and the desperate hustle and hurry. Not only our hurry, but of the river port itself. It was now the supply base for a large army. Safe conduct or no, our barge was badly needed for hauling more provisions further upstream, so it was tied up to a dock and a cargo of rations – beer and salt meat in barrels, beans in sacks, grain – was taken on, loaded by a shambling gang that was working in leg irons. I watched, and Teska watched too, twitching with impatience. When one of the shackled porters fell and didn't rise in spite of blows from the reversed whips of the overseers, he showed only irritation.

'They use slaves up here?' I asked.

'No. Convicts,' growled Teska. 'And at the rate they work we'll be here all night.' He stumped off to have a word with the dockmaster, leaving me to Widow Pila and two soldiers. One of them was watching the loading operation, and I thought that he didn't like what he saw. He shook his head and muttered something to his mate, who shrugged.

Interesting. Could be that not everyone approved of Princc Nathan. I hoped not, anyway – any that I found would be to the good. Could be that I'd need a few of them around me, some day.

I memorised his face, but that was all I could do

for then. Another hour, and we were away. The barge was now deep laden and the current swift, but they'd changed the horses, and we were moving fast. I went below to sleep, with the widow tagging along, of course. There was a sort of cupboard down there, which was called a cabin, with two shelves, which were called bunks. It had no door, only a curtain, and that curtain was in sight of both the soldiers on watch. The two others slept on deck. I went off to sleep as innocent as a lamb.

Morning, and we pulled into a landing that was built into the stream on the western side. There was a muddy track leading down to it, and a harassed gang of labourers was shovelling river pebbles into the ruts, trying to build it up. They were having a hard time of it. Wagons and carts were lined up to take loads off the river craft as they tied up, carters were cracking whips and bellowing for right of way, a line of porters like the one at Conflans was working with the same stumbling urgency.

Teska didn't wait. He waved his paper and got us jumped up the line, charged off into the milling crowd of officials as soon as we tied up, and came back in quarter of an hour with saddle horses and mules. He stood tapping one foot as we disembarked, but there was one delay that he had to tolerate.

I'd named the unicorn Moonlight. As a pit pony he hadn't had a name, only a number, and he rated better than that now. He was led out of the pen on the deck where he'd been, greeted me with

a push of his nose, and stepped on to the landing with the sure-footedness of the pony he'd been. The pale sunlight gleamed from his coat and sparkled on the golden spiral of his horn.

Work stopped. Everybody stared. Teska seized the moment.

'Way, there!' he shouted, and his eyes closed and opened. 'Way for the mage Asta and her gift to His Highness the Prince!'

The pause might have lasted a dozen heart-beats. Then everybody shuffled back and a lane opened in the crowd. I clambered up on the mule that one of the soldiers was holding, and Teska put Moonlight's leading rein in my hand, just so everyone would know it was me he was talking about. Then he mounted, the escort closed around me, and we moved off, everyone watching me. A murmur rippled through the people as we moved through them. Nobody cheered. I rode with my head up, staring over their heads, because I knew nobody would meet my eye. Moonlight ambled obediently after me, all unaware of how he had condemned me. Fair's fair, I suppose. Now we had condemned each other.

CHAPTER

WILL

Armies have stomachs. Lots of them. In this case, to the number of about twenty thousand. Kicking them in their stomachs is a good way to make them fold up, groaning – if you kick hard enough, that is. So we were just winding up to plant a foot in the belly of Prince Nathan's army.

We had a good opportunity to do it. The belly was large and probably unprotected. Large, because the moors are uncultivated, almost. There's no crops, no farms. A couple of travellers, living rough and moving fast, might manage to eat off the country, taking the odd fish from the streams, fern roots, berries, occasional wild goats. But such things bear no relation at all to the needs of twenty

thousand men. Nathan had to supply them, and the supplies they needed amounted to several dozen wagonloads a day. The more troops he used to guard his line of supply, the fewer he'd have to breach the walls of Waycastle. He knew that as well as we did, and he'd skimp on the guards. That was why his belly would be left unprotected. Probably. We thought.

If we thought right, Nathan had made a bad mistake. I hoped he was about to find that out.

There was only the one road, too, which made the job easier. All we really had to do was to find a suitable place on it, and then wait for a supply column.

We'd slipped past Nathan in the night, and were now to the east of him, having looped around to find that road. That part hadn't been hard. To find the road, that is. The marching – well, that had been hard. Silvus had been chivvying us along urgently, and the moors were soggy and unfriendly, a series of fells and dales covered with scrub, with bogs in the hollows. We had to cover our tracks as much as possible, too, which made it harder. I was sore, and I was prepared to bet I wasn't the only one.

He wanted safety, did Silvus, and he was certain that safety involved being far, far away when Nathan learned of the fate of his cavalry patrol. That young cavalry ensign's Uncle Maurice might be as dim as a rush dip, but Nathan wasn't. He'd react, and quickly. We'd kicked over a hornet's nest, up in front of the army. Now we needed to do it

again, in the rear. We'd marched half that night, then rested hidden during the day, and then marched all the next night, reaching this position an hour before dawn.

I scrabbled up a tussocky hill with Silvus, leaving my horse behind to crop, and eased my head over the skyline. The moon was up, just past the full, and I could see plainly enough. We were overlooking the road, the old road we'd travelled before from the valley of the Wydem to the pass at Oriment.

When Silvus and I had seen it last, it was a faint trace across the country, discerned by following a line of slightly lower scrub and looking for a suspicion of a notch on the next hill. Nathan's pioneers had made it far more obvious. They'd cut the scrub and hardened and rolled the surface. They'd built up the crumbled culverts again, and used cut stone to face the bottoms of the fords. Then Nathan had taken his army along it, foot, horse and siege engines. By the time we came looking for it, you could find it a mile off downwind, going by the horse droppings alone. The scout had reported in an hour before, and we'd corrected the line of our march, following his recommendations.

Good man, that scout. Had an eye for country. He brought us to a place where the road curved slightly and dipped to cross a stream. For a few hundred paces, before it climbed the next slope, the hills were on both sides. Ideal.

Silvus called his unit commanders in.

'Very well. This will do nicely. Master Rookwood,

would you dispose your company on both sides, dispersed and twenty paces off the road? Horse-holders one hundred paces to the rear, behind the skyline. Water the horses and feed them, so they keep quiet. You'll need to line two hundred paces, from the stream to the top of the slope. Shoot on my signal. Be alert for it, but apart from that the men may relax and rest once they're in position. Sister, I think we keep your company together, this time. Right about here, behind this hill. Dismounted action, engage on my signal, but leave one section with its horses here in reserve, ready to mount. Off-saddle and rest until dawn, but be ready to move after that.'

He looked about at them in the dim light. 'This time we need not worry about fugitives. The more wild tales that circulate, the better. We ambush the first suitable column that passes. We cut them to pieces, then charge over the remains before they can organise. We pick up what supplies we need, we burn everything else, and we depart. Rapidly. If unexpected visitors turn up, the reserve will be used to cover the retreat, which will be to the northwards. But to reduce the probability of that happening, I don't want the whole thing to last more than ten minutes.'

They nodded and slipped away. I made calculations.

If I were Nathan's quartermaster – and I was grateful I wasn't, because he had a nightmare of a job, and it was about to get worse – I'd marshal my wagons into groups of maybe twenty at a time and

escort each group with as many cavalry troopers as I could lay my hands on. Two such groups a day would keep the army fed, just about.

But that wouldn't be the whole of it, not by any means. By the time the army reached the pass at Oriment, in a week or so, it would be over a hundred leagues from its base, about two weeks' travel for a laden wagon on a road like this. So Nathan would need to have twenty-eight groups – over five hundred wagons – on the road at any one time to bring him his supplies. If each group had a twenty-man escort, that's four full regiments of horse used up just in the train guards. Frightening.

And that's without considering fodder for the horses. No doubt they'd be carrying as much of that with them as they could. But there weren't enough wagons in the Riverland to carry the whole needs of the army for the whole march in one lift. It could only be done if they could come and go.

I settled down to wait, while Silvus stretched himself out on a flat piece of ground. He wrapped himself in the covercloth cloak that he'd been given by the underfolk. It was waterproof and warm, and he was asleep in minutes. I watched him for a while, and then drew the straight, cross-hilted sword that had been my own special gift. It was a better weapon than I deserved, the best blade I ever handled in my life. My sharpening stone was in my purse, and I had oil in a flask. Sharpening a piece of steel as good as that was a satisfactory task, requiring close attention and persistence, but not thought. And who was to

know? It might have been worthwhile. I might need it.

ASTA

We thought it was a campfire at first. In fact, I didn't notice it at all, and the first I knew was when the sergeant of the guards came trotting up to talk to Teska.

Teska was right behind me, on a mule – he never got out of hand's-reach of me. He wasn't any better on a horse than me, though; we both needed something that was smooth in its paces and close to the ground. Widow Pila was on a jenny, and the escort was from some regiment of horse-soldiers or other. Their mounts were big and ill-tempered. They didn't like the mules, so when the sergeant talked to Teska, he had to lean over in the saddle and jag at his bit to stop his horse from biting. I was idly working on the brute's temper, to irritate him worse. Teska had to crane his neck to stare up at the sergeant, and that annoyed Teska as much as the ballet his mule was dancing.

'You see the smoke, sir?' asked the sergeant.

'Yes,' snapped Teska. 'What of it?'

The sergeant's horse frisked and had to be curbed. 'Orders are no stopping during the day,' he explained. 'There shouldn't be a fire up there at this time in the morning.'

'Oh?' said Teska. He shaded his eyes with his hands and stared, trying to look knowledgeable.

'Yes,' said the sergeant, and no more. He watched Teska, sour amusement on his face.

Teska had waved his paper at the harassed officer in charge of transport at the landing, had demanded escort immediately, and had generally thrown his weight about. He got an escort, all right, but not with anyone's goodwill. I watched the sergeant's face again, as he in turn watched Teska. *Your problem, mate,* he was thinking, *and the best of luck to you.* I didn't know what he was thinking from using the gift, mind. I couldn't read his mind. But I had no need of any special talent to know, either.

Teska knew it, too. He stared at the single column of black smoke rising slantwise on the wind a couple of miles ahead of us and chewed his cheek. It was an obstacle between him and his god. I enjoyed the sight, and savoured his uncertainty.

But suddenly his brow contracted, and his face, which had been merely scowling, flattened out in alarm. I turned, and saw that the single streak of smoke had become several, and that they were blending together into a thick black cloud before shredding away on the wind.

The sergeant looked up, saw it too, and he dropped the charade that he was waiting politely for orders. He turned in the saddle and filled his lungs.

'Form on me by fours! Open order! March, you dozy morons! Foulds, Lidlee, get forward to scout. Loomis, you stay with the gentleman and the …

ladies. Sir, I recommend you dismount and ready your weapons. And your magic, if you think it'll help.' A contemptuous glance at me.

Teska nodded and got off the mule. Every man to his trade, he'd be thinking, no doubt. 'Where are you going?' he asked the soldier. He grabbed my arm, in case I might try to run away.

'We'll scout it out. There may be a fight still going on, or we might catch them, if we're quick. At any rate, we'll stay between them and you. If you see me coming back at the gallop, though, run like hell. It's not likely their horses will be fresh enough to chase us far.'

Teska nodded again. 'Very well.'

The sergeant nodded, too, a sharp little dip of his head. He tightened his belt to take the weight of his mail and reached around to sling his shield in front of him. Then he took up his lance, which had been riding in a boot by the saddle. Only his visor stayed up, so that he could see, and he could snap that shut in an instant.

He gestured. 'Forward ho!' And as his twenty troopers got into motion, 'Trot!'

The escort moved out in a column, two men out ahead, and they jingled off down the road towards that ominous pall of smoke. Teska watched them calmly enough, I thought. Merely impatient. It would, I realised, take quite a bit to panic Teska, so long as Nathan was pleased with him. He'd been cool enough to knock me out with a dead man coming for him, before.

'We'll do as your sergeant suggested,' he said to

the trooper who'd been left behind. 'There's a stream just by here. If you water the beasts, we can watch.' He didn't say who or what they would be watching. Not only me, I hoped. 'Rub them down, too, if you can. We may need them as fresh as possible.'

I said nothing. There was nothing to say, and anyway, I was scanning the sky.

The bird in the wood above Etterden had given me an idea. I looked up into the morning sky and searched for another mind, a bird that could see what was going on up ahead. And I found one, a bright, sharp spark of awareness high in the blue above. A kite, quartering the ground beneath, and she was interested in the smoke, too. Or rather in the ground just around it. There was carrion there.

She wasn't interested in the men or the horses she could see moving towards the fires. They were hale, moving easily. I looked at them through her eyes, trying to get my bearings. Everything looked different, colours muted and dim, but every movement as vivid as lightning. Nevertheless, in spite of her excellent eyesight, the kite didn't understand the things she saw in the same way as I did. It took a long time for me to decide that those were our escort, picking their way carefully towards the smoke.

She was much more interested in the dead horses and dead men around the burning wagons, but she was wary of the fires, and hadn't made up her mind yet. I counted. A dozen horses, the wagon teams dead in the traces; a few dead men.

Others hiding in the scrub. Ten or more fires – I wasn't quite sure. But they were certainly bonfires – burning wagons, dead horses. Clearly, someone didn't like what they were doing out here.

Who was that someone? Those someones, rather. I told the kite that there were more kills away from the wagons, and she spiralled out to look for them, drifting north on the morning breeze.

There. Another party, mounted, heading away from the road, moving fast in a column, and already further from the ambush site than we were. More than us, too. Couple of hundred at least. I couldn't tell how many. The kite's mind dismissed it as a herd. Herds didn't interest her. But that was Prince Nathan's enemy, right there.

'What can you see?' Teska's hand was on my shoulder.

I jumped, then shrugged. 'I can't see anything. Even the gift is no use for looking through a hill.'

No good. He just looked thunderous. 'That's a lie. Lies are falsehoods, and falseness will get you that slow fire in the marketplace. I know what you were doing – I've eyes, and I had eyes at Etterden. Now what can you see through the eyes of that blasted bird or beast or whatever it is?' The fingers dug into my coat until I yelped.

'Nothing we don't know already,' I squeaked. 'There's some wagons been ambushed. The attackers are long gone, though.'

'How many of the enemy?'

'I'm not sure ...'

'Don't lie to me again. How many?'

'Couple of hundred, I suppose. How can I know? The bird can't count.'

'And they're long gone?'

'Yes. Moving fast, from their dust. The sergeant won't catch them. He'd be sorry if he did, anyway.'

'Tell me about them.'

'What's to know? The bird isn't interested in …'

'Make it interested. Get closer.'

'I can't …'

'Yes, you can. This is the first test of your usefulness to the Prince. Don't fail it.'

The hand that gripped my shoulder pulled me around to stare at the sky where the kite was only a fleck, rising slightly on the cool wind. I found its mind with mine, and suddenly it felt that it should investigate the riders to the north. It drifted that way on the currents that it knew so well.

I shut my eyes. As the bird moved away, its mind became fainter, and I had to concentrate fiercely to keep the sights it was seeing in view. There they were. I frowned and as I sifted details from the picture, I spoke them aloud. 'A couple of hundred, as I said. Men riding mules and horses. Moving at the best pace they can keep up. Some are in mail, about half … I can tell by the …'

Teska grunted. 'Armour. They'll be sisters, then.'

Sisters? I thought.

Teska spoke again, still gripping me. 'Look for a banner, a device, anything that might tell us who they are.'

'The hawk can't see.'

'I thought hawks had good eyes.' His voice was heavy with sarcasm.

'For movement in the grass. Not for this. It's never seen such a thing, and it doesn't know …'

'Get closer, then.'

'I don't think …'

'I didn't ask you what you thought. Do it.' The hand pinched my shoulder.

She was very reluctant to go lower, and she was far off by now, and out of sight. I could still feel her mind and see what she saw, but my control was slipping. All I could do was to suggest to her that there was meat being dropped, and she did edge a little further down. And yes, there was a pennon, a fluttering little flag on a lance one of the riders was carrying. And another, a square banner, dull blue.

I pushed harder, and the bird drifted closer. The little flag was dull red, and there was a thing like a barrel on it, grey. The other flag had a flower …

WILL

Silvus's head swung up. He'd been riding with his chin on his chest, glum, because he didn't like knocking over helpless targets, no matter how much it benefited us. The wagoneers and their small escort, taken totally by surprise, had been simply targets. That part hadn't lasted even a minute.

He hated cutting down horses, too. We'd taken the best of them, but we needed no more, and there was no sense in simply handing the rest back to Nathan. Those *rhamfias* the sisters carried were poleaxes, too. They'd used them.

So Silvus had been glum, riding away, for all that we had no casualties beyond two lightly wounded, and there was twenty ton or so of Nathan's supplies that would never reach him. But now he looked up sharply, and his nose wrinkled as if he were passing a wayside gibbet.

That was the only use he made of his own gift. Yes, he had the talent, but weakly. He'd sworn to his father he wouldn't use it. He loathes magic, but can tell when someone else is using it nearby. It smells foul to him. I always want to sniff when he senses it, but I never smell anything.

I was carrying the banner. It was just to tell the scouts spread out ahead where the commander was. Same for Sister Informer. Silvus darted a swift glance at it, and then nodded minutely.

'Don't look up,' he said. 'There's a hawk … no, a kite. Behind you, to the left and about sixty feet up. Someone is using it.'

I sucked in air.

'Don't look,' said Silvus again. 'Move up closer to me and try to keep me covered from that angle.'

His hand moved stealthily down to his saddle, where his crossbow hung from a hook. He had to span it, and that took both hands, and then he had to place a bolt on the slide. I tried to keep just behind and to the left of him, and was thankful

that my horse was taller, to be up to my greater weight. Thankful also that Silvus was as good a horseman as he was. He did it all, guiding his horse with his knees. Then he nodded.

'Fall back a little,' he said, and I reined in. 'Signal halt and walk on five more paces.'

We pulled up. Silvus walked his horse forward, as if to investigate something in the path. Then he pulled up, too. In a flash he was off, on the side further from the bird. As his feet hit the ground he turned, the crossbow came up smoothly, paused a moment, and then came the *twang-whoosh* of the release.

ASTA

They'd halted. I wondered why, but that was all. Then, suddenly, there was a terrible, overpowering pain, a blackness came pouring down, and that was all I knew.

Shock. Sunlight. Cold wetness. They'd thrown water over me. I spluttered and clawed it out of my eyes. Teska was muttering. He saw I was awake.

'This is no time to have a fainting fit. What happened?'

Even then I couldn't say at once. They'd laid me flat in the grass by the road, and he came and stood between me and the sun. He stood there, face as hard as the boulders on the hillside.

'I ... they ...' and then I understood, all at once,

and tears came. My face was already wet, though.

'What? Come on, out with it!'

I looked up at him, my sight swimming. Something about him made my mind contract into a tight hard ball. When the words came, they came steadily enough. 'They killed the bird. Shot her, I think.'

'Blast!' He glanced away to the north. 'Is there another?'

I made a show of peering at the horizon, wiping my eyes. 'No. None that I can see that can also see them.'

'Hmph. Well.' He stumped over to his mule, which was being held by the soldier. 'We might as well get on the road again. You can tell me what you saw as we go.'

Widow Pila watched. They were all around me, and there was nowhere to hide. I picked myself up and wiped my face with my sleeve. The man brought my mule, and we mounted and moved on.

'Now,' said Teska. 'Tell me.'

'What about?'

'Don't play-act. Who were they? What did you see?' Again he was looking at me. I groped for an answer.

'You asked me about banners. Well, there was a big square one, blue, with a white flower in a blaze on it.'

'The Order. So it is them. You said half were riders in armour?' I nodded. 'A hundred sisters, then. A fair part of their strength. And the others?'

'Men, I think. Yes, men. The bird couldn't tell

the difference and didn't care, but I remember they had beards. Not in armour. Carrying short spears.'

'For throwing, perhaps. Light troops, skirmishers. I didn't realise the Order had them. Looks like they're changing their methods.' He contemplated it for a moment. 'Good intelligence. The Prince will be pleased with that, at least. More pleased still if there's anything else. Was anyone wearing coat-armour?'

'What's that?'

'A badge with arms on it, like the shields around the gate in Tenabra. No? Or regimental colours, like that?' He indicated the plume on the soldier's helmet. 'Or a sash, anything at all like that?'

'No. In fact they were all dressed very plainly. Grey and green, and rusty armour.'

He grunted again. 'Not rusty. Not the Order. It's been browned, to hide better.' His eyes narrowed. 'Another new fighting method.' He rode a hundred paces on, contemplating. Then, 'Anything else? Did you see the commander?'

I shrugged. 'I don't know,' I said. He turned a sharp, intolerant eye on me. 'I really *don't* know. Unless he was the one carrying the flag.'

'The Order flag, you mean? That wouldn't be carried by a man.'

'No, the other one. The little one.'

'What other one? What little one? Why didn't you say before?' Teska's eye turned blank and sharp, both at once, like a mastiff about to make up its mind whether to leap for the throat or not. Like Fred. And Fred was mad.

I went cold. 'I only just remembered ...' I trembled out, and the eyes hooded over for a moment.

A moment more. Then, 'What was it like?' he demanded. 'The little flag.'

I closed my eyes. It made it easier to see, and to speak. 'It was red, I think. Yes, red. Dull red like rust.'

'What else?'

'It had a barrel on it. Grey, cream, something like that.'

'A barrel.' He sounded unconvinced.

'A barrel. With a jagged top.'

'Jagged? Jagged how?'

'Like the tops of the walls in Tenabra. Please, I don't ...'

'Battlemented. It was battlemented. So it wasn't a barrel.' He was looking right through me. 'Oh no. Not a barrel. A tower.'

'Ah, perhaps,' I managed.

He wasn't listening. '*Gules, a tower argent.*' His face lit with pleasure. 'Oh, this is worth all the rest. The Prince will delight to hear it. The traitor Silvus Castro is here.' He was talking to himself more than to me. 'He is here. A few miles over that hill. We have found him. I have found him. And I am bringing to the Prince the means to track him down.' He turned on me. 'The sooner we get there, the better. And keep this to yourself. The Prince will hear of it from me.'

He kicked his mule into a trot. Mine, tethered behind, picked up the pace as well.

I wondered if anyone else was bothering to grieve over the bird that I'd driven to her death. It seemed not. If there wasn't, I couldn't understand why I was doing it.

But I was, all the same.

WILL

Silvus retrieved his bolt and remounted without a word. We got into motion again.

'That's Nathan's mage, for sure,' I ventured. 'Only he won't try that again.'

'What he won't try is getting that close again,' said Silvus. 'And that's all.'

'We've lost him now, though.'

'For a while, I'd say. We'd better have. That would have been a severe shock to him, and I can't feel any more use of mana. But that puts paid to our raiding career.'

I rode on, frowning. Did Silvus really mean that? I glanced across at him. He turned his head and met my eyes.

'Remember what I said? The whole business depends on seeing but not being seen. We might be able to hit another outlying group or two, but sooner or later we'll run into that fellow again.' He jerked his head backwards, towards the lowering hills. 'And when we do, he'll just keep watching us, and Nathan will hunt us down. We'll never be able to lose him, not with eyes in the sky. Who could hide from an eagle, in this country?'

'Unless we can run him down, ourselves.' It was a thought that had just struck me.

'Yes. But that would involve doing what he's doing. Animals as puppets to do our will. Bending their minds to serve us. Don't you see?' He turned a glance as fierce as any eagle's on me. 'It would be using the Dark. That is the Dark.' His eyes moved back to the line of the hills. A moment later: 'Never!'

I was silent for a hundred paces. The horses picked their way among clumps and tussocks. Silvus's face sank on to his chest again.

'Well,' I remarked, after a while. 'If we can't go to him, perhaps it might be possible to persuade him to come to us.'

I had been speaking, as I thought, purely at random. Slowly Silvus turned and looked at me again.

CHAPTER VII

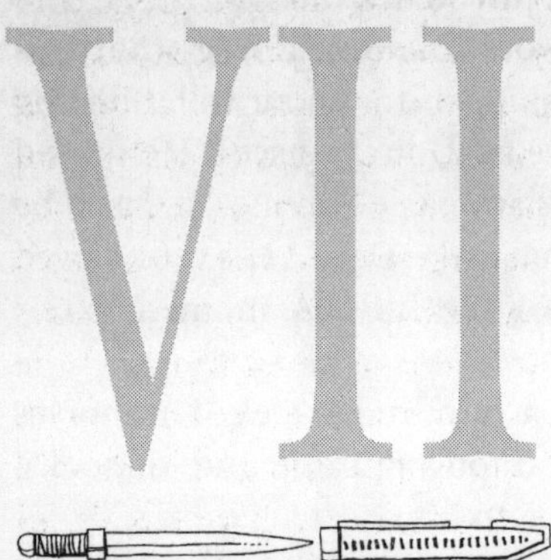

WILL

It took me all day and the next to work it out. I could use only half my mind to do the working-out with, because the rest was occupied with making rapid distance, and with being tired. We were all tired.

No matter how hard we pushed, we were moving slower cross-country than anyone moving on the road. And we couldn't march as if we owned the place. Scouts had to be out and precautions taken against ambush, or at least against running into a stray bunch of Nathan's cavalry. Worse, we had to go the long way around, circling again to get to the west of the main body of his army.

So it wasn't until the evening of the following

day that I had it arranged in my mind. That was after two days of riding around bogs and scrambling up hills leading my horse, two days of snatched hasty meals and insufficient rest and sudden flights into cover on a signalled alarm. But there was one compensation. Nathan's main army was a big one. Just setting up and breaking down camp took him hours each day. So, by the evening of the second day, we were between him and the pass again. The pass was coming closer, though. If we were going to try what I had in mind, we'd need space to carry the plan out. Tired as we all were, I had to talk to Silvus about it now.

A few well-screened fires were allowed, after dusk. The main camp was in a slight hollow, but the hills around were picketed, and we'd see anything coming. Then the darkness fell, and darkness favours the side that sits still and watches. It had rained, and had stopped eventually.

Silvus finished with his supper – sausage and cheese and groat porridge. There was an apple, and we were sharing it with Sister Informer and Master Rookwood. Silvus unsheathed his eating knife to divide the fruit. 'All right,' he said, the firelight rippling on his face. 'Let's hear it.' He didn't bother to ask me what I wanted.

'We have to get this mage alone, or in a small group,' I said, without preamble.

'I won't argue with that,' said Silvus. 'What I don't see is how.'

'We can't walk through Nathan's army and knock his mage over. The mage has to come out

after us. So we have to raid, get him to chase us, and lead him into an ambush.'

'No chance,' said Silvus. 'He won't play.'

'I think he will,' I said, slowly. 'If he has a chance to get you. Nathan wants you very badly. He might risk even his mage to get you.'

Silvus stared me in the face very steadily. You could see him working through the possibilities. Then he glanced at Sister Informer, who was studying the little flames with an air of determined detachment, before looking back at me. At last: 'What did you have in mind?'

I marshalled my facts. 'We can provide remounts for about three-quarters of the auxiliaries, if we use all the horses we have – we took quite a few. We rest them as much as we can, and then you mount a raid – a descent in force on some part of the camp itself. You make as much noise and burn as much as you can, then run, westwards, towards the pass. They'll pursue, with the mage using animals or birds to watch you. And he'll have to ride with the pursuit, to direct it. You lead him towards the spare horses, which will be waiting at a distance that allows you to change over to them when your first mounts are blown. That'll make sure that only the best mounted pursuers – which will include the mage – can keep up the chase. Then you lead him into a spot where a small group is set up, well hidden, ready to spring the trap. We whack him and run away, and meet you back at a rendezvous, where the men we can't remount are also waiting. Simple.'

Silvus stared at me. He shook his head slowly. 'Not so simple as all that. Run away how? The mage would have half Nathan's army with him.'

'No. Only as many good light cavalry as could stay with you in a long chase over rough country, in spite of you changing mounts.'

'Uh-huh.' Silvus handed a slice of apple to Master Rookwood, who accepted it silently. 'You keep saying "us" when you talk about this forlorn hope of an ambush.'

'Yes,' I said. 'You have to be the bait. It's you that Nathan wants. Sister Informer has to command the sisters, who'll cover your retreat if worst comes to the worst. That leaves me, and whoever volunteers for the ambush party.'

'I volunteer,' said Master Rookwood, instantly. 'But you'll need sisters, too. To hold them up, when it comes to blows. So I can't command. It'll have to be you, Squire de Parkin. It's your idea, anyway.'

I hadn't counted on that. I looked at him, dumbfounded.

Silvus shook his head again and looked away. 'That ambush party won't have their retreat covered at all. You were supposed not to be sticking your neck out,' he remarked. But there was consideration on his face, not refusal.

I got my thoughts back into gear, and shrugged. 'We'll have horses, too, and they'll be fresh. Should be able to get away, so long as we don't hang about after doing the deed. This fellow may be able to do magic, but he's not superhuman,

and neither is Nathan.'

Master Rookwood stirred. 'I'll look to the horses and bring them as soon as the trap is sprung. I promised Mistress Brook I'd look after you.'

'There's something you haven't thought of,' said Sister Informer, suddenly.

I watched her. 'What?'

She was staring more fixedly into the fire. After a moment, she nodded to herself. 'I've been thinking wrong. We've all been thinking wrong. We've been calling this mage "he" all this time. But I've known with half my mind that it must be the same one that Nathan caught in Tenabra just last month. And that was an adolescent girl. A small, dark adolescent girl.'

'A girl?' I felt a sudden chill in the pit of my stomach.

She nodded. 'We have to assume it is the same one. Mages don't fall out of every hawthorn bush. It's stretching coincidence too far for Nathan to have found two new ones in as many months, even though two at once has been known.' She schooled her face and shoved a stick a little further into the coals. The last time we'd had a pair, one of them had been the late Prioress of the Order, Merceda the Traitor. The sisters still grieved about it. 'So, the upshot is, you'd have to be willing to cut down a fourteen-year-old girl. From ambush.'

Silvus grimaced. I know I blinked. Master Rookwood's face went blank. He had two daughters. Sister Informer stared at us, and her eyes were calculating. She nodded, slowly. 'Mind you, this is

a fourteen-year-old girl who practises necromancy,' she added.

'Who tried to run away from Nathan.' That was Silvus, in a voice of disgust.

'Who isn't running any more, and who is undeniably the worst threat we face. You said yourself she was using the Dark. It'll only get worse, unless we eliminate her.'

Silence. Silvus stared at her, appalled. She stared back at him. 'I look at you,' she said after a moment, 'and I know why I've always thought that women make better warriors than men. We're more clear-headed, when it comes down to the nasty part of the business. Fourteen or no, female or no, this girl is Nathan's trump card, and our job is to take Nathan down.' We continued to stare at her. She sighed. 'But very well. I suppose we'll have to find some way to accommodate your chivalry. Because we really ought to try this, you know. The longer we leave her in Nathan's hands, the stronger she'll make him.'

'The more difficult it will be to detach her,' I added, chewing, recasting my calculations.

She turned her eye on me, just as calculating. 'Ah,' she said. 'So we're *detaching* her now. Say on.'

ASTA

That big tent was even more impressive, here in the middle of a stretch of lonely gorse and peat bog. Back by Tenabra, you'd compare it to the buildings of the city. Here, there was nothing but hummocks and sweeps of empty land, all coloured grey-green and rust. The colour of it alone, yellow and black like a tiger, shouted at the sky.

His Highness the Prince wasn't at home, though. He came riding up in the gathering dusk an hour after we had dismounted at his door. It had been raining, but the gentlethugs wouldn't let us into his tent without his say-so, and we got wet.

To be fair, so had he. He was wearing an oil-cloth cape over leather, a battered open helmet and riding boots, old and soft and well-greased. He was off his horse before the beast had stopped moving, and he entered the tent with a brisk stride, slapping water off, and giving us a single glance. His escort looked more tired than he did.

A moment later the head troll came out and beckoned us with a jerk of his head. While he searched me, I thought of telling him that talking was invented for times like this, and he ought to try it some day, but I didn't say a word. That bothered me, that I didn't say anything. I would have, once, but I was frightened. And I was getting more and more tired of being frightened.

All the heavy hangings and silk and stuff had been left behind or put away. The inside walls were canvas, now. We were led through a flap in one of them, and there was Prince Nathan, his wet cloak off, drying his hair vigorously on a towel, while sitting at a table. The table was covered with papers, a map, and a dish of bread and meat. I looked at the food, and my stomach growled. The Prince

threw the towel at a servant, picked up a loaf, and tore it open.

'De Teska. What have you got for me?' he asked, around a mouthful of bread. Somebody stuck a goblet of wine in front of him, and he took a pull at it.

Teska was bowing, and I thought I'd better do the same. But Teska was able to talk and bow at the same time.

'In ascending order of importance, Your Highness, I have a unicorn, a mage, and the whereabouts of Silvus Castro the traitor,' he said.

Nathan's face went still for a moment. Then he started to chew again. 'Go on,' he said.

Ah, I thought. *That's got his attention.*

'Castro is about three or four leagues to the north or north-west of us now, sire, with about a hundred sisters of the Order ...' He told the Prince what I'd told him.

When he'd finished, Nathan nodded. 'Useful information. Very useful. That would explain what's been happening. I didn't think they would allow us free rein much longer. I've had to reinforce the pickets, which meant bringing them in closer to camp. It's no use setting out guards of forty or so if the enemy is raiding several hundred strong. But you're quite sure it is Castro?'

'Certain, sire. Asta actually saw his banner.'

Nathan slabbed meat and pickles on his bread. 'Who'd have thought it? Innovation, indeed, and from one of the old families. That man's no more than a decayed limb of the old aristocracy, and most of them haven't the sense to run a pie shop. Like that idiot de Corwell, wearing out an entire regiment of horse charging about in the dark, trying to find his equally idiotic nephew. Do you know, two of his search parties actually ended up fighting each other?' He bit and chewed. I found my mouth watering. Nathan took no notice of that, though.

'So it's no use you telling me Castro's out there now,' he continued, flatly. 'It's dark, and around us there's more leagues of nothing than I ever wish to see. Casting about on the moors in the hope of finding him will simply use up time and horses. He'd love us to do that. We'll just have to be better prepared, next time.'

'We do have an advantage, sire,' said Teska, and he shuffled a little closer to the princely presence, as if Nathan were a fire at which he was warming himself. 'If he raids again, we can follow him until we run him down. Asta brought her host a little close last time, but she won't make that mistake again.'

Oh, I just loved that. It was all *my* fault. I opened my mouth to object, but Prince Nathan's head cocked sideways.

'Oh? How does that work?'

'Well, sire …'

It took them hours to work it out, and I still hadn't had my supper.

WILL

'All right. This is the best place we've seen. I'll be coming from that direction.' Silvus indicated the south-east. 'Set yourself up, and remember, you have to be well concealed – enough to be missed by a hawk. It will pick up any movement, no matter how slight. From the moment I come into sight, you'll have to be covered and as still as a stone.'

'I've told my people. They understand.'

He grunted. 'Which means that you understand too, and you wish I'd stop vapouring. That covered gully behind you should hide the horses, with solid green leaves overhead.'

I nodded. Leather creaking, Silvus leaned down in the saddle and gripped my shoulder. 'Luck,' he said. 'And remember, don't linger. There'll be more of Nathan's cavalry behind me than anyone has any right to fight all at once. Hit her or not, grab her or not, get out while the getting is good.'

'I will. Luck, yourself.'

He nodded, turned, and rode out at the head of his column, not looking back, heading towards the first faint false dawn, towards Nathan's camp. Fifty men, all auxiliaries, all mounted and leading a horse each, followed him. Most of the sisters, already mounted, were moving out in the opposite direction. If it all fell apart, they'd fling themselves across the might of Nathan's army, and hold them long enough for the rest of us to get away. Maybe.

Well, we'd thought of everything we could. Now it was up to me and my fifty. I began to map out the business in my head. What I had was a slightly curving hill, the inner side of the curve facing the direction that Silvus would come from. A stream flowed across my front; the next hill to the east wasn't so high nor so steep. Behind me, over the reverse slope, a gully wandered away westward before turning south for the distant sea. It was choked with overhanging scrub, with a trickle of water along its bottom. We'd picket the horses there.

I disposed twenty sisters, the fighting core of my tiny command, among the bushes and whins near the top of the slope and directly in the path of the oncoming enemy. The auxiliaries were in front of them, scattered thinly along the slope in a line, but with a small group at each end. Every one was under leaves, smeared with earth, prone, some actually burrowing into the soil. It was almost daylight before I finished posting them.

Then, as the dawn broke, I walked that curving line from end to end, checking that I couldn't see them from in front. I was uneasily aware that I couldn't check from above, but I climbed the next hill and looked back. Still no sign of them, but I didn't have a hawk's eyes. We'd just have to rely on stillness and the haste of the enemy.

I stared in the direction that Silvus had gone. Five leagues away, Nathan's camp would be in the morning process of breaking up and getting on the road. Someone over there was due for a nasty surprise. I glanced at the sun, its rim just over the horizon. Just about now, if we had calculated correctly. Time to get into cover myself.

ASTA

'Up! *Up!*' The hand on my shoulder gripped hard and shook me awake. I crawled reluctantly into the world. The hand was Widow Pila's. It hadn't been a bad dream, then.

'Dress. Quickly.' A shift and a blouse were thrust at me.

'Uh? Whazza? Whassamatter?' I wasn't feeling my best. It had been a short night.

Actually, the night shouldn't have been over. There was just the hint of grey light starting to seep into the tent, but that was dawn. I didn't get up at dawn. That was for farmers.

But I was hauled to my feet, the shift was thrust roughly over my head, and it was followed by blouse and robe. It would seem that I did get up at dawn, these days. Cold dawn.

'Is she ready yet?' That was Teska, from outside.

'She's decent.' Widow Pila, saying as little as possible, as usual. She whipped a cloak over the top. Teska swept the tent flap aside and walked in, hunching his shoulders.

'Horses in two minutes. She'll mount with one of the special troopers.' And then to me: 'Get out there now and find a bird, one near the smoke.'

'Bird? Smoke?' I suddenly became aware that there was a lot of noise. Trumpets, running feet, men shouting and cursing, a cry for buckets and water.

'Yes, smoke. Castro has raided the camp itself. But we'll get him this time. If you can find that bird. Hurry up!' He was all of a flutter. It was his plan, prepared with his master. He propelled me outdoors, a hand between my shoulder-blades. I looked around, bewildered.

It was just light, the streaks of grey from the east just starting to show pink. Around us the camp was like a disturbed ants' nest, men running for horses, bellowing orders and responses, tying up points and armour, grabbing weapons, mounting or forming up into lines. A troop of horse came barging past, its officer cursing everyone who got in the way, and trying to work up into a trot, past lines of tents. My eye followed them towards …

There. My eyes went to it automatically. A few hundred paces away smoke rose in the sky, on the side of the camp almost opposite to the dawn, and there was an ominous orange-yellow glow, not the sun. I gaped.

'There's a fire,' I remarked, idiotically.

'Of course there's a fire,' snarled Teska. 'Find a bird. Find the people who lit it. They've been beaten off already, but they mustn't be allowed to escape.' His hand clamped on my shoulder again, not quite painfully. 'Find them, and stay with them this time. Don't get within shot.'

I stared towards the fire, and almost without thinking my mind searched the air above and beyond the glow. There was nothing.

'I can't see one. They'd avoid flame. We'll have to get out of the camp.'

Teska glanced sharply at me, then decided I wasn't lying. 'Here's horses. You mount there.'

Teska pushed me into the saddle, a long way up, and in front of the soldier who was riding. 'Hold on to her for your life,' he told him. I grabbed the horse's mane and tried to grip with my knees. An arm circled my waist.

'I won't let you fall, miss,' said the man. 'Just hang on. Chloe, here, has easy paces.' He clucked to the horse, and we moved off.

I leaned against his leather front. I was further up in the air than I wanted to be, much further than on the mule. The ground looked a very long way away.

'She's very big,' I said, uncertainly.

'Right wheeler for the troop,' he replied, with satisfaction. 'And I ride the lightest by a stone or more. You're hardly enough to signify. Chloe could carry us both to the edge of the world.' Chloe flattened her ears and danced, as a man rushed in front of us, calling for buckets. I grabbed for her mane again, and the arm around my waist tightened. 'Course, she's a trifle flighty. Comes of breeding, that does. Heads up! We're off.'

Teska passed us on his mule, gesturing for us to follow. Chloe lengthened out into a trot, and I bumped and swayed like a sack of peas. I grunted at the bumps, and my mouth opened and closed with every stride.

'You'll get used to it,' assured the soldier. I doubted it. 'Why,' he went on, 'just wait till we gallop!'

The trot ate ground rapidly. Already the yellow glow was coming closer, and at the same time it

was dying down. There was more white than black smoke ahead of us now. We swerved around a pile of cinders and half-burned scraps, and there was a dead man, but I could pay him no mind. We passed a group of soldiers, heard a snatch of talk, '… cut him down as he charged out'.

There were loose horses about now, with men trying to catch them, and more burned tents and other bits and pieces. Then the lines of tents, burned and whole, opened. There was a line of soldiers there, some with wounds, facing out to the open country beyond. Teska bawled for way, and they opened for him.

He hauled up after he had passed the last tent, and we stopped behind him. 'Now,' he called. 'Find them, and hurry.'

I heard horses behind me, but I couldn't pay any attention to them, with Teska staring back at me as fierce as a cornered cat. I looked up to the sky, where smoke still pooled and drifted on the wind, and I searched … searched, and there!

A hawk, the sort that hovers, high in the cool morning breeze, a speck on the wind. I felt for its mind, and felt it seep into me and me into it, full of the touch of the air and the vastness of the space around me and the fierce study of the ground that was passing slowly below. I could see through its eyes, and by those eyes I could see …

The fire like a bright ring, dying now, with a scent like that of burning brush, but sharper and more foul, dangerous, to be avoided. Dead men,

and they were interesting, maybe food. And horses, horses. One group was moving fast away. Another stood still.

I looked up/*the girl looked up*/and I stared myself in the face. Small. Dark. It puzzled me for a moment. Then I realised, and sent the hawk further out to watch the other group, two hills away and moving easily.

'I have them,' I said. 'There's that little red banner, now.'

Teska grunted with satisfaction. 'Follow them. Stay with them.' And then, to someone else, 'Very well, captain. Let us start.'

We jerked into motion again, and I tried to stay with the bird, and to flex with the bumps. Chloe stayed at a trot for only a few moments, though. The soldier clucked again and twitched the reins, and she flowed straight on to a much easier canter. Through my own eyes and those of the hawk, I could see myself and the others around me, and there were many more horse-soldiers coming, a solid column, four wide. And there, across the moors …

'That way!' I called, and we were after them.

After a while I began to find that it wasn't so easy. The hawk didn't want to follow a herd of horses forever. Not for long at all, in fact. Following them too far would bring him into another bird's territory, and he didn't like that idea. But I pushed him as far as I could. When we found another one I let him go and changed to that one. That was all right, after a while.

But riding a horse while looking out through another pair of eyes was confusing, and worse. I had to keep a piece of my attention on the country around me and the riding. My stomach didn't like being told that it was flying with a falcon when it was really being bounced around on the back of a horse. It didn't like it more and more as we went on.

'I think I'm going to be sick,' I said.

'We can't stop without orders,' said the soldier. 'If you must spew, do it to that side, downwind.'

And we rode on. I wasn't sick. I just wanted to be. And I wanted to be out of this.

Hours of riding, and we didn't stop. The moors just went on and on, hill after hill. From the bird's eye I could catch a glimpse of high mountains, purple in the distance, snow on their peaks, far to the west. We splashed through streams and scrambled up slopes. I had to spend most of my time and attention on the birds, but there were snatched conversations, torn by the wind.

'Are we closing?' That was Teska. He had changed mounts, and was riding a horse, not well. He was in pain, his eyes staring. My stomach lurched. Those eyes were mad.

'A little,' I said, hoping it'd calm him. 'They're just following a straight path, though, not curving around, not trying to lose me. Going on at a steady pace.'

'They must know we're here. We're kicking

up enough dust. They must just think they can outrun us.'

'I suppose.' Then, a while later. 'Oh! There's another herd of horses …'

'An ambush. How many?'

'Not an ambush. The new horses don't have riders … the first group is stopping … getting off. They're changing over!'

Teska swore. 'Remounts. Fresh horses. They think they'll lose us.'

'Well, they will. They're riding off. Faster than before.'

I watched them through the bird's eye, as they left their previous horses behind. The new ones were rested and fresh. Ours were already tiring, surely, though Chloe was still going with a swing.

'They won't get away.' There was savage satisfaction in Teska's voice. 'Behind us are the best two regiments of light cavalry in the Prince's army, the horses hand-picked, the loads lightened, and every man chosen for small weight. Castro has to carry food and supplies. He can't run his beasts into the ground, and we can. We'll catch them, if it takes days. They can't run forever, and they can't hide. Not from your sight. Captain!' he called. 'We'll pick up the pace a little.'

I was getting sore. The sun was high, and this seemed to have gone on forever. Head was hurting, hips were hurting. I was hungry, but sick at the same time, so I couldn't eat. Nobody cared about that, though. It just went on and on.

Past noon, and we climbed another hill. The

horses were lathered now, and men were using their spurs. But we came into sight of the chase at last. They were just disappearing from the next crest as we crowned the height. Around me, the riders set up a shout. Down we went into the dip, and at the bottom splashed through a little stream. Started up again.

And then it happened.

I didn't know at first. My mind and my sight were up in the clouds. But the soldier cried out, and his arm tightened around me. Suddenly there were yells and screams, and voices bellowing orders. I was wrenched back to earth, and as I was Chloe seemed to stumble, and the breath was jerked out of me. I would have fallen, but the arm held me. A trumpet blared out, and we swerved, a swift turn.

'Hang on!' grunted the soldier, and there was a buzz like a hornet close by my ear. He reached down, and pulled out a long straight sword.

'What …'

'Ambush! Hold on!'

We swung around and headed back the way we'd come. Behind us now, Teska flogged his horse to come level, bawling orders that nobody heeded. It was up to the soldiers now. Behind, still farther, there was a sudden roar, and a ringing, like a dozen smiths all at work at once.

We were running back for the stream we'd crossed, and Chloe stumbled again. At almost the same moment, the arm around my waist went slack, then started dragging on me. The soldier's

other hand dropped the reins, and they flopped on Chloe's neck. I tried to turn.

'Come on!' I cried. I couldn't turn far enough to see his face, and he was leaning on me more and more. Another whistle past my ear. 'What are you ...?'

Slowly, then with a sliding rush, he dropped out of the saddle like a sack of meal. He sprawled on the ground, his limbs at odd angles. His sword, all bright and shiny, fell from his hand and thumped on the ground. His puzzled face was turned up towards me, and there was blood on it. I looked down at him, about to ask if he was all right. And then he relaxed and the light went out of his eyes.

I had never known his name. I sat there on Chloe's shoulders, in front of the saddle that he'd fallen from, and my innards turned to ice and confusion. Chloe slowed to a walk, then stopped and waited. I stared around, and my mind refused to work at all. I needed someone to tell me what to do. For a moment, even Teska would have been welcome. But he was gone, somehow. I looked around, panicky. There was nothing but dust and yelling and chaos.

Around me, men on horseback and men on the ground were jostling and cursing and hitting out at one another. Another trumpet blared out. Someone bellowed from the press: 'Threes about! Rally on the standard! Form up! Come on, there's only a few of them!'

It was all a blur and a flitting confusion. I

couldn't tell where I was, for a moment. Half of me was still up in the cool quiet airy spaces, spiralling on the wind, and I glanced that way longingly; but there was roaring tumult around me, yells and cries and screams and sudden vivid movement. I scrambled backwards into the saddle and took stock. Two men rolled under the horse's feet, grappling and cursing, and Chloe danced and sidestepped to get out of the way. Another man ran up with an axe. There was a dull thud and a short, choked squeal, like killing a hog.

I had to get out. I had to get out now! I hauled at the reins, and Chloe tossed her head. I squeezed with my knees, and she started walking down the slope. I kicked her and she began to trot.

A man in mail stumbled out of the whirl of murky movement ahead. He had blood on his face, too.

WILL

The trap was failing. There were too many of them. We were at one to three odds, and more of them were coming. The intention had been to close the ends of the line behind them, but it hadn't worked. There were too many of them to fit in the ring, and some of them broke out and rode off, to rally on the peak of the hill to the front, the one they'd just descended. They were collecting more and more as stragglers arrived on tired horses. Tired or not, as soon as they sorted them-

selves out, they'd charge, and we'd go under like a pebble under a wave.

Silvus had passed through, and was at least a half league away by now. He hadn't been able even to acknowledge my presence, and I had to stay as still as a stone in cover while he rode past. He'd looked grim, and had kept going. If he'd stopped, so would they. They'd wait for their stragglers to close up, and we'd never have a chance.

I was at one end of the line, striving to close it, and failing. We'd cut a few of them down, and we'd halted them. Cavalry is always useless, once it's halted. But when they got their wind back and realised how few we were – well. I'd already taken a swing to the helmet, and blood was flowing from one cut eyebrow.

Time to get out. I hadn't seen a sign of that girl. I put my whistle in my mouth to sound the recall, pulled in air to blow … and there she was.

The press of bodies parted as if it were a curtain. Dust rose in clouds, and there, on a tall mare, swaying like a reed in the wind, was a small dark girl, face like a trapped rabbit, trying to look in all directions at once. I gawped, and then lurched forward. It was my mark, all right, and this was my best and only chance. I had a javelin, a throwing-spear, but even then I couldn't use it. I ran towards her, ducking around prancing horses and cursing troopers, and blowing the recall as hard as I could. We'd need every second we had, to get away.

She turned away. Dust blurred my sight, billowing. I parried a slash from someone who got in my way, slipped under the horse and heaved the rider off, popping up on the side he didn't expect. I hadn't time to wait around, though. For a moment I lost sight of her, and looked about frantically.

There she was! She was no horsewoman, for sure; she was sawing at the bit, had lost a stirrup, and was hanging on for all she was worth. I blew the recall again, and it seemed to me that the tumult and chaos around me were changing in quality. Don't ever let anyone tell you that a battle is a *planned* thing.

I was running, panting, blowing on the exhale. I got to her and grabbed for her reins. Filled my lungs.

'Come with me!' It was meant to be a commanding bellow. It came out as a despairing wheeze. For a moment I looked her in the eyes, and there was nothing there but fear and desperation, and no understanding at all. Then the horse tore free, turned and kicked me fair in the brisket, and I folded up like a punctured bladder. Just as well; a blade sang through the air where my head had been. I rolled under hooves, and kept on rolling. Came to my feet, with red spots swirling in front of my eyes, and there was Master Rookwood and one of his men, mounted and leading a horse. My horse.

'Come on! Out, now. It's all gone to pot,' he yelled, and thrust the reins at me.

I looked about, wildly. 'There she is!' I pointed at a disappearing back.

His face jerked up and hardened. A javelin

appeared in his right hand, and he poised it to throw. I was scrambling up into my saddle, gasping and blowing like a foundered ox, and for a moment all I could do was hang on as the horse pranced. Rookwood pulled back and threw.

His horse was prancing, too, and that was enough to put him off. The javelin flew wide; it seemed to pass through her, but it didn't pause. Missed.

I found my stirrups and started to haul the horse around to pursue. Rookwood pulled at my reins. 'Oh no, you don't! I promised Mistress Brook. Come on, or I'll have Gill, here, knock you out and drag you!'

The press closed in front of us again. Now there were troopers in yellow and black, and no sign of the girl, who had disappeared into the swirling confusion.

'Come on!' bellowed Rookwood again, and I wrenched the horse's head around and set my spurs. Mounted armsmen closed up behind us, shooting behind to cover the retreat. We broke into a gallop, and as we did Nathan's trumpets sounded behind us, blowing the charge.

CHAPTER

ASTA

I found Chloe's mind, and I calmed her and urged her to hurry, both at the same time. She was tired, but not so very tired as all that, and I soothed her and fed her courage.

Around us, the battle blurred, and then began to clear. The sides were drawing apart. Men in dull green and men in black and yellow were sorting themselves into groups. There were none on foot now, all were mounting up. One line was behind me, one in front. So I rode out for the side.

I told Chloe which way to go, and she turned in that direction, level with the stream, which I could hear twenty paces to my right. I urged her, talking

to her, and she listened. We turned. Just then a shout came from behind me. There was a sudden movement. A moment later a bright bar of pain blazed across my shoulders. I yelled, the sound lost in the tumult around me, and I felt, rather than saw, a spear slice past. It had scored across my back, and there was a sudden warm wetness there.

But there was no time for pain. I reached for Chloe's mind again and called my hurt to her, and she took it gamely, stretching into a gallop. We dashed a man to the ground and flew across the slope, out into the moors.

I told Chloe how much I admired her, how much I loved her. She loved me in return, and I knew that there was something there that no wild animal could give. Chloe liked people, generally, and would do her best for them. Not like Fred, the mastiff I had healed back in Tenabra. She was willing, and she surged away from the fighting. Up a slope, then down again, and now there was no one near us, and the dust was clearing. She cleared a gorse bush in her stride and settled down into a steady swinging run, as if she meant to do it all day.

Slowly, slowly, peace came. We were over the skyline from the battle, the noise dying away to a murmur like bees, and I eased her back a little. My shoulders were stinging now, a steady sharpening pain, and I had to get some sort of a binding on them soon. I could feel the wash of blood, and I knew that I'd need bandaging.

Get me over the next hill, I told Chloe, *and we can rest.* She snorted and ran on gallantly. And now,

well behind me, came the high scream of trumpets and a sudden thunder of hooves, followed by a ringing crash. I rode on, not looking back. I'd had enough of battles.

WILL

We rode breakneck over the hill, and Nathan's army was after us. That was bad enough, and it was worse that we'd failed. But there was worse still to come.

I was flat to the horse's neck, getting the best pace I could, when I passed through the line of my twenty sisters, mounted now. There was something in the face of the file leader that seized my attention – a fierce joy and an acceptance. I knew then what she was going to do, and I started to pull up.

'No!' That was Rookwood. 'They'll buy you ten minutes or so. Let them.' He grabbed my bridle.

'They'll die in the doing of it. I can't ...'

'They know it. You can't stop them now. Do you want them to do it for *nothing*? Come on, dammit.' He hauled me along, and I went, shamefaced, staring over my shoulder.

The file leader had moved a half-length or so in front of her sisters. Now she peered down the slope at an oncoming yellow-and-black multitude that outnumbered her people by tens to one. Her sword flashed as she drew and held it high.

'For the Lady!' she called, and her voice rang clear and glad. Her sisters drew steel. It was as if

the line had suddenly been blessed by shafts of sunlight.

'For the Lady!' they answered as one, and they set spurs and started forward. Walk, then forward into trot, and as they left my sight and the sight of the world, their sword points were lowering into the charge.

I was riding down the reverse slope, free and away, my life bought and paid for, when the crash came behind me, the song of steel, the cries and bellows, the screams of horses. Not a few of Nathan's cavalry would rue the day they chased the Order across the moors.

I started the prayers, and kept them going. Not that the sisters would need my prayers, and I thought it likely that the Lady wouldn't listen to me, anyway. I needed them, though. And I needed to be doing something that might conceivably be useful, as we fled from our defeat.

The afternoon wore away. Around me the remains of my first command closed up and joined together as we rode. Nobody spoke. We just prodded our horses along. They'd been rested, and that saved us. That, and the start the sisters had won for us, and the approach of night. The pursuit never really got started – they were too busy licking their wounds, I suppose. No dust followed us.

We reached the rendezvous as the darkness closed in. Here was Silvus, and Sister Informer, and the rest. They were waiting for me, and all I could report was failure and loss.

Silvus learned all he needed to from the look on my face. But it was Sister Informer that I feared. She was searching the ranks as we came stumbling in, searching for her sisters. I pulled up and let the rest pass me. The last rider shambled by between us, and then she straightened and lifted her gaze to me. I could only shake my head and then hang it like a schoolboy. Her eyes closed briefly, and her lips moved. There was nothing I could say.

Around us, fires were being kindled, all of them behind screens. Scouts were out a mile away downwind, so we would not be served as we had served Nathan's men. The dusk reduced detail, showing only outlines, and thus made it possible for me to look people in the face.

I dismounted, off-saddled and walked the horse around until he was cool, then hobbled and started to groom him. Somebody dumped feed in front, and a little warmed water. Nobody spoke.

A hand on my shoulder. Silvus, and behind him Sister Informer.

'Master Rookwood told us,' he said. 'I knew it wouldn't work, as soon as I realised how many of them there were. Master Rookwood estimates a full cavalry regiment, and Sister Informer reckons from his description that it was one of Nathan's new Horseguards, the best he has. And more, they were stripped down for the chase. They were set up to do it, specially. No wonder they pushed us so hard. If it hadn't been for you, they'd have caught us.'

'If it hadn't been for the rearguard, you mean.

The one I left behind.' I finished the horse's feet and started brushing him down.

Silvus took the brush out of my hand, pulled me around by the shoulder, and looked me in the face. 'It's not your fault. You couldn't have done any better. For what it's worth, Master Rookwood also says that he's certain that you dropped over fifty in the first volleys and the melee. And if I know the sisters, there's many more than that with their faces to the sky.' I bowed my head. Silvus's voice came all the same, dry and hard as a bleached bone. 'But that isn't the point. The point is that I need you. And, though I know this is no comfort, what happened is what rearguards are for. The sisters knew it, and they accepted it. So must you, Will. It's part of command.'

'In that case, I don't want to command,' I mumbled. Silvus shook his head. There was a moment's silence. Sister Informer broke it.

'Fine,' she said, and her voice was dangerous. 'Fine, Will Parkin. Go ahead. Reject the Lady's gifts to you. Deny your abilities. Forget about your competence. That's fine. But I tell you this: you are our armsman for a year and a day from last October, and like every last novice in the Order, you'll obey. If we say you command, then by the Lady, you command. And we say you command.'

I stared at her. 'I got your sisters killed!'

She pushed a hand out in emphatic rejection. 'Wrong. Nathan got them killed. It was for us to predict what he might do, and we didn't. He's a sharp one, and no doubt. But …' She stepped

forward and stared me full in the face, light from the nearest campfire making shadows of her eyes and glistening on the trails that tears had made down her cheeks. 'No matter how sharp he is, he failed. He failed to take Silvus. He failed to break your people, and you brought most of them back. And just at this moment, his cavalry commander will be feeling as if he reached down a rabbit hole and found a wildcat.'

I looked away. She watched me, steadily. I tried to find words. 'It might have worked,' I said. 'It so nearly did. I had a hand on her bridle ...'

'Ah,' breathed Silvus. 'That I did not know. Master Rookwood said that you pointed her out to him in the press.' He stroked his goatee. 'You should know that Master Rookwood is blaming himself. Said he had a fair cast at her, and missed.'

'Not an easy cast. And he was possibly thinking about his daughters.'

'He said something like that,' said Sister Informer. 'One of them is just that age. Scana's thinking about the novitiate next year. This mage looks rather like her.'

I grimaced. 'I did no better. I couldn't take her, and I couldn't just kill a child, and then the horse kicked me. Probably on command. By the time I got up, she was twenty paces off. Master Rookwood knows the rest.'

Silvus and Sister Informer glanced at each other. 'That's what we need to talk to you about,' said Sister Informer. 'Rookwood says she wasn't making for her own lines, the last he saw of her.'

I frowned, and tried to remember. I had been rolling on the ground, not the best position to get one's bearings. 'I think … yes. As Rookwood threw, she was moving across him. He only missed by a fraction. There was a lot of dust …'

'Always is,' remarked Silvus.

'… but before she disappeared she kept on going – and that was across the slope, now I think of it. Once I was in the saddle, I tried to follow her, but Rookwood hauled me back …'

'Good for Rookwood,' said Sister Informer.

'… and we ran for it, heading uphill. Nathan's line was reforming beyond the stream at the bottom.'

Pause. All three of us reviewed the picture in our minds. 'So,' said Sister Informer carefully, 'the last you saw of her, she was running away from *both* sides.' She looked at me, eyebrows raised.

I screwed up my face. 'Maybe. I can't be sure.'

She nodded. 'No. Of course not. But we know she has run away before this. You may have pulled off an unlikely victory, Will de Parkin. If you have, then doubly my sisters have been justified. They would say the same.'

ASTA

I tore a strip from my shift and bound it across my shoulders, knotting it in front, wishing that I could see how bad the cut was. There was blood on the blouse. Not as much as I feared, but still.

So far, the world was a very unfriendly place. Nathan and Teska wanted my gift, and they had been nasty about it. But so had the man in the green-and-brown mail. He had grabbed my bridle and commanded that I follow him. I'd had enough of following people. Browned mail. That was the Order, Teska said. I wondered what the Order was. Whatever it was, it threw spears at you. I had better stay away from them. There must be some people in the world who weren't fighting each other.

There were some docks, and I found a handful of spider webs, and shrugged them under the makeshift bandage. Chloe was tired and getting hungry, but we had to make some more distance before dark. Teska would be going stark mad, and Nathan would be looking for me, very soon now. He'd look very hard indeed. I didn't intend that he should find me.

Where could I go, though? I looked around, and saw a land that was as strange to me as the other side of the moon, all brown bracken and low dull-green bushes, rising and falling, swept by the wind, empty and lonely under a vast and open sky. One thing I'd learned in my travels with Teska – that Prince Nathan ruled most of the world, it seemed. But most isn't all. The moors, now. He didn't rule here, and I felt fine about that. I needed to find people who weren't on anyone's side. Or perhaps not. Possibly they disliked Dark mages, too. I began to think that perhaps it was up to me alone. Then I thought that it had always been that way.

I took up Chloe's reins and started walking, to

spare her. She'd need grass before long. Oats or something, too, if I could find them.

Choose a direction. Not east; that led towards Nathan's lands, where I'd come from. And both those armies were somewhere off in *that* direction, south by the sun. North, then, and after that I would bend around to the west, hoping to find where the other people came from.

We started off along the ridge, Chloe and me. High in the air, a hawk was circling. That was how we spent the afternoon.

Late in the day I found fodder for Chloe, at least. There was grass and water in a hollow by one of the streams. I did what I could for her. I'd held horses for gentlefolk before now, but I didn't really know how to care for her. I got her saddle off, after a while. She liked to be rubbed down with handfuls of slightly scratchy leaves, and I cleaned out her hooves the way a stableman had once showed me. I let her wander, knowing that I could call her.

Then there was the problem of supper for me. I hadn't eaten all day, and the day had been a busy one. I was used to missing meals, though not recently.

The saddlebag provided half a loaf and a piece of cheese. Enough for one meal. After this, I'd have to find a rabbit or a bird, or something. I could make it stand still, I thought, if I stopped it from fearing me. But how to cook it? I had no fire. There was no flint and steel in the saddlebag,

either. I gave up on the question, after a while. There was a blanket strapped behind the saddle. It was enough for the night.

I was rolled in the blanket before the sunlight left the sky. I already knew that Nathan's men would not continue the search in the hours of darkness, and that was my best chance of travel. I would sleep until the midnight chill woke me, and then go on until dawn. I was sore, though the bleeding had mostly stopped, and it took me a while to find sleep. I kept an eye on – or in – the hawk, and that in turn brought me news of anyone moving on the moors. No one came my way. Eventually I slept.

When I woke, shivering, there was a half moon, and enough light to see by. The moors were silver and shadow under a sky of stars, but the wind had turned and was coming from the south, and that would mean rain soon. I had to find shelter.

My back was worse, a steady hot ache. My teeth chattered, with more than the chill of the wind. I hoped the cut wouldn't go bad on me. I cleaned it at the stream as best I could, and the cool water was good on the sore place. Then I called Chloe – she was off by herself on a patch of grass. She was a little rested, and had some grass in her, at least. We set off, me leading her. I thought it was best to spare her as much as I could. I might need her speed yet.

There were animals about in the darkness, even now. Little minds, sparks in the dim vastness of the moors. I tried to use them, from time to time.

Owls were best, I found, giving a sight of the night as if it were a shadowless picture, black and white and stark like a snowfield. We picked our way northwards, Chloe and me, under the stars.

Dawn brought the rabbits. And a stream. Sart could tickle a trout, or at least he could before his hands got too shaky. I knew the theory, but I had a better way.

Fire, though. The gift was no use in making it, and I had no tinder, flint and steel. The dew was falling, and everything was damp. But Chloe found a salt lick, and fish can be eaten raw. It just needs a certain attitude. It was enough.

In fact it was a little too much. The light improved, but there were dark clouds coming up from the south. And that cut was bothering me now. The pain had spread to my head, and I felt hot and dizzy. I didn't want the second half of the fish. To go on, I had to scramble up on Chloe's back. She stood for me while I did that, and we walked on together.

It was a painful morning, and a worse noon. Teska was sometimes behind me, and sometimes he wasn't, and I seemed to hear his voice in the sigh of the wind in the gorse, chiding me and threatening. Sometimes Prince Nathan was with him, and once the sky itself took on the semblance of Nathan's face, looking down on me as if I were an insect crawling across his table. I came out of that knowing that I was wandering in my mind, and knowing also that I must find someone soon.

Sometime later, I woke with a jolt as Chloe

moved down a sharp little slope and her gait changed. She was picking her way less cautiously. I looked around, groggy, my eyes swimming, and it seemed to me that we were walking along a track, a rough rutted pathway winding among the gorse. Ruts. Ruts are things made by wheels. I dismissed it as another dream, and indeed the track seemed to melt and be remade in front of my eyes. The sun was lowering between the clouds, mid-afternoon, and my head hurt. I was wet, too, but the rain had passed for now. The light hurt my eyes, too, and it was all I could do not to close them and retreat into the dreams again. But the track meant something important, though sometimes I couldn't remember what it was.

The next I knew, the scrub and bushes I had been blundering through were gone, and I didn't know why, and I couldn't say what had become of them. Suddenly we were walking in cleared land, and there was a man a way off, ploughing, and a woman walking in front of the ox team. I waved to them in case they weren't a dream, and they seemed to wave back. But waving was a mistake. Pain broke over me like a wave, and the wave pulled me under into blackness. The last I knew, with a greater jolt of pain still, was the ground growing large before my eyes and my own shadow coming to meet me.

WILL

We broke camp the following morning and set off for the pass, moving as fast as we could, so as to get there well in front of Nathan's scouts. It was raining by the afternoon, steady and soaking. Rain was good. It would wash out our tracks and scent.

The mountains were close now, and we had to push to reach them. I hated this part. Every time I came this way I was tired, and every time I walked with danger and failure dogging my steps. The first time it had been with Count Ruane, and I hadn't picked him for the Dark mage that he was. The second time it had been me; I had pushed Arienne into using the Dark, to the peril of both our souls. And now it was as bad. Nathan was behind me, and if he caught me the only thing to do was what the sisters had done. I wondered if I would be able to, if the moment came.

I was beginning to hate the sight of the entrance to the pass at Oriment. Which was silly, really, because in daylight and a warming day, it was a sight to raise the spirit and stop the breath. The Brokenbacks are ragged buttresses and knife-edge ridges rising like the waves of a frozen sea out of the high moors. Those ridges lay athwart us, and out of them rose peaks that no one had ever climbed, great towering sawteeth with names to break the heart: The Watcher; Nilbogrim; Shehanna; Mount Tresonor; Icefast; Oriment itself. They scowled down at us, the eternal snow that crowned them as white and unmarked as a

shroud. Creeping towards them, you felt like an ant crawling across a lawn.

There, notching the ridge line, was the pass. The trail led across the blank face of the mountain, climbing, climbing, and then dived into the chasm between Oriment and the next. It wound, continued to climb, and then finally debouched into the narrowest of vales. Beyond that, where the trail turned into a road and the valley widened a touch, stood Waycastle, the cork in the neck of the bottle. It was a cork that Nathan would have to draw. I hoped he would find the wine bitter and strong.

We were well ahead of Nathan by the time the pass came into sight – I'd have estimated three days, perhaps four. The Order had mounted a watch at the entrance, and the sun being high, they flashed us a light signal as we climbed the long slope towards them. Silvus groped in his pack, pulled out a mirror, and returned the proper response.

I wondered what the Order would think, and I hoped only for their usual practical charity. The Order always believed that you'd done your best – they couldn't conceive of anyone doing less. Well, we'd done our best, and we'd touched Nathan up a little, but it came down at the last to an ignominious retreat and a loss we could ill afford. It was no use saying the enemy had lost more. Nathan had more to spare, and in the end we were probably the worse off. That was why we were shambling in before our expected time, and there was no laughter and little talk in the ranks.

We passed the place where Silvus and I had camped twice before: 'camped' meaning that we had fallen exhausted to the ground there and then managed not to die during the night. It was just a slightly more level piece of the mountainside at the meeting of two ridges, and there was nothing particular to mark it. But I knew something else about it: just up the slope, and in the side of a little gully, no more than a seam in the face of the mountain, there was an entrance to a warren of the underpeople. The folk we used to call goblins. Ruane the traitor had found it, the first time we had passed here, and we had walked their halls to pass under the mountain. I glanced in that direction, wondering if they would help. It was Arienne's job to talk to them, and perhaps she would bring them over. But they distrusted us. Well, who could blame them?

We trailed on, up the mountain to the entrance and then the peak of the pass. Here the sisters met us, for we had some wounded, and they escorted us in. I saw the slightest, most fleeting glance pass between Sister Informer and the commander of the escort, a shake of the head, the same closing of the eyes and the movement of the lips. The commander's face went very still. Then she nodded and gestured us in. As Silvus drew level with her, with me a length back with his pennon, she reached out a hand and smiled.

'Welcome back,' she said, and no more. Silvus took her hand and bowed over it in the saddle, graceful as a gentleman should be. She turned

her horse and rode on with us. Charity indeed.

Waycastle, I realised, was different every time I saw it from this place. It lay a mile off below me in the valley, a little after the peak of the pass. It had been ringing with the bustle of departure last time I had approached, tents around it, the bailey choked with carts and wagons, the hall stacked with farm tools. The Order had been sending out young couples from the land west of the ranges to settle the moors to the east. I wondered how that was prospering. Spring was advancing. They must be about their ploughing by now. I hoped, briefly, that Nathan wouldn't find them, or would leave them alone if he did. There was nothing we could do to protect them.

But now Waycastle had closed in again, stronger than ever. The motte it stood on had been scraped bare, and the ditch I had helped to dig ringed it, deep and grim. The approaches were pocked with sharp little pits, each with its stake. We had to ride carefully, led by the escort, and in single file to the gate. The Order had built new buttresses to brace the curtain wall, and a massive new earthwork bulked in the gateway, crescent-shaped so that it wouldn't shelter attackers from crossfire from the flanking towers, but would hinder a party trying to swing a ram against the gate. A ram would be little use against that gate, anyway. It was covered with a portcullis of hammered iron the weight of a house.

Inside the outer wall was the bailey, and inside that the massive keep, tall enough to look over

the outer wall. This was the citadel, and it would be defended to the last.

And here was Arienne. She was waiting in the bailey for me.

CHAPTER IX

ASTA

Light came and went. So did the pain. Somewhere I understood that it was better to feel the pain, because that meant I was still around to feel it. I was hot, and I couldn't stand the covers on me; cold, and my teeth chattered together. Sometimes there was a bitterness in my mouth. Faces came and went in the dreams.

But the dreams gradually drained away, becoming phantoms, shards of colour and shapes of things that weren't there, drifting against the solidity and sureness of the things that were. The faces became real faces.

One of them said to me, 'Your fever's down.'

My mouth was as dry as ashes. I swallowed, and

she brought a clay cup with a drink, holding it to my mouth, supporting my head. I drank. It was cool and faintly bitter.

'Thank you,' I croaked, and her eyebrows climbed.

'Well,' she said. 'You're healing, then. That's the first sensible thing you've said in three days.'

It was also a tiring thing to say. I couldn't summon up the energy to speak again. I could move my eyes, though. I looked around. I lay in a bed made of sacking stretched on a wooden frame. The bed was in a house, and the house was a very simple one. Its floor was clay, and the beams that held the thatch up were just peeled poles. The walls were wattle, roughly plastered with mud. They kept the wind out, and that was about the limit of it. In the centre of the floor was a smoking fire pit with an iron rack for a pot.

She saw what I was doing, and smiled. 'Yes. Rough, isn't it? But we'll have a proper byre before winter, and the year after that a chimney, even if I have to build it myself – I'll not have my babies crawl about in the muck, nor choke in the smoke. And it's ours. The house, two ox gang of cleared plough land, a yoke of oxen and seed corn to plant.'

I managed a word: 'Where …?'

She rose and went to stir the pot. A young woman, dark-haired, straight as a rush, dressed plainly. The house was clean, however bare it was, and there was lavender in a bunch above the doorframe, scenting the air.

'You are in my house,' she replied. 'I am Jonna, and my husband is Pers Rudlan. He's out ploughing, and won't be back until late. We are shareholders in the Hundred of Newcombe. Welcome. Can you eat?'

I realised I was starving. But at the same time my stomach felt uncertain. 'Is it soup?' I husked.

Soup it was. I ate, and fell asleep before I'd finished.

I was sore when I woke, and there was soup in the pot, still. No one was in sight. The sun was different – it was morning, a spring morning, and the larks were singing. I was free.

Free. Free. It was like a song. And I was hungry, and I needed the privy. Getting up was a slow, dizzying business, but I managed it. There was no one around outside, either.

Instead there was the earthy smell of new-ploughed fields, and sunlight like a kiss. I was free.

Evening, and I had managed to peel some turnips and cut a little bacon from the side that was hanging from the roof beam. There were dried peas in a bin, and pearl barley. A farm loaf had been left on the board. It was enough for supper for hungry people, and I was glad to have been of some use, in having it ready for them when they came in. It was almost full dark by the time they did, and they were tired and grimy from hard work in the fields.

They were surprised at the supper in the pot, and Jonna thanked me before asking if I would

share their meal. After it, she looked at my back and clucked. Then she nodded. 'The cut is drained and healing. Still angry, but healing. Next time remember this: spider webs can be used to staunch bleeding, but they must be clean. Dirt only poisons a wound.'

Her husband said something in a tongue I didn't understand, and she answered him. He nodded, emptied his bowl, and held it out for a refill. There was plenty.

I was sitting on the frame of the bed, weary, for all the little that I'd done. Jonna came and sat beside me, while she wiped out her bowl with a piece of bread. I realised that they'd given me their only bed. They must have slept by the fire, wrapped in whatever spare blankets they had.

'Well, now,' she said. 'You're from the Riverland. That much we know from your speech. I was the only one who could understand you.'

My head swam. I had trouble concentrating on her words. And yes, she did have an odd accent. 'Are you from Tenabra, too?' I asked.

She shook her head. 'No. I speak the River-speech because I've been to an Order school. They teach it there. It's still spoken among them.'

Order? Where had I heard …? I groped among memories, some of them false. Order. It had been said in Teska's voice. In response to something I had said about rusty armour.

'The Order?'

'Yes, the Order.' And then, seeing that I didn't understand, 'The Order of the Lady of Victories.

The swordswomen. You must know of them. You've come all this way to meet them.'

'Not me,' I said. 'It was Prince Nathan who came. I was brought.' Jonna looked at me out of one eye. 'You must know of him. He owns most of the world.' That was one 'you must know' apiece.

'Does he, now? Well, I've heard of him, all right, but he doesn't own me. Nor anyone here. Nor the Order. Nor' – and here she turned and faced me fully – 'a certain fine big mare, no matter that she's carrying his brand.'

'I didn't steal her,' I said, and it was too quick. At that moment it came to me. Order. They were the people who were fighting Nathan.

'No,' she said. 'I didn't say you had. Though it's true you ride with a long stirrup for your size. No, she's your horse, all right. She was very reluctant to leave you. You must have had her a long time.'

'Some time, yes.'

She nodded. 'So. We thought as much.' She seemed as if she might go on, but she stopped, rose, and crossed the room to dip up water to wash out her bowl. The man – Per – had already slipped out.

I roused myself. 'At least I can let you have your bed again. I'm quite used to sleeping on the floor ...' That started a polite argument, which I won.

I was better again the following day. Able to do some serious thinking. Even did some digging and weeding in the garden plot, which was planted

to peas and cabbages and greens. So, when they came home again after another day's hard work, I had questions ready to ask.

Everything was new, you see. The houses – there were another three within sight, all like this one. The tools. The pathways. Even the fence palings, new cut and planted in the raw earth. There were no children, no old people. All I saw were young couples like Jonna and Per passing on their way to the fields, all intent on working all the hours the day had. And they all knew about me, all greeted me with a sharp dip of the head, though they couldn't speak.

Evening again.

'Well, of course it's new,' said Jonna. 'That's its name – Newcombe.' *New vale*, I thought. She looked across at her husband, who was whittling a leg for a stool. 'We're settling the moors for the Order. We hold our land from them.'

'You hold from the Order?' I knew enough about farmers to know that the question of land, who had it, how, from where, how much, what sort, with what rights, loomed large in their minds.

'Yes. But it's our land. We'll pay taxes to them for it, starting in the third year.' She sighed, contented, sleepy now. Supper had been bulked out with a rabbit that Per had hit with a slingstone. No hunting laws here: no lord to enforce them.

'But the Order rules here?'

She seemed surprised. 'Of course. The Order gave the first winter's food and the tools and the beasts and the seed and all the rest so that we could settle land of our own. We hold from them. But it's ours.'

I nodded and smiled, and set to my supper again. My stomach had stopped complaining. When we went to bed, I could think.

Seemed like this Order was just as keen on ruling as Nathan was, though maybe they went about it a little different. No wonder they were fighting each other.

And I was the chaff between their millstones. Both of them wanted what I could do. I remembered the big man who had shouted at me in the battle, and I remembered the blood on his face and the spear blazing its trail of agony across my back. Only an accident they hadn't skewered me.

I couldn't stay here. They'd find me. The village wasn't big enough to hide from them. But sleep came over me before I could get any further than that.

There were spring greens to pick the next morning, nearly a bushel basket from the patch we had. Jonna had stayed behind to do it, and I helped her, and when we'd finished she eased her back.

'Too much for just us,' she said. 'The soil's good. And the neighbours have done as well. We'll trade some.'

I looked around. The houses in sight made little flecks of white lime against the brown of the soil. Beyond, not far off, the scrub and low thickets of the moorland lined the sky. Further away, the blue of mountains loomed. Who was there to trade with, if not the neighbours?

In the afternoon, Jonna hoisted the bushel basket on her back. She had added some other things to it, herbs picked wild from the open country, sharp and balmy by turns. She wouldn't hear of me carrying anything with any weight to it. Which reminded me.

'We could put it on Chloe,' I said, 'if she's anywhere near.' A way of asking what they'd done with her. I'd called her, and found she was nowhere near.

'Chloe?' asked Jonna.

'My horse.'

'Ah. Well, we have no stable here, nor a way to care for so fine an animal. So we sent her on. The Order will look after her. There's stables at Waycastle, and good grooms.'

And people who will want to know how one of Nathan's horses came to them. Gods.

'Waycastle?' I asked, looking unconcerned.

She nodded, shrugging into the straps that carried the bushel basket. 'Their nearest place. Just beyond the pass at Oriment. About four or five days' journey.' She waved vaguely towards the mountains. 'We must go, if we're going. The day's getting on.'

Four days there, four days back. I could expect them tomorrow or the next day. I was just in time. I went with Jonna, thinking hard.

We climbed the hill behind the house, along a boundary between two fields, where a footpath led upwards. Towards the middle of the slope the fields ended and the path became steep. The soil

turned thin and stony. But the footpath led on towards the top of the hill, a track worn by many feet already. I wondered at that. Why would the people hereabouts be trudging up here, away from the fields that they had won and were tilling with such labour?

The day was warmer than the weather up till now, and Jonna wiped her brow when we came to the top. Then she unslung the basket and stared around. So did I.

There was a good view, but nothing in sight except the fields behind us and the moors, rolling on into the haze-blue distance. Earthen colours behind, with slight differences made by the different ploughing patterns. Beyond and before, russet and dull greens and browns; the mottled colours of the moors. They were higher and steeper towards the mountains. Perhaps that was why the people had settled here, four days out from the last place. This was the first piece of reasonably flat land.

Jonna took her basket and set it down on the ground. No, not on the ground. On a flat stone that lay flush with the surface of the hill at the very peak. She gestured to me to place my bundles of herbs next to it. I did, wondering.

'Are we making an offering to the gods?' I asked. I knew some people did that.

Jonna smiled. 'No, not that. Not today. Now, we need to go down the hill a few steps and wait.' And she turned away and led me down past the first thicket. We sat on a stone, side by side, and stared out over the fields, not towards the hilltop. I sat with her, puzzled. I knew what would happen to goods if you left them out unwatched in Tenabra. All right, perhaps it wasn't the same here, but nevertheless, what was the reason for putting them out on the hillside?

On a venture, as we sat, I cast my mind upwards, to find a hawk. There was one high in the blue above, and I had him stare down where I thought I was, while I looked up at him. The experience I'd had, looking through the eyes of a bird and seeing my own face, was interesting, and I thought I'd do it again.

But as he looked down, and I used his eyes, I could see not two people on that hill, but three. The third was at its peak. We sat thirty paces away downhill, behind a thicket, staring off into the other direction.

'Jonna,' I said urgently. 'Someone's behind us. He's taking – I'm sure he's taking – our things.'

Her face didn't change. 'Shh!' she cautioned. 'Wait. No matter what you hear – and you must have sharp ears – stay here and say nothing.'

I blinked. Then I cursed myself. I'd almost given away that I had the talent. Jonna was nice, and these people were nice generally, but I didn't think their goodwill would stand knowing that I was a Dark mage. I straightened my face and used the hawk's eyes.

The person on the top of the hill was small and dark, and moved slowly. The hawk could see detail, but he was looking down from on top, and there's little you can tell about a person's face from that angle. I concentrated to see him clearer, and as I did, I slowly became aware of the current of his thought.

What? This wasn't right. I couldn't enter a person's mind the way I could an animal's. People's minds were like fortresses, hard like stone, slippery, unable to be grasped. But this …

It was a male. I could hear his mind, in a way. Not the words, but I could track his feelings. He was calculating, and he was weighing the greens and the herbs in his hands, and flitting pictures of other goods and ideas about them whirred in his head like the flicker of sunlight on water.

He was thinking of what and how much to offer in payment. The sun was warm on his neck, and it irritated him. I didn't think at all, but sent to him the pleasure I felt in the gentle glow. It was suddenly as if he saw it a different way, and he felt what I felt and thought in that moment as I thought.

Then I remembered Teska's words: *You can change animals … their minds and their bodies – and animals includes goblins.*

That was a goblin. I could change him, mind and body. I could make him love me and obey me, as Chloe loved and obeyed me. He wouldn't care about me being a Dark mage. Well, maybe he would, but it wouldn't matter.

I sat and thought, and as I did he finished his work. He groped about the rock on the top of the hill, and I heard his thought: again not in

words, but as a series of movements with hand and fingers. The key to his hole.

And the stone lifted like the lid of a chest, and there was a passage, narrow and low, that led into the hill. He packed the goods into a basket and selected his payment from a stack just inside: a saw blade, a flask. He laid them out before the stone, and retreated inside to the cool and the dim, with a sense of relief I could feel. The stone dropped shut behind him.

I was on fire to see what would happen next, but Jonna sat on until she was certain that the trade had been made. The wind sighed over the hilltop, and the grasses fluttered and rustled. I fidgeted.

Finally she rose, and we returned to the height. Our goods were gone, and I remembered to be surprised, and more surprised still at those that replaced them. Jonna was pleased.

'The underfolk give good trade,' she said. 'A fine blade, this, and we need one for the planks we will cut as soon as we can send the wagon down to the nearest stand of trees. And this is even better.'

She drew the cork from the flask and sniffed. *Wine?* I thought, but no. The whiff that reached me was acrid and oily.

'Lamp oil,' said Jonna. 'The best there is. The underfolk know the secret of making it, and it gives a steady clear light without smoke. Much better than candles or slush.' She packed it away, padding it with cloths. 'Come. The day isn't over, not yet. There's still work to do.'

She began to pick her way down the trail. I

followed, looking back. There, behind me, were the people who would shield me from Nathan and the Order alike. I knew that, now. The only problem remaining was how to meet them properly.

WILL

'Nathan's own brand,' said Silvus. 'She's not from a private regiment, then, nor is she a hired animal. Belonged to one of Nathan's regulars.' He cradled his chin in his hand. 'Trot her back again,' he said to the groom.

The big mare moved with an easy flowing gait, her hooves hardly seeming to touch the hard-packed earth of the bailey.

Silvus nodded. 'Not a knightly destrier either, Will. For one thing, a mare. Much better tempered, and schooled for lighter aids.' A nice way of saying her rider didn't have to spend half the time fighting with her. 'She can carry weight, all right, but the saddle she was wearing was a light horseman's.' He picked it up. 'See – no cantle.'

I watched her move. She had been poorly when she came in, but a single day's rest and grooming had restored her. Her coat shone, lustrous and even, and she tossed her head. Suddenly I knew that toss. It had come just before the hoof landed fair in my brisket.

'No wonder Nathan's Horseguard nearly ran us down, if they were riding mounts like that,' I said.

'Yes. That's another thing that's different. She's not far off the size of a destrier, but she'd have three times the endurance. Camarg blood – look at the amount of bone and the dished face …'

He could go on all day on this subject. I thought I'd better cut straight through to the essential part. 'And she was being ridden by a small dark girl.'

'Um. Wounded across the back. Yes.' Silvus ran a hand through his hair. 'Well, there's no doubt.' He turned. 'You were right,' he said to Sister Informer, who was standing, arms folded, three paces away. 'Our mage is in Newcombe. We must try for her, and that as soon as possible. It seems she's run away from Nathan again, and she clearly has no love for him, but we can't take the risk he won't find her again and force her. We must take her first and hide her from him.'

Sister Informer nodded. 'So. We'd best tell the Prioress.'

That was no problem. Sister Informer had the ear of Prioress Winterridge, at any time of the day or night. The sun was a full handspan above the horizon, which would mean that the Prioress had been up for four hours already.

We found her flexing a blade at the new forge. The swordsmith, a youth who had been making hoes a month before, stood blinking while she bent it out of shape and let it spring back, then sighted along the spine. Behind her, Arienne stood in the shadows, hands clasped before her.

'It warps a little,' she said. 'But it's much better than the last batch. The new charcoal?'

The smith mumbled an assent.

'Good. Well done. The pattern welding shows great skill.'

'It was good of the underfolk to help him learn that skill, Sister Prioress,' said Arienne, pointedly.

'Amen to that. It proves they are coming to trust us. For all they know we might end by using it against them. That is your doing, Arienne.' The Prioress nodded at the smith, looked around and saw us. 'Ah. Sister Informer, Ser Silvus, Squire de Parkin.' Then she saw the looks on our faces. 'Excuse me, if you please.'

She ducked her head to pass under the lintel of the door, for she was tall, and walked with us across the busy bailey, hands behind her back, and we told her.

At the end of the recital, she nodded. 'We must send to bring her in, certainly, but Nathan's scouts are already observing the pass, though his main body will not be here for a few days yet. I have just been discussing this with Arienne. There is only one way to slip past him now.'

My ears pricked up. 'One way?' I shot a glance at Arienne, who nodded in agreement.

'Yes,' she said. 'As Sister Prioress says, we must go the way you went before, but this time with the consent of the underpeople. We can slip past Nathan by walking under the mountain.'

Silvus pursed his lips. 'I seem to keep on making this observation, but nevertheless it is a correct one. You young people use the word "we" a great deal.'

Arienne's gaze slid to me. 'What else have you been volunteering for?' she asked, frost forming on the words.

'Me?' I protested. 'Speak for yourself. What's this thing *we're* going to do?'

She shrugged. 'I have to go, obviously. Someone has to talk to the underpeople.'

Silvus and I glanced at each other. 'I hate it when there's a good reason for doing something I don't like,' he muttered.

'And,' continued Arienne inexorably, 'clearly I will need someone with me who can force the mage's compliance, and someone who can speak for the Order.'

'We can do that in the same person,' remarked Sister Informer. 'I will go.'

'And I,' added Silvus.

The Prioress considered. 'Very well. There is no reason to send more than we need. But we do need three, plus Mistress Brook, to share guarding her. This mage will have to be watched all the way back, girl or no. She has already escaped Nathan.' She smiled at us. 'Mind you, some of my favourite people did that. But she must not escape us.'

'She's wounded,' Silvus reminded her.

'Yes, she replied. 'And not likely to be fond of us for that reason. After all, we did it to her. All the more reason to fetch her quickly. You said that she was fevered, raving. Let us hope that her recovery has not yet taken place. Or else she'll turn the underfolk against us.' Her face took on the lines of chiselled stone. 'She must not be allowed to do

that. No matter what. She must be prevented from going to the Dark, by any means necessary.'

She and Sister Informer exchanged glances. In other words, if we couldn't stop her any other way, we were to kill her. I thought of the small figure, surrounded, panic in her eyes, struggling with that horse. She had looked lost and helpless. I couldn't have done it then. I grimaced.

The Prioress was watching me. 'You have doubts, Squire de Parkin, which do you credit. I would not set anyone to such a task. In truth, it weighs heavily on my own soul. You need not ...'

'No,' I said, before she could relieve me. 'No. I failed then, and because of that I condemned your sisters for nothing. Please, Prioress. Let me try to make up. She will not go to the Dark if I can stop her. My word on it.'

She considered me, head on one side. 'Very well,' she said, eventually. 'The word of a gentleman I will accept. And you, Ser de Castro?'

Silvus bowed his head. 'I will serve you in this, Prioress, by my word and gage.' He sounded unhappy, but what Silvus said, that he would do, or die trying.

She nodded. 'Very well. This will be on foot. The tunnels of the underpeople will never pass even a pack pony. You still have the covercloth?' We nodded yes. 'You should start as soon as Mistress Brook has obtained permission and arranged for guides.' She started across the bailey, headed for the keep. 'I have some explaining to do to the Lady. Perhaps She will show me a better way. I hope so.'

But the Lady was silent. When we passed through the gate of the fortress, carrying provisions for four days on our backs, Prioress Winterridge came to the outer steps of the keep and saw us off with a face that was already harrowed.

We crossed the narrow valley by a way that I remembered without pleasure, for all that it was a pleasant walk in the hills. The last time Silvus and I came this way, we had been three parts dead. For Arienne, though, it was different. She was going to visit friends.

We climbed the opposite slope. Waycastle sat on a spur of the hillside to the north of the little stream, a brook which raced down the valley to join the Ladystream further west. Once we'd climbed far enough, we could look down on it, a mile off and more, like a toy castle set down on a green. The walls and towers, so strong and tall when we stood next to them, seemed puny and frail when set against the ancient bones of the mountains.

Arienne breathed in and touched rocks, trailing a hand over them. I knew what she was doing. Even here, even where humans walked, there was mana in the stones of the mountain, like little chips of light.

We plodded up the trail until we came to a bend in it, no different from a thousand other bends.

'Turn your backs,' said Arienne. We obeyed. She had given her word not to tell others how she worked the underpeople's doorknocker, and Arienne, like Silvus, kept her word. There was a faint scrape of fingers against rock, and then a different quality in the breeze. Not a sound from latch or hinge, but the wind played hollow around a hole in the mountainside.

We turned back. Arienne gestured us in, and we ducked our heads and walked into the darkness.

Inside, she groped in her pack, pulled out a lamp – the make was the underpeople's – and lit it. A tug, and the rock door swung shut without a sound, counterweighted beautifully. We were in the warren.

This was a made entrance. The underfolk used natural caves wherever they could, but they linked them with shafts and drives that they cut over slow generations with pick and patience, for they were marvellous miners. The floor was dry and sanded, and the worked walls were braced with iron beams. Iron that didn't rust, for they were marvellous smiths, too. It was low, so that I had to stand with head bowed. They were smaller and broader than us, on the average, with leathery skins that didn't sweat and were best suited for the unvarying coolness underground. They had lived underground for uncounted years.

But the underground gave few sources of food, Aricnne had said. Cave fish, some mushrooms. They had galleries, their most secret places, with openings to the world above most artfully concealed, to bring sunlight in so that they could grow vegetables in trays. They had to line such places with silver mirrors, and the soil had to be scraped from the floors of caves where bats roosted. No wonder they would trade for the food we had for the growing; and they had much to give in return.

We straightened our faces and waited. Not long, for the underpeople were polite. It would not have done to plunge off into the further tunnels ourselves. Apart from being rude, it would also have been dangerous.

Around the farther corner came a glow, and then the meeting party. Three guards with crossbow and shortsword, and a guide. All dressed in the underpeople's loincloth and vest.

It wasn't cloth they wore, but soft leather. Bat skin, I had learned. I wondered at what ways of life they had, here under the hills. Did they farm the bats?

Arienne stared at the last of them, the guide, her face as blank as a gambler's, and he stared back at her. This was good manners, to the underpeople. I tried to copy her; Silvus and Sister Informer, too. After a moment, Arienne began to talk to them.

I had some idea how she did it; I knew I couldn't, and not only because I didn't speak the language. I didn't have the talent, and Arienne did. She could read what they felt, and they could read her, if she wanted them to. But there were further signs, tiny gestures and fleeting slight variations of face and stance, that added meaning to the stream of emotion. You had to stare closely at a person to notice such things at all.

Arienne relaxed after a few moments. 'They saw the signal from the castle, and have already given

permission. They will take us to the exit closest to Newcombe.'

'They don't run all the way out there?'

'No. This is a large warren, but not that large. They're not saying, and I'm not asking, how large it really is. They can set us a long distance on our way, and Stillpeace, here, says that it's an easy walk, with only one set of stairs. There's a millway, he says.'

'What's a millway?'

'You'll find out.' She paused. 'He also says ... there's a small warren near Newcombe. He's worried about them, if there's a Dark mage in the offing. They have no defence. He urges us to hurry.'

'Let's go, then.' We shouldered our packs and moved out.

The passages were low at first, and we walked hunched over, down a steep, narrow drive that led straight into the mountain. Then we joined a larger way, and walked on, the guide – what had his name been? – Stillpeace? – in front. Behind, the guards followed. We were accepted, not liked. Possibly I had killed fathers, brothers, sons of theirs. I tried to remember that.

We splashed through little rills from time to time, water that emerged from the walls. The passage curved and jinked until I lost all notion of my direction. Somewhere there was a low rumbling that rose by degrees to a dull roar, the walls reverberating around us, louder as we went. I felt like a mouse in the soundbox of a bass viol.

We turned into a long gallery and descended a stair. The noise shook the walls. At the bottom was the strangest thing I ever saw.

It was a long, narrow platform with wheels, pieced together out of sheet bronze and leather, with four bench seats on it. But there was no team to pull it. The underpeople used no draught animals.

Instead, a steel rope – a rope made out of steel strands twisted together, not a chain – ran through guides on the floor. It was moving at a steady rate, gliding from the darkness of the left to the darkness of the right.

'The millway,' said Arienne, with satisfaction. 'Sit on the benches and put your packs under them.'

We took our places. Stillpeace gripped a lever that jutted up from the side. He eased it forward. There was a faint grinding sound, and then a jerk. The carriage began to move forward, faster and faster. Stillpeace pushed the lever all the way forward, and we were moving into the darkness of the tunnel before us. It was just large enough to take us.

I just sat and gaped, but Silvus had to know. 'How does it work?' he asked.

'The lever tightens a clamp on the cable. We are pulled along by that.'

'What moves the cable?' He was really interested.

'It's a continuous loop, miles long. It passes around a mill wheel that is turned by an enormous head of falling water, fed by mountain lakes a mile or more above us. That water powers everything in a warren, which is why the underfolk are mostly to be found in the mountains.'

Silvus nodded, and watched the walls, close enough to touch, moving past us as fast as a horse could trot, while we sat at our ease. From his face he was working out all the ins and outs of how the thing was made to work. I was content just to wonder.

We descended and ascended. From time to time we passed a light in the passage, and Stillpeace would release the lever. We would roll a few moments, and then another light showed and he would close the clamp again. Again we would pick up pace.

'Changing cables,' remarked Arienne.

Silvus nodded again. 'I suppose they counterweight the cars on the slopes by compensating on the opposite run of the cables,' he said, and she nodded in her turn.

The motion was smooth, swaying slightly. The air was cool, unvarying. I thought about how much craft was needed to make this place, to bring food and air down this far. I thought about it until my head ached and I went to sleep. So much for wonder.

CHAPTER

ASTA

It was after midnight, so far as I could tell, and time to be moving. They'd be coming for me soon, Nathan or the Order or both. Let them fight it out among themselves. I wouldn't care. I wouldn't even be here.

The house was dark, and quiet except for Per's snores. I gathered my bundle and slipped out, not making a sound. Practice. Teska had said I was a poor sort of thief. What would he know?

Sharp, fixed stars with points like spears glittered among drifts of fleeing cloud. Behind the sleeping village, the hill frowned down.

I found the way up, straight as a stretched string between the field boundaries, winding

around the wild slopes above them.

I came to the place where we had sat, and went on, passing the thicket. At the very peak of the hill I found the stone, and walked around it once. No obvious handle, but I had seen it open. I remembered the sequence of hand movements the guard had made, but I had no idea where to start. Well, this spot was as good as any. I pulled at it to open it.

It wouldn't. I groped for a better finger hold, and found none. I hauled, and it was as if the stone was attached to the roots of the world. I fell back.

All right. It was locked. Well, I had dealt with locks before. Time to think. Through the hawk's eyes I had seen the rock open like a trapdoor. It opened that way, hinged from that direction. All I needed was to find the hinges …

An hour later, I was still scrabbling and niggling at the base of the stone. Nothing. The goblins hid their doorways well.

I drew off a way and sat on the ground, contemplating the irregular hump of the stone against the bright stars. Another two hours of this, and I'd have to slink off and either hide or else return to the house. Jonna and Per were early risers.

I searched for a mind, and found only tiny points of animal awareness in the grasses and the thicket. Nothing that thought in words, even words so strange as the ones I had heard only yesterday. And I remembered other words, the words of Teska again, may he rot: *You need to see the animal you control, at least at first, and the talent rapidly decays with distance.*

Think. Think. The goblins traded here. Well, what would cause them to open their door but trade goods placed outside it? Why not offer them some? They wanted food, it seemed. I had that.

I'd taken some of Jonna's dried and pounded fruit and a bag of grain. Not much – I didn't want to rob them. But they owed me for a day's wage and a fine horse. Now I took it from my bundle and laid it on the ground. Then I walked away down the hill. There was a fox, not far off. I convinced him that a new vixen was in the offing, and he was soon watching the stone with attention.

For a long time, nothing. I became stiff, and stretched very slowly. Dawn was not far now. The slab of rough stone lay quiet under the stars. Then a slow change began in its outline, a gradual humping up, and little by little it yawned open. I watched through the fox's eyes, and a head poked cautiously up, and as it did, a current of thought flowed into the pool of my mind. Caution; that was a habit. Then pleasure in the coolness and dark; a certain nervousness about the wind in the heather and the odd noises from animals. Then calculation. He was considering what price to give for the things I had left, but he was thinking about it in words that meant nothing to me.

I let him prattle on to himself, and listened to the thoughts under his thoughts, until I knew him. And one of the thoughts at the wellspring of his mind, at the very roots that formed him, was a need to protect the young, the helpless of his people.

After that it was simple. I made a noise like a

crying child; he tensed, but I took away his nervousness. Out he came step by cautious step, until he saw me, and in a moment I had told him the tale, and poured out my deep need and love of the goblins.

He had no choice, after that. What's a learned thought beside the deepest of needs and the most urgent of feelings? He stroked me as I sat on the ground and nothing could stop the pity and the love. I looked up into his face. There was something in it that reminded me of Sart, the flat bones underneath the flesh. I sent that back to him, and he was lost. He had never been allowed to breed, and it gnawed at his spirit.

We sat there together until the black of the night was just starting to be tempered with the grey of the earliest day. There were shouts below. The village was awakening.

WILL

The warren under the Brokenbacks had a name which in the nearest human words meant *The Place of Youngest Stones.* But stones are all the same age. Aren't they? Arienne only shrugged when I asked her.

After the millway there had been a stair, a long sweeping passage with steps hacked out of the living rock, and it had brought us to a junction and then a narrow corridor and eventually to an outlet. The last two hundred paces they blindfolded

us, and I have no idea how the exit door worked.

Arienne said: 'They ask your word and bond that you will not take off the blindfold until the door has closed and I have told you.'

'My word on it,' said Silvus.

'Mine, too,' said I.

And so we stood, and there was a grinding, and the cool breath of evening swirled around us, and Arienne took my hand and led me forward.

'Step up here; once again. Now step straight ahead, two full strides. Good. Now stand.'

We waited, and there was a silence. Arienne was talking to them. Then the grinding again, and a soft impact. Quiet again, except for the sighing of the wind in the gorse.

'All right,' she said, and we gave ourselves sight again.

We were standing on a long roll of hill, above a swale through which a slow stream ran. Across the little vale was another hillside like a green wall, and along its face ran a track, a wagon trail, clear as a fingermark on a frosty window. Already roads were snaking out into the moors once again, challenging the endless leagues. I looked behind me. I knew there was a doorway of the underpeople here, but I could find no trace of it. The hill looked the same as every other, rolling, irregular, spattered with thickets and brush.

Arienne pointed to the left, roughly north by the low sun. 'Newcombe is that way,' she said. 'Four or five leagues. We can be there by tomorrow morning if we hurry.'

Silvus and Sister Informer exchanged glances. It was fairly close to dusk. The millway had brought us three days' distance in one. And we had slept.

'Very well,' said Silvus. 'You think it necessary to hurry?'

'Yes,' Arienne replied tightly. 'If she recovers and suborns the underpeople before we get there, they are lost. The Dark will corrupt her and them.'

Sister Informer nodded. 'And there's Nathan,' she agreed.

Silvus grunted and lengthened his stride. He listens to sense from anyone. We were already stepping out. We splashed through the little stream, turned on to the road, and commenced to make distance.

I'd made night marches before, and under worse conditions than this. The night was only a little damp, for the moorland. There was a shower or two before midnight, clearing later. The road was clear enough, two wagon ruts and a centre strip, snaking through the scrub, and trending a little east of north, as I found once I had sighted the guiding stars. The slopes were steep at first, but we were moving mostly across them, and later they flattened out.

We walked in single file, not talking. There was no need to hide tracks once we were on the road, though we had taken care to conceal the place where we had joined it. And Arienne could use night birds and animals in the thickets to scout for us. She allowed that, so long as she wasn't

forcing them or deceiving them. The Dark is the practice of warping things for one's own benefit – warping anything. Minds, bodies, nature. It isn't warping the nature of an owl or a wildcat to watch through its eyes as it watches a hillside. Night hunters will do that anyway; Arienne was simply piggy-backing on them, without weighing them down.

Thus it was we made good time, as if able to see in the dark, avoiding the wet patches, looking ahead to see the difficult bits. The night was starlit and quiet except for the sweep and rush of the wind, and the moon set early.

Nathan was some leagues to the south. His scouts would see and report the rough track that wandered away northwards from the pass, and he might be moved to investigate it. Certainly he would picket it, and send riders to see where it led, sooner or later. We had to be there first. That was another reason to step out.

It was on the tail of the night that we came to the fields of Newcombe, new plough land still scattered with stones, unfit yet for much more than peas and beans and turnips. But there was some bottom land, and that would make meadow some day. We passed it as the frogs began their last choruses.

A house – a hut, rather – loomed up by the road. 'We'll have to enquire,' said Sister Informer, and she knocked on a doorframe. The folk were abroad already. She had a few words in the western speech with the householder, and then turned and pointed.

'The next house but two,' she said. 'A few hundred paces, and off on a branch of the track to the right.'

We nodded and followed her. The cocks were crowing, and the first streaks of daylight were creeping up into the sky. There was the morning star, the Lady's own herald. Good. I know that 'Dark' is just a figure of speech, and that the night is no more evil than the day. All the same, I like to be able to see. We are people of the sun, just as the underfolk say.

Here was the house, but we were still a long hundred strides from it when the plank door opened and a man came out.

'Asta,' he called, hands trumpeted to his mouth. 'Asta!'

ASTA

No more time to waste. They were calling my name, now.

They have taken me and will lock me away, I thought, and let my fear flow into him. They will make me unfree, and make me work for them. I felt again the bar of fire across my back, and I fed that pain into his mind, and he flinched, and became angry that they should do that to a helpless child.

He would shelter me. He would protect me. The need to do it was more than a duty; it was a necessity.

We climbed to the height together, and below, somebody shouted 'No!'

The rock was open, and he gestured me in. Still I had to turn and look down the trail at them, like a rabbit at the entrance to its burrow.

Four of them, running up the hill, fit to burst. I had expected horses, like lords. That they were on foot nonplussed me for a moment. One I recognised – the big man who'd had blood on his face. Another Teska. Behind them, also running, waving at me to stop, were Jonna and Per. Well, I was sorry, and I liked them and all that, but I wasn't going to become a slave again for their sake.

I turned away. They were still a hundred paces off, downhill, and blowing like that they'd have to be great marksmen to hit me with a crossbow bolt. The old man who led them held up a hand. They halted.

'Wait,' he cried. 'Wait! Please.'

He sat abruptly on a rock by the side of the trail, gasping. 'Please!' he called again. 'We mean you no harm.'

No harm. That's what Teska had said. I shook my head and stepped down into the hill, and the goblin pulled the door shut and did something inside it. It was dark and cool and slightly damp.

Up above, night was ending. I had hoped to see the sun again, once more, but if not, well …

The goblin – his name was something like Bargainer – lit a small lamp, and we turned away from the door. I had others to meet, and there was, as Jonna would say, a great deal to do. I followed him into the dark corridors ahead.

WILL

The door closed silently behind them. I had the feeling that it ought to have boomed like the drums of doom. For a moment all I could do was gasp and blow. It seemed that every time I saw her I was like that. Well, you try running a thousand paces uphill in armour, yelling your head off, after a long night march.

Silvus croaked a curse, then apologised. Sister Informer and Arienne both ignored him.

A silence, while we sat and despised the morning, the world, the entire condition of the human race and the universe in general. Then Silvus stirred and stood up.

'Well, that's that,' he said. 'Unless you can think of something.'

He was talking to Arienne, whose face was as pinched and as white as his own. That was the Dark up there, the manipulation of minds for the profit of the mage, and both of them were reacting to it as to the opening of a charnel pit.

'Not I,' she said, and her voice was strained.

I cleared my throat. 'You can't, um, counter her effects? Prevent the underpeople from assisting her?'

Arienne grimaced, a rapid downward flexing of her lips. 'Only by doing what she is doing. Changing their minds back again, to what I think they ought to be. But who is to say what they ought to be? Who am I to say that?'

Silvus nodded. 'It is the Dark, the most subtle

temptation of all. To mind-lie to a person, and only for his own good.' He turned his back on the slab of rock at the top of the hill. 'Never!'

We walked down the hill again, a great deal more slowly than we came up. The young couple who had sheltered her watched us with stricken faces. Sister Informer gave them a rapid shake of the head, and they glanced at each other in dismay.

'You couldn't have known, and you did very well,' said Sister Informer. 'But it seems that there will be an end to your trade with the underfolk. Probably.'

The goodwife wrung her hands. 'Who'd have thought it?' she asked. 'She seemed so nice. Helped us in the house, and worked in the bean patch …'

'Yes.' Sister Informer glanced upwards at the height again. 'But she is with the Dark now, and we should bring the news back to Sister Prioress as soon as may be. We must rest a few hours, though, and eat.'

'Please, come to our house. We have food.'

'Thank you. So have we, and we will not take from your store. But we beg a length of your floor and peace for a few hours.' She couldn't help her eyes sliding towards the peak of the hill again. 'If we are permitted it. You and your neighbours must look to your defences.'

'Would she attack us? She seemed grateful …'

'Who knows what a Dark mage will do? And to our shame, the Order cannot protect you.' Sister Informer bowed her head. 'Fealty cuts both ways.

If we cannot do our duty by you, you owe us nothing in return.'

'It hasn't happened yet. And you did not tell us to harbour a Dark mage among us. So come. Be welcome in our home.'

We hunched down the hill again, tired and discouraged and miserable. The little hut among the fields had a cheerful fire in the grate and breakfast on the hob. We ate and tried to make small conversation. Then we rolled ourselves in our blankets and slept.

Noon, and someone was shaking me awake. It was Silvus.

'We're moving?' I asked. I hadn't realised I'd let myself fall so deeply into sleep.

'Not exactly,' he replied. 'She wants to talk to us.'

'Who? Sister Informer?' She and Arienne were sleeping in another house.

'No.' That was a voice through the door. Arienne's voice.

I scrambled to my feet and started looking for my shoes and my wits. 'Who, then?'

Silvus smiled grimly. 'Who do you think?'

Outside, larks sang, and the air was rich with clover and harebells and buttercups. The sun shone, willing new growth from the freshly ploughed fields. We climbed the hill together, not speaking, Silvus and I and Arienne.

Near the top, by a thicket, stood Sister Informer.

'I woke early, so I thought I'd bring some goods up here to see if the trade was continuing,' said

Sister Informer. 'A good sign, if it is.' She turned her head, to stare up the slope. 'And what do you know, she came as far as the door and asked to parley.'

'The mage?' asked Silvus.

'In person. Our safe conduct is guaranteed, she says.'

'Word of honour?' asked Silvus, wryly. Silly question, and sillier still to trust any such thing.

But Sister Informer merely nodded. 'She wanted us to go within. I proposed an alternative. We are to approach to within hailing distance of the entrance, leaving any bows or slings behind. She is to come to the entrance, no farther, able to retreat at the first sign of trouble.'

'We could be making ourselves targets instead,' remarked Silvus.

'Mm. But in that case, all she has gained is a corpse or two at most, and the village's undying enmity. And the Order's.' She shrugged. 'We might as well find out what she wants.'

Silvus nodded, in his turn. 'Very well.'

In the back of his mind was his oath. I knew that, because my oath was in the back of mine. But we walked together up the track, passed the last bend, and came into sight of the rock at the top.

It was open and waiting for us. In the opening was one of the underfolk, squinting in the light, keeping to the cool shadow. And behind him, shielded by him, half-seen in shade that was black against the brightness, a small dark figure stood.

'Stop there.' We were twenty paces off. The

young voice was sharp, but self-possessed for all that, and we halted. The air crackled with tension.

'Put your hands out so I can see them.'

We showed our empty hands, even as I revisited in her speech the tones and vowels of the Tenabran streets. But this was no street urchin, not any more. She might have nodded. 'Good enough,' she called. 'Now. Who speaks for the Order?'

Sister Informer took a half step forward, and the girl in the cave mouth tensed, as did her guard. But the sister only nodded at her.

'I do,' she said, quietly.

'You?' There was suspicion in the voice. 'Not the old man?'

Silvus bridled visibly. Sister Informer almost smiled. 'Ser de Castro and Squire de Parkin are our men. The Order speaks for itself.'

Silence. Then, 'And the other lady?'

Arienne spoke for herself, too. 'Arienne Brook. I am a student, sponsored by the Order. Studying the talent. The gift you have. And I speak to the underpeople.'

'Teska studied the talent, too.' The voice was flat with dislike.

'Who?' Arienne's brows drew down.

'You don't know him? Be thankful you don't.'

Arienne nodded, as if she understood. Sister Informer cleared her throat. 'What do you want of us?' she asked, speaking clearly across the gap.

My eyes were getting used to the shadow in the cave by now. I could see the girl who stood there, looking over the guard's shoulder. Her face was

small, dark, sharp-featured, with bright, quick eyes. The guard gripped the hilt of his shortsword with one hand. The other gripped something on the underside of the shell of rock over his head, ready to drop it in an instant.

The girl's eyes narrowed. 'I want to tell you that you'll have peace from me if you leave me alone. I have nothing against the people here. They can trade, and live in peace as they have done, so long as nobody tries to bother me. Live and let live.' Sister Informer was silent. 'What do you say?'

Sister Informer shook her head, regretfully, firmly. 'No. I cannot grant you peace and law. It would be against my vows. You are using the Dark.'

'I am not!' Her voice was shrill, like the voices raised in playground arguments. Sister Informer folded her arms, not offering an answer. After a moment the girl went on: 'Anyway, you just want me to do stuff for you. Like Teska. To make things. To help you. And I'd never be free again. *Do it or burn,* he said.'

'Ah,' said Sister Informer. 'I begin to see. This Teska, he would be Prince Nathan's man?'

'Yes.' The answer was sullen. 'Just like those two lugs are yours.'

Sister Informer nodded. 'Well, consider this. Prince Nathan, our mortal enemy, is perhaps ten leagues from this spot with an army far larger than ours. If he discovers where you are, he'll come and dig you out as if you were a badger.'

The young face of the mage twisted with scorn. 'He can try.'

'Oh, he'll succeed. This is only a small warren, not well defended – because it hasn't needed to be. He has engineers and sappers enough, and you would be worth any amount of time. He could use you to recruit the underpeople as well, you see.'

'The underpeople?'

'You probably call them goblins.' Silence, except for the wind wailing in the grass. 'So you see why we can't leave you alone. Once Nathan finds you, you are lost, and so are they. If you continue to use the Dark, you're lost anyway.'

'If I give up, I'm lost, too. I'd just become your slave instead of Nathan's.'

Sister Informer sighed. 'I don't suppose you'd accept my oath, by the Lady's name and by my hope of Her garden, that we would never force or even allow the use of your talent as Nathan has done?'

'No, I wouldn't. Would you?'

'No. I don't suppose so. I, too, would want guarantees. The fact that you won't use your talent in Nathan's service is much in your favour, though.'

'I wonder if you'll think this is.'

'What?' asked Sister Informer, and at the same moment Arienne gasped and whirled. Silvus and I followed, and our hands went to our hilts. There were eight warriors of the underpeople behind us, and their steel crossbows were levelled.

'Don't try it,' said the voice, triumphant now. 'There's another exit to the warren in the thicket. Don't move. You won't be hurt. But I want a hostage. Not you. I want you to take the news back.

Not one of your enforcers, either. You'll do, lady, since you speak goblin. Step forward.'

She meant Arienne. I moved in front of her, and drew. I was wearing mail, but mail won't keep out a crossbow bolt at that range. Silvus moved up beside me, steel clearing leather.

'No,' said Sister Informer. 'I think not.' She drew as well, completing a circle around Arienne. 'Now you must kill us, shoot us down in cold blood.'

'Don't make me do it.' The voice was ragged, now, with an emotion made up of fear and despair and dashed hope.

'I will not.' Sister Informer's voice was as cool as glass, and as inflexible. 'You will do this thing of yourself, and will account for it yourself. The Order of the Lady of Victories does not bow to the Dark. Do what you will.'

I saw the mage glance at her puppets, and for a moment thought that it was all over. But nothing happened. We all stood there staring at each other.

In the breathless silence, Arienne tugged on my sleeve. 'Will you stop posturing for just one moment, Will Parkin?' she demanded.

Cool wit provided me only one reply: 'Eh?'

'You're so busy rescuing me that you haven't thought this through. And you, Sister Informer. Is martyrdom so attractive? I'm surprised at you.'

Sister Informer shot her a swift glance. 'What are you talking about?' she asked. Then: 'Oh. Oh! Ah, I see. Yes.' A pause. 'I agree. It's the best we could do.'

'So let me pass.'

Arienne stepped past me, and I grabbed her elbow with my free hand. 'Not so fast,' I said. 'What's going on?'

She sighed. 'Think, Will. I know you can, when your chivalry's not thinking for you. This girl has no idea of what the Dark is, nor what the talent is, nor what the Order is. If we are to save her and the underpeople, we must teach her. Who better to do it?'

I blinked. She gently disengaged herself. 'I'll be all right. She really isn't a bad person. If she were, we wouldn't still be standing here. She's just frightened and angry, and she's been hurt. I will bring her as soon as may be.' She stood tall and kissed me. 'Farewell for now.'

And I stood there like a plough ox while she turned and walked steadily up the hill to the opening in the earth. Shadows closed over her, and then the dark swallowed her up and the stone shut on her and she was gone.

CHAPTER

ASTA

he door closed. 'This is the Dark, you know,' said the tall girl.

'There's a lamp. It's not so bad. You'll get used to it,' I replied, not understanding on purpose.

She shook her head. 'You know what I mean. And I am used to it.' She stopped and stared at the goblin who was guarding me – Doorkeeper was his name. Suddenly her own thought was as open to me as a temple door. She spoke the words as she thought them, for my benefit. *People-of-Youngest-Stones greet. Lack (you) (anything)?*

He stiffened slightly, and that was the only thing I could see. But I could hear him, in a way.

Again she translated. *Satisfaction for now,*

unhungry. Trading-with-sunpeople needed, good.

She nodded to me. 'You understood?' I nodded, in my turn, still rigid with surprise. 'They built here because of the settlement at Newcombe. If they stop trading, they'll run short of food.'

'I won't stop them trading. I've already said so.'

She smiled faintly. 'You also *said* we had safe conduct.'

'So you have. I won't hurt you.' I felt uncomfortable about that, but she took no notice.

'Unless matters don't suit you. Your would-be master – Teska, wasn't that his name? – he must have said much the same before he bound you to service.'

She was shrewd, this one, for all her ladylike ways. What she was saying was that I had turned myself into a version of Teska. Well, he was doing it for profit. I was trying to live free. There's a difference. Still, I couldn't say anything for a moment.

'You see why this is the Dark?' She was quite matter-of-fact about it. 'You've already warped these people's minds, because you needed to; broken your word because you think it necessary. And now, you'll keep me hostage, just as Teska kept you ...'

Enough was enough. I was tired of hearing about Teska. A plague on him. 'Quiet!' I snapped. 'Shut up about Teska.'

'He'll be here soon, you know, with his friends. I wonder if you'll be able to ignore him then?'

'I've had all I can take of this.' I looked at Doorkeeper, and sent to him how I was unhappy

with this person, that she was threatening me, and I was frightened of her. I caught nothing but confusion in return.

That was the trouble. She could speak to them. I could only tell them how I felt. I must have looked annoyed, because she laughed.

'I'll tell him you want me put away. But if I promise to keep quiet about you-know-who, will you allow me to tell you one more thing?'

'What is it?' I snarled.

'Only this. This is the Dark, the use of the talent to change minds and bodies for your own ends. The Order and its people do not trade with the Dark.'

'You mean you'd rather let them starve? You've got a neck, telling me *I'm* the bad one!'

She looked down at the floor, then up. 'No. They shall not starve. But think, please think, what you are doing to them.'

She nodded, picked up the hem of her skirt, and started down the narrow steps, with me behind her. Doorkeeper followed with the lamp. This was crazy. She was supposed to be the hostage around here. Wasn't she? And I was the boss. Wasn't I?

WILL

I was getting tired of failing. I seemed to be doing it a lot lately, and other people were having to take up the slack. First the sisters, then Arienne.

I must've looked as if it was getting to me. Sister Informer and Silvus exchanged swift glances as we started out on the track for home.

'Arienne can manage,' remarked Sister Informer after a while. 'Remember that this chit has no idea of the talent, Arienne's or her own. If all else fails …'

Silvus nodded grimly. At the last, the only restrictions on the powers of a mage were the mage and the powers themselves. And, if needs must, a foot of steel where it would do the most good.

'There's nobody in the world better to look after her than Arienne,' agreed Silvus. 'And nobody more likely to retrieve her.'

I nodded. It didn't change the way I felt about it.

I had to shelve it, though, because we had to keep our wits about us. We were on the road back. Sister Informer was risking travelling in the open day for the sake of bringing the news back as soon as might be. We had no scouts, no forewarning. If Nathan was picketing the road, we'd be in trouble.

We almost were. We heard horses, about an hour after noon, and took to the scrub. A patrol passed us at a jingling trot, following the track north.

'There'll be more,' said Sister Informer as we emerged, listening to hoofbeats dying away. 'Fortunately our earlier raiding has probably persuaded them that it's a good idea to keep together. Still …'

'I'll take point,' I volunteered.

She nodded, and I moved out ahead to just within sighting distance. We went on, slower and more careful. Just as well. We dodged two more parties during that afternoon before we found the point on the track where we'd joined it, by that entrance to the warren.

It wasn't hard to find a place to hide, using the covercloth capes. We concealed our tracks carefully and waited, eating bread and cheese.

'How do we tell them we need to get in?' I asked.

'They know,' said Sister Informer. 'Arienne said they keep a watch on this entrance, and they'll have seen us. They won't open until full dark, though, with Nathan's men on the road. I don't blame them. They'll be nervous that Arienne isn't with us, too. Take it very gently.'

The sun descended very slowly. Spring was in full flight, and the heather was in bloom. Bees worked busily, hurrying to make the most of it. Having little else to do in the bright sunshine, I worried.

At last the shadows lengthened. As full dark approached, we moved up to the spot on the hillside, slightly more exposed, where we had been when Arienne removed our blindfolds last time. We faced away, down the hill, and I at least had a suitable strip of cloth to bind my eyes. It was Arienne's favour. Silvus and Sister Informer closed theirs.

The doors of the underpeople work silently. I tried not to jump when a cool, hard little hand touched my forearm. I moved as it directed, and the sounds of the world took on a different quality after a few steps. There was only a pressure on my ears to tell me that the door had shut behind me.

They led me along a way and down three steps, before the hand tugged off my blindfold and gave it back to me. I opened my eyes, and found myself in a narrow tunnel, lit by the tiny lamps that the underpeople carry with them. Silvus and Sister Informer still had their eyes shut, and I knew both of them well enough to know they had not peeked.

'It's all right,' I said. 'We've arrived.'

The underpeople speak, but not as we do, and not with sounds. There was no way to tell them what exactly had happened. Arienne was a friend of theirs, but we were at best not enemies. At least not enemies any more. Yet Silvus had a touch of the gift, too, and he had once passed through a test they'd given. He was staring at the gate guard and his two fellows with intensity.

After a moment he sighed. 'I think he's saying he'll pass us on. I get worry and a certain wry displeasure. That's all I can make of it. It'll be the millway again, I think.'

It was the millway again, but not at once. We passed two bracing columns, wedged, but with sledgehammers leaning by them to knock the wedges out. If the entrance were discovered, the underpeople were ready to drop the hillside on anyone who forced it.

They led us through descending narrow corridors and into a grotto, a long avenue between standing coloured stones. It was lit with bags of the glowing insects the underpeople used for a permanent light source. Underpeople were in niches and side-chambers, some simply squatting, others working on benches, cutting or polishing stones, or shaping metal – strange confections of wire and enamel and coloured glass. Pictures, I think, except that they weren't pictures *of* anything. I thought of a crafter's workshop, or perhaps a bower where ladies worked on tapestry, or embroidered; and then of a garden where scholars walk as they discourse about the stars.

All of which were probably wrong, but there was a strange solemnity and peace about the place, like a shrine. It calmed me.

We walked through, the jewelled colours glorious in the strange light, descended again, met a turning, and came to a long drive and the millway.

It was as it had been, except that this was the opposite run of it. The guard's two assistants got on the carriage with us, and after a moment another two appeared. We jerked into motion, and I got on with the worrying. You can get used to anything that's not actually painful, and there was little else to do.

A day; well, a night anyway. We came at length to the place where we had boarded the carriage that first time, and there coasted to a stop. The surface was not far from here, and we climbed through half-remembered passages to reach it.

At the top, we were checked. There was an open chamber, also prepared for collapse, apparently

a cave mouth that had been masoned up. The entrance was a door that opened outward from the top. A gate guard halted us. He must have known something about human gestures, because he shook his head and pointed to a port, a little keyhole-sized window. Silvus applied his eye to it. Then he hissed on the inhale, and yielded place to Sister Informer. She hissed too. I had to wait until last, hopping from one leg to another.

When I finally got a chance, I could see the vale before Waycastle, a narrow green meadow with a fast stream down the middle of it. It was several hundred paces off, down a sharp slope, and it was full of soldiers. I was watching Nathan's army setting up its siege works and camp.

The castle stood on the opposite slope, frowning down into the little valley. It looked untouched, the banner of the Order floating from the keep, the bare mound beneath it, the earthworks, the gateway.

Nathan's camp, below me, was laid out as if on a plan. I could observe it. *Come on, Will, there'll be questions later. Find out all you can.*

All the troops were infantry, so far as I could see. No horse lines. He must have left his cavalry to guard the pass, and to patrol the roads and watch his lines of communication. Probably have a screen pushed down the road towards the west, too, to warn if there was a relief army coming. Fat chance.

But that left plenty. I estimated five thousand infantry in the vale itself, his shock troops. There

was no room for more. The rest must be camped back to the pass itself.

'We can't sneak through by daylight,' said Silvus.

'We can't pass them at all without a diversion from the garrison. Or from someone,' said Sister Informer.

I straightened myself up. 'Master Rookwood's men are in the hills somewhere. They were going to raid the camps. I'll bet anything you like that the Prioress will hit them from the other direction when they do.'

'Probably tonight or tomorrow night,' supplied Sister Informer. 'We have to be ready, then.'

'We have to be allowed,' said Silvus. He turned and stared at the guard.

Well, it took a while. The underpeople don't measure time by the sun. Fortunately, they were quite able to understand that we didn't want to go out in the light. It was far more difficult to get the idea across that we would try by night when there was some kind of a battle going on. I'm not sure that they understood, in spite of everything. A runner went back and returned, to stare at the door guard, passing a message we couldn't read. However, they were prepared to allow us to rest by the exit, and to leave freely. So long as they watched us.

We showed them the food still in our packs. It would appear that they didn't care for sausage or cheese, but they were more than willing to trade for our twice-baked bread and dried apricots. The nuts – Sister Informer had brought hazelnuts –

were especially welcome. As for me, after a sleepless night, I spread my cape and bed-roll out on the floor, and prepared to sleep. The guard stared at one of his mates, who went away and came back shortly with three of the underpeople's bed-rolls, thick slabs of something soft. We thanked them as best we could. Silvus and I slept, and Sister Informer watched for a while.

They let me sleep. When I woke, there was Silvus glued to the eye-glass, while Sister Informer slept.

'It's late afternoon,' said Silvus. 'If you need what I think you need, it's down the hall.'

I did. When I came back, he was still peering. 'Nathan must have been pushing them hard to get here,' he remarked. 'They're tired. Nobody's digging, and they're taking their time setting up. The units on guard duty look dusty and weary.'

'I'll bet Sister Prioress can see that, too.' That was Sister Informer, who was sitting up. We turned our backs politely while she rolled out and went down the hall. She returned, having washed and dressed.

'It would seem that tonight's the night, then?' I asked.

'See for yourself,' said Silvus. 'The light will be gone soon, and I doubt that they'll ever be more ripe for a raid. Give him a day or two, and Nathan will have them throwing up a ditch and earthwork wall right around the camp.'

Sister Informer looked and nodded. 'Now, if I were Master Rookwood, what direction would I come from?' she asked, apparently of the air.

'Will?' Silvus was looking at me.

I shrugged. 'Down the steepest slope, of course, to get there fastest and to give the light foot the best chance to get away.'

'Of course.' Silvus took on the air of a savant discussing philosophy. 'And that would be?'

'The side of the camp opposite to us. Behind the castle, on the other side, where the mountain comes down to the motte.'

'Yes. And the time?'

'Well, you'd want the enemy to be well asleep. You'd do it in the middle of the watch, when the sentries are least alert. Not before dawn, because you want as much of the night as possible to get away in. Say, four hours after sundown.'

'Precisely. Let us therefore prepare ourselves to move. I think we can probably slip out in a couple of hours' time, and perhaps get as far as the stream. We can wait there. It's only a few hundred paces to the ditch from there.'

'A few hundred paces through Nathan's camp.'

'Yes. But I think we can count on there being a certain amount of confusion. You still have that sling?' I patted it where it hung on my belt. 'Good. Well, now.'

He laid himself on the roll, took two breaths, and was asleep.

Darkness came slowly. I realised it had arrived when the fires from the camp had become bright flickering points, and the tents and wagons were vague shadows. Silvus woke. We watched for a

while longer, looking for those fires that winked occasionally as sentries passed in front of them. Then we nodded at the gate guard.

Silvus stared at him, as well. 'I don't know how you think "thanks" if you don't know the word. I've done my best,' he said.

The door opened a crack, from the bottom, and we slithered through. The evening air was sweet, with a breeze stirring in the clumps of scrub clinging to the side of the mountain. A trail, apparently made by goats, meandered down the sharp slope in the general direction of the mountain meadow that was now covered with Nathan's tents.

You can't move silently, unless you're a ghost. You can't move invisibly at all. The great advantage sentries have is that they can wait, silent and still. But given a couple of hours to cover a few hundred paces, it's possible to be very quiet. Given darkness and the covercloth capes and enough cover – there was plenty of that – it's possible to be very hard to see. And it gives you something to do. A sentry can get tired of sitting still.

One of them did. He eased his seat, and for a moment I could see his spearhead outlined against the stars. It took me ten minutes to work around to where I had a fair shot. A sling is almost silent.

It was a risk. If I were an ensign in charge of night pickets, I might have had another one in sight, just in case. I used an egg-sized stone, rather than a bullet, on the off-chance that I wouldn't crack his skull. He dropped like a shot rabbit, and there was only a dull thud.

Nobody made an outcry. When I reached the place I got a shock, though, because Sister Informer was there before me. I'd lost sight of her. Which was, of course, to the good.

She shook her head. He'd been wearing a helmet, but it was only a pot, and ill-fitting at that. I'd broken his neck. I took the helmet, though. It had a plume on it that identified a regiment.

She was whispering the prayers as we shoved the body under a tussock where it wouldn't break the skyline. They wouldn't find him until dawn, and by then there would be other things on their minds.

I looked a question. She inclined her chin in the starlight, and by that I understood that Silvus was a little further down the slope. We followed him, heading towards the chuckle of the little stream. There were campfires on the nearer side, but we were hoping to thread ourselves between them and reach the belt of small timber on its banks. Hiding there would be easier, but with a problem: anyone else could hide in it, as well.

That meant that the approach had to be very cautious. We never completed it.

Far off, over the other side of the camp, there was a sudden flare of light in the sky. It was enough, with my night-sight fully operating, for me to catch a blink of Silvus's face. He stood up, shrugged slightly, and walked casually into the stream. I pulled on the dead man's helmet, which fitted me worse than him, and followed, trying to look like a man coming back from the latrine.

We splashed through, and started up the other bank. Now we were among the tents, and trying not to call attention to ourselves.

There was distant yelling now. I gestured Sister Informer up, and nudged her ahead of me. In her cloak, she might pass as a camp follower, and my errand became easier to explain. We moved up the slope towards the castle.

A few of them were beginning to become aware that there was something wrong. Now we were passing tents in regular lines, not clumps. A head stuck out of one of them, and asked me in aggrieved tones what was going on. I shrugged.

'You with the doxy! Get moving! You think I've got all night?' Silvus had not addressed me in those tones in a number of years, but that was his voice, all right. I jumped most realistically, then smiled apologetically. Sister Informer giggled, and we stepped out. The head disappeared, grumbling.

We were almost in among the siege engines – gaunt wooden derricks, half-assembled, with their ammunition lying in piles – before anyone tried to check us. People were running about and trumpets were sounding assembly. An engineer, I guessed, grease in his beard, stepped in front of us, ten paces ahead, holding up a hand. Silvus spoke first, though.

'Rinaldi, Lord Runkin's regiment,' he snapped. 'We're covering you against the sortie.' He continued sauntering forward.

'Sortie?' The man's head automatically swivelled towards the castle. 'What sortie?'

Silvus pointed. 'That one, you dolt!'

And the funny thing was, he was right. The ditch I had helped to dig was just ahead. In the shadows beyond its lip, a sudden yellow glow showed, and then a volley of lit torches looped up over the rampart. Figures started to appear, thrust up from below.

'Run!' bawled Silvus. The engineer looked once and ran for his life. As he passed Silvus, the latter tripped him, making him the most surprised man in Nathan's army. A point flickered in his eyes as he rolled over. All he could do was glare.

'Believe me,' remarked Silvus, 'you'll thank me for this, given the alternative. Rose!'

The last word was a bellow. Someone ahead answered, in alto tones. 'Garden!'

Now there were people in mail around us in the darkness. Sister Informer dropped her cloak, showing her mail.

'You've about five minutes, I should think, Sister Celestin,' she remarked, calmly, addressing one of them. 'Most of the enemy are heading for the other side, but they'll be here as soon as Nathan sees the fire. Those there, I think. The ropes are tarred.'

The Order's fire cannot be quenched, and it lights by itself. They splashed it here and there on siege machines, and it caught immediately. The engineer muttered and squirmed, watching his charges burn. Silvus frowned at him, and he subsided.

Troops were formed now, to the rear of us.

More trumpets were pealing. A few more engineers appeared, and were dealt with.

'Didn't they have any screen at all?' asked Sister Informer of her colleague.

Sister Celestin grinned, a flash of white teeth in the starlight. 'Some,' she admitted. 'Light infantry in the ditch. I don't think they saw us coming.'

'Evidently.' Sister Informer turned and assessed the noise and activity behind us, then turned back again. 'But I think it may be time to depart now. I trust you can cope with leading us through the booby traps.'

The machines along a fifty-pace section of front were blazing now. Sister Celestin paired off one of her party with each of us. We scrambled down the wall of the ditch, careful of the stakes at its bottom. I might have placed them there myself. Stupid to impale myself on one now.

My shepherdess turned to me. 'Hold on to my belt, now, and step where I step. And don't bother me. This is tricky.'

We set off up the steep slope, walking at a measured pace, she counting under her breath and me making sure of where my feet went. The things hidden in the covered pits we had dug on the approaches were excessively unpleasant.

The motte that Waycastle stood on was steep, and that was all to the good. I climbed it in sections that night, so many paces forward, so many to the side. By the time we both arrived before the gatehouse I was breathing heavily.

But the gate stood open, the portcullis up.

There was a strong guard just in front of it, in case Nathan should want to throw some men away on a counter-sortie, and we were challenged again there. Below, down in the darkness in front of the burning engines, someone howled in pain. I hoped it wasn't one of us.

It wasn't Silvus, anyway. He and his guide loomed out of the darkness a minute after me, followed by Sister Informer, followed by the rest of the sortie party.

'All well, Sister Celestin?'

I knew that voice. Prioress Winterridge, in mail and helmet with nasal bar.

'All well, Sister Prioress. Two slightly wounded, and one nasty burn.'

'Very well. Bring them into the infirmary at once.' The Prioress nodded at the blaze, like a housewife appreciating a warm fire. 'You've done well.' Her glance took us in. 'Ah, Ser Silvus, Squire de Parkin. Always a pleasure. Sisters, shall we withdraw?'

An arrow arced into the ground just by her left foot, shot at high elevation by someone below – out of sheer exasperation, no doubt. It hit with just sufficient force to stick in the packed earth. She ignored it and gestured us past her, following us in. The portcullis grumbled down on its chains, and the ponderous gates boomed shut. Massive bars were instantly levered into place.

She waved at the roof of the keep, far above. A string of lanterns was hoisted up the flagpole, held, and then dipped once.

'Recalling Master Rookwood, who will now melt into the hills,' she explained, to Sister Informer. 'We improved the hour while you were away by concerting a code of signals, sister.'

Sister Informer nodded. 'It will be interesting to observe the enemy camp again in the daylight, Sister Prioress.'

Prioress Winterridge began climbing the steps to the guard walk on the wall. 'Yes. Or even now. Shall we go and see if they've managed to put the fire out yet?'

She sounded like a young girl, eager to assess the cloth available for a new gown. Silvus and I were used to that. We followed.

ASTA

It took me a couple of days to find out the truth. No, actually, that's wrong. It took me maybe an hour to find it out, and a couple of days to swallow it.

The trouble is, the underground is boring. I couldn't go out. There's no sky. The air always smells the same – dry, slightly metallic, slightly dusty. The food is tasteless.

I got to missing the sun. I even got to missing Tenabra on a Highday night, when the streets were full and smelly and loud. You had to dodge drunks and keep out of the gutter if you could, but at least there was a laugh to it, and a sharpness, a feeling of change and a taste to the air. The goblins – the underpeople – had a sort of a laugh, a faint twitch

of the face just under the eyes. But I never knew why they laughed, or at what. And a good deal of what they thought was sad. You can get tired of that very quickly. I did, anyway.

She was right. I couldn't live in a hole forever. I had to think of something else, and she was the only person I could talk to about it. So on the second day, I went to see her. She seemed perfectly relaxed about it, too, as if she'd been expecting me.

'You comfortable enough?' I asked.

She was being kept in a sort of guest room, a space that doubled as a storage place for trade goods. There was a bed and a washstand in the wall, one of the underpeople's that filled and emptied at the same time. There was a privy next door.

'Yes, thank you.' She nodded at a goblin who got up and left as I came in. 'Maker of Curd was just telling me that he hopes to bring another bean bed into production soon. Almost half as much bean curd again. It would solve many of their problems.'

More bean curd. Hooray. It looked like junket and tasted like jellied air.

'Not all their problems, of course,' she went on.

I had to bite. 'What else is there?' I asked.

'Why, Nathan, of course. If he comes here, they'll sell themselves to protect you, and their lives will come at a high price. But it's a price Nathan can pay. And will, if he knows you're here.'

I shrugged. 'Who'll tell him?'

She looked at me, unwinking, and there was a certain impatience behind those eyes. 'The

villagers. They know who you are, now. He'll follow the road to see where it leads – another conquest for Nathan is like offering a strawberry to a hog. They'll tell him because nobody likes the Dark.'

I winced, and attempted bluster. 'He'll never get me.'

She tutted, impatiently. 'He'll dig his way in within a fortnight. There's only a couple of hundred underpeople here all together. It would be different if this were a big, well-established warren, well defended.'

'All *right*! We'll just have to work it out when it happens ...'

She was shaking her head. 'You can't. Not with Nathan. He knows what's what. He'll call any bluff you can run.' Her voice was as soft and as pitiless as falling rain.

We sat in silence for a while. I was looking the future in the face, and thinking that it didn't seem to go on for very long. I couldn't stay, I couldn't go. If I ran out, the villagers wouldn't help me, and I'd starve. If Nathan grabbed me, I'd be his slave or burn. I watched the rock wall, dim in the lamplight, and felt like crying, for the first time in years. She watched me.

I had just about decided that I could always die, when she spoke.

'I told you that what you are doing is the Dark, Asta, and so it is. Interfering in a person's mind, that is the Dark. But there are things you haven't done. You haven't tried to use the underpeople to attack. You haven't filled them with hate for others.

You haven't twisted their bodies, or grown monsters. You haven't even considered killing folk so that you can use their dead bodies. The way back is still open to you.'

I blinked. She smiled. 'You can do all of those things, Asta. All of them have been done by Dark mages. But I don't think you want to.'

I blinked again. Of course I didn't want to do those things. There was a sort of thrill in using the talent, a feeling of power, but ... those things ... and I knew what that thrill was, and where it came from. Still, I had to protect myself. Protection was what I needed, and the underpeople could provide it.

A thought struck me. 'You said it would be different if this was a bigger warren.'

Her eyes widened, just a touch, and she might have hesitated. But she answered readily enough. 'Yes. Or better defended. A big warren is a maze of tunnels and passages and drops and blinds that can swallow an army.'

I nodded. 'Well, there's my answer. Let's go find a larger warren.'

She gestured impatiently. 'It isn't an answer. You can't live in a warren forever. I like the underpeople and know them, but I couldn't do that, not for long.'

'Better than being a slave for Nathan. Or for you.'

'I keep telling you. The Order wouldn't ask you to use your talent at all, and wouldn't even allow you ...'

'Oh, yes, sure. Uh-huh. But let's see if I can find a safe place to stay before I start talking to them. Where's the nearest one?'

She bit her lip. 'I won't tell you. I won't allow you to enslave my friends.' But it was said as if she was trying the idea on for size, and not liking the fit.

'You'd rather these here died, and I died, and you died.' I sighed. 'I'll just ask them here.'

She caved in then, as somehow I knew she would. 'All right, then. I hoped you wouldn't think of that. Anyway, I can't allow Nathan to take you, and I can't afford the risk that you'd surrender to him, if it came to that.'

'I'd rather die,' I said flatly.

She nodded. 'Perhaps you would. But if you won't trust me, I won't trust you.' And with that, I had to be content.

Being the boss allowed things to be decided quickly, and action to be taken as fast. A glimpse outside showed that it was bright morning, a bad time to be travelling, but giving enough time to sleep while things were made ready. A cape like Arienne's – that was her name, Arienne – for me, and some food. We would have to make for the mountains that could be seen from the hilltop.

'A night's travel. As quick and as silent as we may,' she said. 'Nathan might already have sent soldiers down the road.'

I nodded. 'The goblins will be better in the dark, too.'

'You're taking guards?' she asked.

'What do you think?' I replied. She only smiled.

We set out as the sun sank below the western peaks, from a door in the hillside a little away from the village. Arienne had been right; this was the farthest extent of this warren's tunnels, and it was no more than a few hundred paces on. Like all the works of the underfolk, it was well hidden, under a stone in a fold of land outside the reach of the village's fields; but Nathan had lots of soldiers with lots of shovels. Arienne spent a moment getting her bearings, and then pointed to the left of the setting sun.

'That way, until we strike the road.' We shouldered packs and moved out.

The road wasn't hard to see, in the moonlight, an hour or so later. I was watching through the eyes of the underfolk, who see well in the dark, and Arienne must have known the country well, because she went confidently forward. We turned more to the south and walked on through the night.

The moon was setting by midnight, and we had nothing but darkness after that; but it was some time later that Arienne stiffened and held up a hand.

'Soldiers,' she said, low and urgently, and motioned us off the road.

I had been relying on the senses of my guards. They had seen nothing, even with their night vision. 'How do you ...' I started, and then stopped. There was a whiff of smoke on the night breeze.

We circled around them. Just a few, a patrol, camped in the scrub beside the track. But it meant

we couldn't stay on that track. Sooner or later we'd walk right into the arms of one group or another. Once we were past them Arienne beckoned and pointed towards the looming mountains, black shadows in the starlight.

'We'll have to go straight,' she murmured. 'There's an adit, but we'll be pushing to get there by dawn, across country.'

I nodded, reluctantly. I was getting tired of having someone else in charge. I'd been in charge of myself for a long time. 'The quicker the better,' I said, though, and she nodded.

'Then let's step out.' She squared her shoulders and stretched her pace.

There was grey on the rim of the sky, a long time later. My legs were aching. The hills were getting steeper and steeper and more and more bare, and the night wind was chilling. Hard before us now, the mountains reared into the sky.

We halted – for a breather, I thought – in a sharp little dip in between two long slopes. Above us was a long rocky scarp leading up to a real peak. 'Trollface,' said Arienne, glancing at it.

She was looking up, towards the brightening sky. Larks were rising in the clear air as the dawn came up.

'It's here, somewhere,' she murmured. Then, 'Ah. Up that way, and into the next slope.'

She must have seen something I could not, because she turned a little to the left, walked up the steep incline, and then down the other side. She cast about, looking for something, and the

two guards looked around as well, glancing nervously at the sky. Dawn was coming fast now.

They found it, between them. There was a big flat stone lying in the dirt, a stone like a million others, and when you picked up another one and tapped against it rap-rap, rap-rap, someone would hear it. So she said.

'Now we wait,' she went on.

'We can't wait forever. It'll be broad daylight soon, and we stick out like a sow at a soirée.'

Her lip twitched. 'Roll yourself in the covercloth cape. Go to sleep if you like. The only way anyone would find you then would be to step on you.'

I did that, and was tired enough to sleep, with the sun rising for warmth and the day coming on. When I woke, Arienne was talking to the underpeople.

CHAPTER XII

ASTA

The shadows were shorter when I woke. It wasn't voices that woke me, though. The underpeople make no sound when they speak.

Arienne was staring one of them in the face, another guard with crossbow and shortsword. Her lips compressed. I could hear her speech. She was talking in parallel to her thought. … *choice none. Sorrow. Must keep from other king, Dark-king, greedy termite. Or go (we) to the earth. For custom-refuge, stand (I) guarantee. Head (mine) on it.*

He didn't like the idea, I could tell. I reached for his mind to convince him.

'No!' Arienne's shout was sharp with worry. 'Let it be! I have given the guarantee, and it

should be enough. Custom-refuge is sacred.'

The guard hesitated, all the same, custom or no custom. I could feel his fear of me.

No more. Arienne looked at me. 'You hear? If you use the power on them, I am forsworn. You will then have to kill me, or I will kill you. To do that, having had my word broken already, I will do whatever I must.'

What did she mean by that? But whatever it was, she meant it. Her face had turned to a mask. 'All right,' I said. 'If they let me in, I'll only try to keep my skin in one piece. I won't touch them if they help me. It was the only way, before. I won't do it again.'

She nodded. 'Good enough. They are going to help, on my say-so.'

'They must like you a lot, then,' I offered. All that talk of killing had me wanting to make peace.

'They trust me. Don't break the trust.'

The guard gestured behind himself. A piece of the hill, complete with a bush, opened and we walked in.

Again, the passage was narrow and low, and steep. The underpeople like to keep their outlets to the surface as cramped as possible, for good reason. After the first three or four paces it drove into hard brown rock, hacked out with picks.

At the bottom there was more of an opening, and the passage joined a cavern, a place that looked more natural. Here there was a group of underpeople to welcome us.

Or maybe not to welcome us. They were pleased

to see Arienne, that much I could tell. They weren't so pleased to see me. Even my own guards weren't sure any more. I bit my lip and resisted the temptation to feed certainty to them. It was like Sart looking at a half-full bottle. I shook myself. I didn't have to reach for it. I was in charge, not the talent. I wasn't like Sart, and I didn't have to go that way.

But still I understood. For the first time, I understood how it was for him, and something inside me slackened off. It had been screwed up tight for a long time, but now I could forgive him. Funny. I never thought I had anything against him, before.

They turned, all at once, and led the way. The floor sloped. We were going deeper into the hill.

This was a grander affair than the warren outside Newcombe. They'd connected up a number of caves and caverns. In places the lights they carried were not enough to see the roof, and we walked among pillars and trunks made out of stone, like strolling in a shadowy forest. In others the passage walls crowded close on each side.

At length we came to another cave, and through it ran a stream. It wasn't deep or wide, and I had lost all notion of direction by then. The flow was from right to left and fairly slow, and that was all I knew. There was a chain of boats tethered together, shallow-draught, with flat bottoms, in the middle. They were pulled over, and we all stepped in. One of the underpeople in each took up a short pole to fend us off, and we shoved off.

Nobody spoke. There was barely a ripple on the

water, and the slope was gradual. After a while we came to a pool where the banks meandered away out of sight, and they poled us along. The roof receded far overhead. Stony islands jutted out of the dark water, and our lights made long pale streaks, scattered and rejoining as our small wash passed over them. At one place there was a side current, water dropping away into some depth beyond imagining, and after that the steersmen leaned into their poles a little harder, as if the current was against us now.

Arienne had been talking to them. I hadn't tried to eavesdrop, sticking fairly to my bargain. Now she spoke. 'There's a lift lock ahead. Just sit still and wait.'

I didn't ask. When we came to it, I gasped, though. It was a waterfall – a sheet of water falling over a rock shelf from an upper cavern. Fixed to the face of the rock was what looked like an immense pair of balance scales. One pan of the scales was in the water before us. It was big enough to contain all the boats, and we drew into it and waited. A gate shut in the front of it, to hold the water in, and then the waterfall stopped running. Instead, the stream was diverted and water rushed into the upper pan of the scales, fast at first, then slower as it came near to balancing. Then the pan we were in began to rise, and the other to sink. We rose straight up the cliff face, dozens of feet into the air, and the other pan dropped past us, and came to rest in the lake below. As it did, we reached the top. The beam swivelled a little, and

we were set down in the pool they'd blocked off. The other side of our pan was let down, and we poled into the upper stream.

The boats rocked and went on, and the darkness was complete around the little puddle of light that we made. Once the roar of the falls had dwindled behind us, there was no sound but the lap of the water. After a while I slept.

When I woke, the boats were drawing into a landing, no more than a shelf of rock squared off and jutting into the current. It was only big enough for one boat at a time. We gathered up our things and stepped off in our turn.

They gestured us on. Some of the people that had come thus far with us left us here, and others met us. Arienne exchanged greetings, and then stiffened.

'What's the problem?' I asked.

Arienne's face flattened into a mask of dislike. 'Nathan. I'll say this for him, he can move when he wants to. He's at the pass and is laying siege to the castle already. I thought he'd be another few days, at least. So did we all.'

'What castle? What pass?'

She turned and stared at me. 'Don't you know?' Then she shook her head. 'Stupid question, as Ser Silvus would say. The Castle is Waycastle, and the pass is the pass at Oriment, the only way through the mountains. The Order's land is mostly on the other side of the mountains, and the castle guards the pass. Nathan must take it if he wants the Order's land. And he wants the Order's land.'

I shrugged. What did I care which lord had what land?

Arienne was watching. 'You might not think so, but it's a problem for us. With Nathan's army in the way, we can't get to the castle.'

'I wasn't going there, anyway, remember?'

'I thought we'd talked about this, Asta. You can't stay with the underpeople forever.'

'The war won't last forever, either.'

She nodded, slowly. 'I suppose that's reasonable from your point of view. But the trouble is Nathan. For him, the whole world consists only of his subjects and his enemies. He won't stand you as an enemy. He won't treat with you, not in good faith. You're his bond-slave, or dead, as soon as you come out.'

She let me think about that, and turned and talked to our reception committee. Again, I kept out of it. Then she nodded.

'Very well,' she said. 'Let's get on.'

From the landing a drive led upwards, dim in the lamp light. 'Watch your step,' she remarked. 'We're being accorded trust here. They wouldn't normally show their halls and pathways to sun-people. But that doesn't mean they'll use more light than they must.'

'They can use all they like, for all of me,' I said. 'I couldn't find my way back for a kingdom.'

She spoke to them again, and I thought to see that faint twitch under the eyes that means laughter. I didn't check their minds to make sure, though.

From the pull in my thighs, I became aware that we were walking up a slope. The stream had led generally upwards; after the first bit, we had been poling against the current. Now we came to a length of cleft natural cave, uneven and rugged, but with steps cut every few paces. We began to climb in earnest. I began to count steps.

At one hundred I was feeling it. At three hundred, I was a walking ache. At four, with me just about to plead for a halt, we turned aside and crossed another cave, walking over a bridge hung from chains. I looked over and down. There were spots of light far below, and small figures that worked in the glow of mighty furnaces. Hammers could be heard, ringing like bells, and there was something that made a continual dull pounding, a throbbing in the air.

Arienne looked back at me. 'Not far now. This is a place I've been before. Not all the way down to the bottom of it, but I know their main workshops are down there. Now we can take the lift.'

She had said it with relief. Good. I was glad I wasn't the only one.

The lift was a platform on a cable, moving slowly up the face of the opposite side of the cavern. It was guided by iron rails set in the rock. We had to step on to it from the bridge, and it carried us up the walls, up and up and up. The noise of the workshops and the glow of the furnaces receded into the darkness below.

'This was the first of all their places,' said Arienne. 'The cave that sheltered them after they

left the light behind. Something happened, out on the moors, something their oldest stories only hint at. But here they have found peace over the ages.'

I nodded. It was something I never dreamed of. Mind you, the world was full of things I never dreamed of. The lift, for one.

'Get ready to step off,' said Arienne. An opening in the wall was coming up. We stepped off, tallest first, and the platform ascended past us, into the unseen heights above.

Up until now the passages had been rough, the pick marks showing, and only cleared enough to pass. But this was different. We passed through a set of doors, and suddenly we were in a tiled hallway, sloping up, lit with softly glowing lanterns every few paces. The light was green as summer leaves, and it glinted on gems in the walls, cut and polished, and on mirror panels set up to double it. Twenty paces of this, and we halted before another set of doors, bronze, heavy-looking. My thief's eyes saw that their hinges were silver, set with gems that looked like garnets, and the doors were adorned with enamel panels in patterns of swirls like running water. The swirls were outlined with wire that certainly looked like gold.

'The lord's house?' I asked.

'The council's,' replied Arienne, 'but not a house. The nearest word is "space".'

The doors opened. Light flooded in. Not lamp-light, and that was a relief. It was light from mirrors set at different angles around the walls,

and they in turn reflected the beams of the sun which slanted in from tiny niches high under the ceiling on three sides. We were close to the surface here, perhaps a cave mouth that had been masoned up and hidden. The floors were tiled with little pieces of gem-like glass, and the walls were faced with a pale glazed frothy stone like frozen honey.

Around the walls were the most unusual things to be found in all the warrens of the underpeople: trays of soil supporting green plants. They were on swinging arms, so that they could be swivelled to catch every shaft of light, and the plants were peas and beans and tubers. A carefully trained row of strawberries was just starting to set fruit. There were no flowers, except for plants that would produce food later. Not even in the Great House could the underpeople afford gardens that were only pretty to look at.

When I'd finished gawking, I could look at the underpeople who were waiting there.

Arienne went down in a deep curtsy. I couldn't curtsy, but I did my best. They looked at me without expression, then at each other with fleeting little glints of their eyes, and back at Arienne again.

She held her head high and she spoke to them and spoke her words aloud at the same time, for my benefit. '*Fear and ignorance. Not-know different from lust-for-power.*'

Uncertainty. Fear. I didn't have to read their minds to see that.

Arienne spoke again: '*No use of power-to-enslave, after seeing (me). Serve greed-king refused (she). Head (mine) on it. Watch (her) (me).*'

They glanced at each other again, then at me. I kept silent, and didn't listen to their minds, though the need was like an unscratched itch. Sart, I thought, you'd have been proud.

She relaxed. Then she spoke to me alone.

'They grant sanctuary as long as I am here to watch you. They don't trust you. That means that when I leave, you leave.'

'Not if it means becoming a slave. I won't do it, and they won't be able to make me.'

She turned and looked at me, considering, head cocked on one side. 'It doesn't matter now. We're stuck here for some time at least.'

'How much time?'

'It depends. There's a way out being prepared. But if you want to know why we're stuck here, look in that glass over there.'

She pointed to a piece of glass like a small window pane set in the wall. I went and peered in it – it was at a goblin's eye-height. Then I blinked.

There was a field in the glass, all covered with tents and flags and soldiers in blocks. It was a long way away, as I could see from the shimmer and ripple in the air.

It was Nathan's army. I could see the black-and-yellow tent in the middle. 'Can they see us?' I asked, in a husky whisper.

'No. Not unless they're prepared to look under every stone on the mountainside. On all the

mountainsides. Twist the knob on the side to move the field of view.'

So help me, the view changed. I found myself looking beyond Nathan's camp. There, clinging to a part of the hillside, was a castle, with other banners floating from its towers. Blue-and-white banners.

Arienne had come to stand beside me. I looked up at her. 'Yes,' she said, and nodded. 'The siege has begun. Will's over there, and Ser Silvus. And the sisters.'

'I'm sure they can manage without us.'

She looked at me, and it seemed to me that there was something odd in the way she did it. 'I hope so,' she said, grimly. 'I certainly hope so.'

We were placed in new quarters, down a corridor and a set of sculpted stairs, the passage rich with coloured stones and with hangings made of metal and glass, like tapestries on the walls. Some had the green lights hung behind them, to shine through pieces of the glass, which changed the colours of the lights. Coloured shadows followed us. I think they were meant to be part of the effect, which was as strange as it was – well, beautiful, I suppose.

The rooms were a guest suite, Arienne said. She showed me how to work the privy and the wash basin. There were two bed pads, rolled up.

'My word was that I'd watch you,' she told me. 'I have to do that. So I'll put my bed across the outer door when we sleep. I don't think you can pass me without waking me.'

'I could cut your throat in the night,' I said, sourly.

She stared at me, and slowly shook her head. 'Do you know,' she said, considering, 'I don't think you could. It's a silly thing to stake my life on, that the Dark hasn't taken you, but I will.'

I glared at her.

Time passed, and there was nothing to do. I got tired of twiddling my fingers. The air was cool, even and lifeless, without sunlight or movement. Tombs were like that, and that made me think about the call of the dead, how I had heard it and let it take me. Somehow I knew that had been the worst of all the things I'd done. I wondered what I might do to make it up. In fact, I began to wonder whether life was worth living at all; and there was only one person to talk to. It took only a few hours of that sort of cool, quiet nothing to make me cave in.

'What's this Dark you keep talking about?' I asked. Blurted it out, actually. That's what that sort of thinking does to you.

We were both sitting on the floor. Arienne was writing in a flat book that she'd been carrying all this way in her pack. The pen and ink had been supplied by the underpeople. She had to sit with the book against her knees, her back against the wall. The underfolk didn't go in for chairs.

She closed the book and frowned. 'It's the power used for your own ends, in a way that hurts something else, or is wrong in itself.'

'I didn't hurt anyone.' But that sounded weak,

even to me. I remembered the bird I'd flown to death; the pit pony I'd warped.

'You took away the free will of the underpeople. That's hurting them.'

'It didn't actually damage them, though.'

'Like Teska didn't actually damage you. Why, then, do you hate him?'

I had nothing to say to that. I went back to thinking.

More time passed. Thinking got more and more painful, worse and worse. And then, for some reason I couldn't understand, I found hot, sharp tears sliding down my face. I wiped my nose on my sleeve, and with the soft green glow of the room shivering into sharp splinters of light, put my head on my knees.

And then there was an arm around my shoulders, and a quiet voice in my ear. 'Come now, Asta. Dark mages don't cry. They can't.'

But I cried, turning my head into her shoulder, and she held me and rocked me, and we sat together in the dim, quiet room.

It seemed like a long time after that when the outer door opened. There was no knock. The underpeople don't, for some reason. A face looked in, and when Arienne made a very slight movement, the underperson entered. Another one followed, and I stared.

The one who followed was smaller and slighter, and wore more clothes. Not many more. Not enough to disguise her femaleness. She was the

first female underperson I had seen. That was why I was staring. Mostly, though, I was staring at the bundle she was carrying.

She was upset. The faces of the underpeople are still, unless they laugh or … cry? Was she crying? Was that slight quiver of the mouth and narrowing of the eyes the same as my tears?

The first was staring at Arienne, and Arienne's face creased in concern. Another faint gesture, and the other came forward and laid the bundle in Arienne's lap.

It was a baby. A sleeping baby. But Arienne's face creased further. Her eyes became distant, as if seeing things hidden. She frowned. She looked at the other two, and gave the slightest, tiniest nod. Then she stared down at the baby again.

It was a quiet baby, very quiet. And then, as you looked at it, you suddenly realised there was something wrong. It wasn't breathing as often as it should. And its colour was odd. The underpeople have a skin like red leather, thick and creased – but this child was almost purple-blue, strongest at the lips and ears. Surely a baby should be a lighter shade?

I looked a question at Arienne, but she wasn't looking at me. Nevertheless she spoke: 'There is a hole in her heart. She will die of it, unless something is done.' She was staring at the child, and her face was as blank as snow.

'What can you possibly do about …'

She didn't reply. She just sat there with the baby in her lap, and the room became quiet and still as before.

Teska's voice sounded as if in my ear: '*You can alter their bodies as their minds ... and that includes the goblins.*' I pulled in breath, opened my mouth to speak and closed it again. Arienne was far away.

The stillness went on and on. Arienne's face did not change except for fleeting shadows that crossed it like clouds across the sun. She stared at the baby, and I stared at her in the wan light. It seemed to last a very long time, though I have no idea how long it really was. Arienne took a sudden breath and held it, and breathed out, long and hard. Then her shoulders slumped and her eyes closed, and weariness and relief washed over her.

The baby flushed pink and wriggled. It took a deep breath and began to wail. The cry cut the silence like the first temple bell on Sunreturn morning, the day after the longest night of the year.

Arienne leaned over the child, kissed it, and handed it back to its mother. The woman – yes, she was a woman, as the other one was a man – took it. Her face had no expression that I could read, but she took the baby, held it with one arm – it was squalling lustily – and seized Arienne's hand. She stared into Arienne's face, and for a moment as they stared at each other, I could understand what she was saying without hearing her mind. Without violating it.

It lasted a few moments only. Arienne made the smallest of nods, the tiniest smile, done without showing her teeth. Then the other two backed away through the open door behind them, and the man bowed low before closing it softly and so leaving us.

The silence remade itself and stretched out. I stared at Arienne, and she at the wall. I had to make several tries before I spoke again: 'You never told me you have the talent yourself.'

She shook herself. Speaking seemed an effort for her, too. 'It never came up.'

'Don't be …' I searched for a word.

'Disingenuous,' she supplied.

'That's it. Don't be disingenuous.'

She made a weary gesture. 'I didn't want you to know.'

I nodded and understood. 'You could have cancelled out my talent at any time; at least stopped me from influencing the underpeople. You could have done for me, if you'd wanted.'

'Yes. I suppose I could have.'

'But you didn't.'

'No.' She hitched her back up against the wall again. 'I wanted you to come away from the Dark, and towards … the Light, I suppose. You had to do it yourself, though.' She looked up at me. 'And you did. You are no Dark mage, Asta Harrower. Never again.'

CHAPTER XIII

WILL

We needed the morning light to see the full extent of the damage we'd done, though we watched late into the night as the fires flared and then gradually died. That was fun.

But when the sun came up, what had looked like a major defeat for Nathan revealed its true size, and I tried not to be despondent about it. A bite had been taken out of the park of siege machines set up just out of ballista range, beyond the ditch. Blackened frameworks and charred beams showed where the fires had cut the number of stone throwers by half, maybe. That was important, and I looked at it and cheered up a bit, in a conscientious sort of way. The losses would slow

Nathan down. Dots were swarming over and around the remaining devices, assembling and salvaging. In spite of their efforts, he wouldn't be ready to start his approach for a couple of days.

Over on the other side, Master Rookwood's raiders had burned tents, wagons and supplies and left a litter of yellow-and-black corpses, and very few of their own. The result looked like a black spot a few hundred paces across. Burial parties were working already. Beyond them, more figures were digging, working to throw up a ditch and wall right around the outside of their camp. Another raiding party wouldn't find matters quite so easy.

And that was that. We'd killed off a hundred or so. More important, we'd decimated his siege engines. Fewer engines meant fewer stones thrown, which meant lower rates of damage to the castle, which meant we'd have more chance of keeping it repaired. Good.

But there was an awful lot of Nathan's men left. A couple of new units marched in during the morning, called up to replace losses. They set up tents on the burned ground, and in a few hours there was nothing to show for the efforts of Master Rookwood at all.

That day went quickly. There was always something to see. The big yellow-and-black tent rose in sections out of the ruck of lesser accommodations, on the meadow by the stream. Twice we identified Nathan himself, a sparkling dot on a white horse, surrounded by a yellow-and-black entourage, going or coming.

He was a busy man. The field was seething with activity. Already the small stands of timber were being hacked down for firewood, and the stream where it flowed out of the camp was an unpleasant brown. Sister Prioress watched and ground her teeth, though you'd have had to know her well to see it. The Order prizes land and cares for it well.

Still, things were going to plan. Nathan's army was stalled outside the ditch, more than a ballista-shot away, five hundred paces or so. During my watch, I passed the time of day with one of the ballista crews on the wall. They had their machine ready, but not wound up. You can't keep those things at full tension for long – it tends to snap the frame.

But nothing happened all day. Nothing we could do anything about, anyway. The besiegers dug their ditch, nearly completing it by dusk. Darkness fell, and when the watch changed I went to supper with Silvus, moped around cleaning gear without saying much, and then went to bed. Sleep was easy enough.

Morning brought some changes. They'd used the night to dig away a section of the rampart of our ditch and remove the stakes. The result was a ramp, a slope they could get a machine down. If Nathan could establish a stone thrower on the mound itself, he would be able to reach the bailey of the castle, which would make life difficult for those within. Stones, bundles of blazing tarred straw, long-dead horses to promote disease – that sort of thing.

Well, he tried. The first piece was a heavy mantlet, a wooden shield like a section of wall faced with wetted hides, ten paces wide and five high, slightly curved. It rolled on wheels set behind with a tongue to steer them, and it was pushed by twenty men with levers. They trundled it down the ramp they'd made and started slowly up the mound.

We watched and waited. There was nothing else we needed to do. They reached the upslope. Sooner or later … sooner or later … any moment now … and … ah! There it was. One of the wheels hit one of the steep little pits we'd dug, and the iron-shod spike within made a mess of its rim. The mantlet lurched, dropped and snagged on the ground; and at that moment some unkind person within the castle released liquid fire from the sluice directly above. The stream of fire rolled down the mound, lapped around the mantlet, and wetted hides or no, set it alight. Black clouds of oily smoke began to arise.

It was crowded behind that shield. Somebody got a hot foot almost at once and ran for the rear. He took a slightly wrong path, or he wasn't watching where he was going, because he found another pit and we could hear his howl from the wall. The mantlet was burning merrily now.

They all broke and ran at once. The distance was still too long for archery, but the ballistas picked off three or four before they got out of range. The mantlet burned to ashes, and that was that. Score one for us, and that was all the play for that day.

Nathan had pushed a finger into the pie and found it too hot to eat. So he started trying to cool it. The second night brought more digging, and in the morning there was another length of ditch dug away. They'd keep on doing that until there was enough removed to launch a general assault from several directions at once.

Meanwhile the largest machines – big trebuchets with a long counterweighted throwing arm – had been assembled, and they began to throw stones. It was extreme range, even for them, and the missiles had to be lobbed. The first few were too heavy and fell well short, but they could reach the outer walls with lighter stones, and we began to bless our new bastions and reinforcing. There was no significant damage.

They even threw a few fire-bundles right over the wall and into the bailey, where everything that would burn had long since been removed. We just let them go. So long as the engines were kept at that range, knocking a hole in the wall would take forever; we could shore it up as fast as they could bash it down. If they tried to bring the engines closer, they'd be in range of our own machines. This went on for days.

And so on. The trouble with sieges is that they're more or less predictable. It's a waiting game. The main question was, could we keep Nathan waiting until winter? The answer, so far, was probably. For every move there's a counter-move, and the only way to change the course is to introduce something from outside.

And Nathan tried to do just that.

It was the fourth night, I think. Sister Prioress looked at the ring of earthworks that now surrounded the enemy camp and shook her head. A raid from outside, even in the darkness, was a perilous proposition now. She made the flag signal that meant 'Try an alternative', and Master Rookwood would be turning his attentions to Nathan's outer pickets – that bunch of cavalry further down the road to the west, for example.

So we knew that it wasn't due to us that there was a sudden hullabaloo across the river, two hours after dusk. Flaring flames in several places, and so much yelling that we could hear it from the walls, a faint piping and squeaking like nestling birds.

Silvus looked a question at the Prioress. She shook her head.

'It isn't Master Rookwood. The possibilities are two – it's the underpeople, which would mean that Arienne has brought them, or it's Nathan himself. A false alarm, to try to tempt a sortie from us. He may not realise that we can communicate with our raiders.'

Silvus squinted into the darkness towards the distant fires. 'It isn't the underpeople,' he said. 'It's too small. If they were to attack, there'd be fires all along the perimeter.'

'There are that many of them?'

Silvus shrugged. 'There must be thousands, at least. The warren goes for ten leagues. It is their oldest, Arienne says. They are reluctant to come above ground, but if they did …'

'They'd give Nathan some trouble.' I put in.

Sister Informer and Prioress Winterridge nodded, both together.

'A pity,' said the Prioress. 'But it appears unlikely. They have little cause to love us. Still – ' She turned to Sister Informer. 'Ready a sortie party anyway, sister. Anything could be happening.'

ASTA

Grey cool dimness. We slept, eventually, but for how long I don't know. My eyes weren't gritty any more when I woke up.

After that, there was a sort of soup with mushrooms and strips of something that looked like spinach and tasted like beans. We were halfway through it when there were footsteps outside the door. It opened and a face looked in. We jumped to our feet, as was polite. The elders had come to call.

It was a full party. The elders, plus what might have been an honour guard. A dozen or more. The room felt full once all of them were in.

Arienne started to curtsy, but as she did the one at the head of the group took her hand and drew her upright again. I knew he was an elder, though how I knew it I'm not sure. His skin was a little paler, maybe, a little more wrinkled. He moved carefully, as old people do, when he raised her. Then he stared at her, and she stared back in silence, meeting his eyes and watching his face as he watched hers.

I waited as long as I could. I was beginning to be able to see the tiny signs that the underpeople used, but I still had no idea what they meant. The silence of the conversation went on and on until I had to say something, or scream.

'What is it? What's he saying?'

Arienne waited a moment more, a faint play of expression crossing her face. The other might have nodded, and then he let her hand go and stepped back. She breathed out sharply, and shook her head.

'What, for the gods' sake?' I asked.

Arienne faced me. She allowed relief to show on her face, mixed with something else. 'They are grateful for the baby. Children mean a lot to them. They've made what is a very hard decision for the elders of a warren, for it means handing us their heads. They'll show us the secret ways. Some of them, anyway.'

That was news. But – 'Why bother? And aren't all their ways secret?'

'No. "Secret ways" is a pale misunderstanding of the term. These are tunnels not known to most of the underpeople themselves. They come in varying degrees; some are known to very few indeed. What a person doesn't know cannot be found in his mind, not even by a Dark mage. As for why they'll show us, it's because one of them leads under the mound of the castle itself.'

I blinked. This was getting stranger and stranger. 'So you can go home straightaway.'

She seized my hand and gripped it. 'We go

home together, Asta Harrower, when we go, you and I.' She hesitated. 'Mind you, there is one problem …'

Somehow I knew there would be. 'What?'

She looked back at the elders, who were standing patiently by. 'The tunnel doesn't go all the way to the castle. They say that the work was stopped years ago – or they may mean decades – when hostilities between them and the Order died away. There was a sort of uneasy informal truce for a long time, you know, before the Order realised that the underpeople have nothing to do with the Dark. That they had been forced to serve.'

Forced to serve Dark mages. Forced to serve people like me.

No. No. That wasn't right. People like Teska and Prince Nathan.

I shook myself. 'So how close does the tunnel go?' I asked.

'As far as the ditch at the base of the mound. It actually opens into it. The underpeople blocked it off and concealed it when the ditch was being dug, and it was never noticed.'

She communed with the head elder again. I waited. Then she spoke again.

'It will have to be in the night. I know the pit-falls and the password; so long as we're quick and quiet, there shouldn't be any trouble. We can scoot up to the castle, avoiding the booby traps, and even if we're spotted – not likely – they'll never be able to catch us.'

'Us?'

She bit her lip, and then faced me steadily. 'I have to go, if I can. I'm needed. Watching the camp through other eyes, especially by night, giving warning, scouting. It might make all the difference. You can't stay here on your own, and I promised to guard you. So you have to come, too.' That was the cool, reasoned explanation. Then: 'Please come, Asta. Sister Prioress will be so pleased. You'll like her, I know you will. She's a bit like you.'

I nodded, trying to look like I knew what I was doing. Outrunning the pursuit, dodging through the dark. I was supposed to be good at that sort of stuff, after all.

It takes no time at all for your head to get out of pace with the sun, if you can't see it. We'd just had breakfast, but when we went up to the room where I'd first met the elders it was already afternoon. One by one the underfolk withdrew, until only the elders were left. We watched Prince Nathan's camp for an hour or so, and then gave some close attention to the hill that the castle sat on.

'It's only partly natural,' said Arienne. 'They had a spur of the hillside to put the castle on, but they built up the top of it by taking from the bottom and squaring it off. It's a sharp climb. And you'll have to follow me pretty carefully. There's pitfalls all over it, like raisins in a slice of fruitcake.'

'The Order doesn't like visitors, then?'

'The Order doesn't like Nathan. And it's mutual.'

The day got on. The sun went west and dropped behind the hills. When the castle had become a black square block against the sky and the vale was covered in shadows, we shrugged into our cloaks. The packs we would leave, with the little food remaining in them. The underpeople needed all they could get.

Still we waited. Night came slowly, but the stars were out and bright at last. No moon, and there was the promise of cover later – high cloud was forming around the peaks. We looked at each other, breathed out once, and nodded to our hosts.

Out again, by the same way we came in. This time we took the lift down, past the bridge and into the depths beyond. Only the elders had come with us to guide us. The secret ways were secret indeed.

'Get ready,' said Arienne. An opening in the wall was sliding up towards us. 'This one.'

We stepped off. I'm lucky, because I'm no taller than an underperson. Arienne is tall. She had to bend. It was narrow, too. After a few paces we could go only in single file, two of the elders in front, then Arienne, then me, then the other elder.

Fifty paces of this – the tunnel was lit only with the backlight from one lamp – and the elder in front of us stopped. The one at the head of our little column went on, and the one behind me turned and fell back a few paces.

'To warn if anyone comes,' said Arienne. 'No one without the secrets can see this.' The first bent down. Arienne stared at the ceiling, an awkward

pose, since she was bent to get under it. 'Don't look,' she warned.

I didn't. There was a tiny click, and the elder straightened. He made the slightest of gestures. A piece of the rock wall opened. We scrambled in, and he followed us, and the door closed behind us.

Black darkness, thick as treacle, and the air smelled earthy, rather than cool and faintly metallic, as the air in the warren usually did. There was a scrape and a flare, and it revealed the elder putting a flame to a tiny lamp. He squeezed past us and went on; we followed.

We were descending. The passage was just high enough and just wide enough to let us pass. Arienne, slim as she was, had trouble in some places. Twice we went on hands and knees. Every few paces there were braces, iron posts in the walls and iron rafters in the roof.

We passed openings on either side. The tunnel curved unexpectedly, and divided more than once. After a while and several turns I couldn't remember the way back again. If our guide wanted to lose us here, we'd never get out. I began to wonder if that might not be his plan. Every turn and every junction made me more nervous.

Then our footfalls changed. I looked down in the dim light, and I could see earth, not stone, beneath my feet. At the same moment I became aware of a chilling damp in the air and a low rushing sound.

The roof dipped, and even I had to sidle to get past. Arienne went on all fours. There was water

dripping, and a puddle on the floor, although the walls and the roof just here were sheathed in a grey smooth cement.

'Uh … we're under the river … oof!' Arienne got past the tight place and stood up again. 'Not far now.'

There was an upslope now, though, which made it harder, and the tunnel got even rougher and less finished underfoot. Again side passages led off. The underfolk must have mined right under the meadow and the road. I said as much to Arienne.

'Yes,' she replied. 'Even I had no idea how much they'd done. And some of this work is recent, though much is old. They must have been preparing exits and pop-outs and pits for years.'

'Why?'

She shrugged, and that made her hit her head on the roof. 'Ouch! It may be just mine workings. Or for water. But I think – narrow place coming – I think (oof!) it was in case a Dark mage fooled a gate guard. At least some of the underpeople would escape into holes that were unsuspected.'

I scraped past a corner where a wedge of sharp rock jutted into the narrow way. 'And they're telling me about it?'

'They trust me. And you're coming with me. See the dilemma you caused them, though? They don't want to show you this at all, but they don't want to keep me against my will, and I've given my word to watch you. Which I am.'

'They don't trust me.' That was clear, anyway.

'No. Put yourself in their place. Would you?'

'I suppose not.' I thought about it some more. 'And here I am, trusting you, too. Because you didn't use the talent on me when you could have. And because of that, I have to trust your precious Order as well.'

I couldn't see her face as she sidled past another intersection, peering ahead into the darkness, but her voice was wry. 'Learning not to use the talent is the most important part of learning to use it.'

I snorted. 'Deep. Very deep.'

We went on, slowly. Then the tunnel roof got lower, and we had to go on hands and knees. Ten paces of this, and then there was a heavy door made of iron, and beyond that, an open place. We could stand up.

It was a sort of a bubble that had been dug out of the earth, and it had been braced with beams that were different from the others. Not iron – they were a curious reddish-grey in colour, and they felt slightly waxy. They were thicker, too.

Strangest of all, there were glass bottles balanced on shelves at the head of each one. The bottles were full of an oily yellow liquid, and they were tightly stoppered. The shelves they stood on had braces that were hinged in the middle, and a wire ran from each to a big lever by the iron door.

The elder stared at Arienne's face. Even she looked puzzled as she translated: 'Three-burning-metal, is the nearest words for it. A metal that burns. If the shelves are dropped, the bottles smash against the beams and the liquid … I can't

explain this ... sets fire to the metal. A white flame that is hotter than ordinary fire.'

I nodded. Why not? It was no more crazy than anything else down here.

'It's the last piece. Just beyond there – that braced place on the wall where the spade is leaning – is the break-out. He says it will only take a few strokes. That's the reason for the special precautions.'

I nodded again. If anyone were to crack into this place by accident, the underpeople would burn the braces and it'd fall in, leaving nothing. They'd probably seal off the crawlspace, too.

Arienne spoke again. 'The elder says he'll do the digging. But he'll have to put out the light and go by ... feel, I think is the only word. And he needs to listen first, to make sure nobody's around, up top.'

'Just a moment.' I moved up as close to the place Arienne had pointed to as I could, without being in the way. 'I wouldn't want to joggle one of these bottles in the dark.'

'Gods, no.' She pressed herself to the wall beside me. 'All right now?' I nodded. She stared at the elder, the light went out, and the darkness was like a solid wall.

Silence. Silence. I strained to hear, holding my breath. When I realised that the faint regular crackle I could make out was the blood in my own ears, I knew I had heard everything I was going to. But the elder waited another full minute before he started scraping at the soil with the spade. It

sounded like a cavern full of miners, cheery songs and all. The patter of earth on the floor was as loud as a galloping horse.

Scrape, scrape, chunk. Some more earth fell in. And then there was fresh air, scented of heather, on my face. I could see a star. More earth fell in, and three more stars appeared; four; six. And, moving my head a little, I could see the sharp angles of walls and towers on a hill, far above. The castle.

It was enough. I touched the old man on the shoulder, and he stopped digging. We listened, and there was nothing but the night wind.

I eased my head out of the hole. In front of my nose was a stake, sharpened at the top. Nasty. Right above me and behind me was a wall of earth. I glanced right and left, and made some sense of it. It was the side of a trench, and we had emerged at the bottom of it, in the angle between wall and floor. I slid a little forward, quiet as the stars, and twisted myself to get around the stake. The night stayed still and calm.

Arienne followed me. As soon as she was out, the hole was rapidly blocked up. I heard the scraping of the spade and the thud of the earth, rapidly fading, then dying completely away. We were on our own now.

No sense in waiting. I moved forward on elbows and belly, and Arienne moved farther, passing me. Then we set still and looked and listened with every eye and ear we had.

I searched the sky and the earth for something that could see in the dark better than me. No such

luck. Army camps aren't good places to find owls or cats. There'd be a mews for falcons in the castle.

Arienne moved off first, and I followed, both of us creeping like worms. Fifty paces up the hill, maybe, we would be able to walk, but just here, with Nathan's men just over the other side of the ditch …

And then it happened. A sudden flare of light washed over the ditch, distant and faint, but it looked as bright as a sunrise to us. There was an actual shadow where the line of the trench wall behind us cut it off, and we were only partly in that shadow. Most of me wanted to get back into it, but I knew that was silly. In that dull green and brown cape I was hard to see, so long as I stayed still. It was movement that people saw, at night.

But now there was yelling and commotion behind us, a way off, but somewhere in Nathan's camp. Someone was getting upset, and I hoped it was him. There were trumpets blaring, as well.

I looked at Arienne. She was looking at me. 'It's a raid,' she hissed. 'The Order is raiding Nathan's camp. Come on, and follow me. This couldn't be better for us.'

'The light?'

'The further away we get from it, the better. And the noise covers us. Come on.'

Indeed the first flare of it had died away a little. A tent burning, likely. Arienne wriggled forward, heading up the mound, feeling ahead of her. Then she rose to hands and knees, and went on more confidently. I followed. The light died away

completely. We scuttled upwards in the dark, feeling more secure.

That was how we actually fell over somebody who was lying on the ground, feet pointed down the slope. There was a muffled exclamation, a thud, and a whirl of half-seen movement against the stars. I had been seeing Arienne as a black creeping shadow; now she disappeared. A voice hissed out of the blackness ahead, 'Sarge!'

Hiss or no hiss, that wasn't Arienne. I reached into my boot-top, where I had put one of the goblin knives. Another voice, another hiss, three paces to my left and ahead. 'Shut up, Baines, or I'll have you for breakfast.'

That decided me. I pulled my boot-knife. Arienne let out a sob, apparently around a hard hand.

'It's a girl, sarge.' The owner of the hand seemed pleased with his discovery.

The other one wasn't. The whisper was exasperated. 'I don't care if it's the regimental band, you bloody fool. If it isn't a sortie coming down from the castle, you keep quiet about it.'

Feeling ahead of me, my fingertips found a boot-heel. It would be fair to say that most boots cover feet, and feet are generally attached to legs. It wasn't Arienne's boot. It therefore belonged to whoever had nabbed her.

It would also be true to say that most men cannot run fast with three inches of steel in their calf muscle, and will tend to clutch such an injury, rather than hang on to a captive.

He shrieked, and I jumped up. I pulled Arienne loose and pushed her ahead of me. 'Run!' I told her. It was the only thing I could think of doing.

She shot me a look, and ran. I followed. Ten paces, fifteen. I thought we were away, but I looked back, and just as I did that she jinked.

It was my fault. I saw her not quite ahead, and I cut the corner. My side-step was almost good enough, but not quite. I trod on the edge of the little pit, broke through the earth-covered matting that hid it, and my foot slid in, turning my ankle. Pain shot up my leg, but there was worse to come. There was a steel-pointed stake in the pit, and it ploughed up my shin, a line of fierce anguish. Black blood was welling out.

I flung myself to the side, clutched my leg and rolled in pain. Ten paces ahead, Arienne ran on, thinking I was behind her. I bit my lip to stop from crying out. No sense in both of us …

Steps behind. Another stumble and a curse. A scrape.

'Here's one, sarge,' somebody whispered hoarsely.

'Forget about whispering, Alson.' The voice was weary and disgusted. 'They must have heard Baines yelling in Tenabra. Grab what you've got there and let's go. And watch your step. There's more pitfalls than you've got fleas.'

'It's another girl.'

'Lucky old you. Now *move*, before somebody up there decides to find out if we've got our fireproof breeches on.'

I was hauled up, my arm was jerked up behind me, and I was frogmarched – slowly and carefully – down the mound and into the ditch. They didn't notice my leg until they'd thrown me up on top of the rampart. I pointed it out to them by screaming and fainting.

CHAPTER

WILL

I’m not entirely sure that I got the biggest shock of my whole life when I saw Arienne running up that hill. I’m not dead yet, after all. I only hope I never have a bigger one, though. Any bigger, and it’ll be the last.

Our sally-party – Silvus and I had tagged along, for the practice – was outside the gate. We were snuffing the air but ready to retreat at a moment’s notice, and the portcullis was ready to drop with a run. There’d been some sort of commotion out on the mound itself, somewhere near the ditch, and no doubt the Prioress was tempted to pour some of the liquid fire down towards it, partly for the light, partly to discourage their nonsense, and

partly for the entertainment value. But she didn't, thank the gods. Nevertheless, the noises seemed to confirm the general opinion that this was just Nathan playing tricks, and a wicked attempt to deceive.

We weren't using torches. There is no better way to advertise yourself. In fact we were sticking to the star-shadow of the gatehouse, hunkered down and listening, still and quiet.

The commotion in the camp subsided. Out of the darkness came the sounds we'd been listening for – footsteps. I saw the outline of Sister Informer's face change as she lifted her head. I think she was about to order a javelin volley, but something stopped her. Perhaps it was because there was only one set of sounds, and that one was irregular – not someone at the military double, but one person fleeing, pelting at the top of their pace, exhausted, stumbling now and then.

She challenged, instead. 'Rose!'

'Glory! Sister Informer ...' The rest was a sob.

'Arienne! What are you ...?' Sister Informer shut her mouth with a snap. It was obvious what Arienne was doing here. She was running towards us, and there was something badly wrong. She emerged from the darkness, another shadow in a shadowed world, running like a drunk. How she missed the pitfalls I'll never know.

It takes a lot to upset Arienne. She was badly upset now.

In fact, she was distressed, gasping, not only with the long run uphill. She crashed into us, and we had to hold her up. 'Sister Informer, Asta's down there.' She was gasping and whooping for breath. We looked at each other. Arienne shook her head. 'Oh, I'm not … making sense. I brought her, and … I lost her … There's soldiers on the slope. Nathan's.'

Sister Informer nodded grimly. 'There would be. That whole thing' – she swept an arm at the distant fires – 'is a play put on for our benefit. They're out there waiting for us to take the bait and sally out in support of a non-existent raid.'

Arienne's face crumpled. She made a sound that might have been a denial, but she looked back. 'I left her there,' she said. 'I thought she was … just behind me. I came on, but she wasn't …'

Almost I thought she was turning back into the darkness to search. I moved in and held her. She was shaking.

'There's nothing we can do about it now.' That was a new voice. The Prioress was in the gateway, tall and spare in mail and helmet. 'Inside, quick. I wouldn't put it past Nathan to have archers on the slope. They could be stalking us even now.'

I had to tug at her shoulder to bring Arienne in.

The gates thudded shut behind us. Arienne pulled herself away, and I followed her. The Prioress had come in last, as was her habit, and Arienne tried to explain again, in bits and spurts as her breath returned.

Prioress Winterridge listened carefully. She doffed her helmet and pulled the mail coif back. Her braided hair fell from its coil on the top of her

head, down past her shoulders. She dragged her fingers through the roots of it, and stood, still listening.

Arienne ran down. It would appear that she had lost the mage out on the mound; that neither of them should have been there in the first place; that it had been a folly, and that it was all her fault.

'We should have stayed with the underpeople,' said Arienne. 'But I was so proud of myself, how I'd handled it, and I wanted to show you ...'

'You don't think she deserted?' The Prioress had eyes as sharp as a winter wind, and they glittered in the light from the flambeaux on the walls of the keep. Somehow she had extracted the gist of the situation. 'The Dark arose too strong in her?'

Arienne considered it, even through the shock and pain, then shook her head. 'No. She broke me loose from one of them, helped me on. I ran, and she followed, but I had to keep my eyes on the ground, looking for the pitfalls.' Prioress Winterridge nodded, and pulled her gauntlets off, dropping them into her helmet. 'When I looked back, she was gone.' The last word was a wail.

We all looked at each other, the Prioress grim-faced, Silvus stroking his goatee beard, Sister Informer with her head on one side. Arienne's eyes closed, remembering that mad scramble in the dark, and she shuddered. I moved up behind her and held her shoulders, and this time she leaned back against me.

Prioress Winterridge tallied opinions without asking anyone what theirs was. She knew at a glance, and anyway it was for her to say what we would do. She chewed her lip, and made up her mind.

'There's nothing we can do about it now.' Arienne made to speak, but the Prioress shook her head, total authority in the gesture. Then she sighed. 'I'm sorry,' she said softly. 'But we have no more idea of where she might be than you have. She might have escaped, and be lying low. She might be injured, out on the hill somewhere. She might have found her way back to the under-people somehow. Whatever one it is, I'm not sending people out to look for her. Nathan wants me to do just that very thing. I'd be sending them into a trap which I have no doubt is well laid and well sprung.'

Sister Informer cleared her throat. 'There are, of course, other possibilities for her fate, Sister Prioress.'

The Prioress acknowledged the delicate way it was put with a sharp dip of the head. 'Yes. She might be dead. They might have taken her but not recognised her. She might have convinced them that she's harmless – passed herself off as a camp follower. Or' – she lifted her face towards the distant stars and seemed to request aid from them – 'she's been taken, they know what they've got, and will force her.'

'Yes.' Sister Informer spoke for all of us. It was reluctant, but it had to be faced.

The Prioress nodded, and the night wind moaned in the angles of the bailey. It was cold.

So was her voice, when it came. 'In that case, we must be prepared for the underfolk to attack us, dragged in by Nathan's mage. They're wonderful miners. We must take further precautions. Water in shallow bowls, set out to detect digging underneath us. Countermining parties. We'll consider it in Conclave tomorrow.'

I grimaced. Countermining was the dirtiest of all the dirty jobs given to a soldier, excepting only burial detail. It meant digging into the mine that besiegers were trying to drive under the walls and scragging the miners there in the darkness, a murderous free-for-all fought with anything that might be to hand.

But soldiers get used to dirty jobs. What made me scowl was what I had been thinking about sieges. You can predict them. If Nathan could add the underpeople and their mining skill to his attack, he had just swung the balance a long way – his way. Could we hold him until winter?

The answer was now *no, probably not.* It depended on the underpeople. And on Asta Harrower, the Lady be with her. I held Arienne while she wept.

ASTA

This wasn't how it should be. There shouldn't be so much pain.

There was a flash of it so bad it woke me. Someone was pouring something into the score along my shin, and it burned like fire.

'Waste of good wine,' he grumbled. 'I'll bandage it up. Should be rebandaged each day. Not too tight. The ankle will be all right. Only sprained, not badly. I'll bandage that, too.'

He was, I realised, a little drunk. Not enough to be helpless, not actually swaying. Just a little over-finicky in his speech and a little clumsy with the bandage. It was rough cloth, and it hurt, too. I gasped with it.

'Hello,' he said. 'She's awake. There y'are, Hedley. She'll live until they hang her.'

Hang me? Panic. I opened my mouth, but there was nothing to say. Just like last time.

But he was smiling at the other man, bad teeth showing, red face and wine-breath, greasy face and fingers with dried blood under the nails. A surgeon. More likely a farrier. One that had one joke, and had just cracked it.

'Thank you,' said the other. 'For your trouble.' A coin passed.

'No trouble, Hedley, no trouble. What I'm here for. Evening. Evening, all.'

I was lying on a folding bench in a tent. Just a plain canvas tent, not yellow and black. There was just me and Hedley now. And a basin and a cloth. Hedley was looking at me and frowning. A young man with a fluffy brown moustache, leather back-and-breastplate and a helmet that had been made for him, with a smart plume to top it off. A cloak, heavy and good quality.

A gent. A soldier. Put them together. They'd brought me to their officer.

'Oh, thank you, thank you so much,' I gushed, doing the distressed maiden.

He frowned and harrumphed. Another decade would see him red-faced and crusty, thickening in the middle. 'Not at all. I have sent for the captain. He'll know what to do with you, Miss ...?'

'Hardaker,' I said. 'Lovita Hardaker.' How do I know where I got the name from? Maybe I read it somewhere.

He frowned again. Something seemed to be teasing at the fringe of his mind. Time to get out quick, before he worked out what it was.

I didn't need to work it out. I knew. He'd seen me. He'd been the young fellow that Teska pulled rank on to get a cavalry escort, down by the river, all those ages ago.

I sat up – there was a moderate pang from my leg – and began getting off the bench. He made a move to stop me, but it was polite, and I could ignore it. I swung up to a sitting position, and my head didn't swim too badly.

I smiled at him. 'You've been most kind and gallant, but I really mustn't trouble you any more.' I was using Arienne's tones. She spoke like a lady. 'And they'll be worried about me.' Who *they* might be, I wasn't saying. 'So, if you'll just excuse me ...'

Too late. Footsteps outside. A face looked in and scanned me briefly. It was the sergeant who'd been in charge of the escort. 'Yeah, that's her, ensign,' he said. 'How'd she get here, anyway?'

'I really don't know. But I think you'd better take this message to the aide-de-camp of His

Highness. You'll find him …'

That was that. A half hour later I was in front of Nathan.

The tent really was yellow and black this time, and there were lanterns standing around, shedding bright yellow light. Nathan sat on a folding chair, and I stood in front of him, just like that first time we'd had a little chat. A small crowd of goons and flunkeys stood around, in case I should try an assault. Somebody was holding a knife to my throat, but not quite allowing it to touch me, in case I should turn it into butterfat.

'So,' said Nathan, 'you became separated from Teska in the skirmish and you panicked. The horse picked it up, bolted, and you were miles away before you could get it under control. You've been trying to get back ever since, dodging the Order and moving by night. The horse died on you. Uh-huh.' He leaned forward. 'Who was the other girl? And why'd you stab the soldier?'

'I don't know her name, Your Highness. She said she'd help me get to your tent. Seemed to know the way. But we snuck down the ditch, and then she started leading me up the hill towards the castle. I knew that wasn't right. And it was her stabbed the man, not me.'

Prince Nathan stared me in the face. Then he sighed. 'And whoever she is, she has now disappeared. Well, it's a story. I don't believe it, but I'll give you a chance to prove yourself. It's your last one.'

Oh dear. He leaned back. A shadow, a coldness, came over his face. It had been merely shrewd and calculating before, but now he was putting on a crown that he kept always in his mind. It was a rich crown, but Nathan wanted it to be richer still.

He spoke, and the words were like stones, cold and hard and falling to harm. 'You can do something for us. Do it, and there'll be rich rewards for you; fail or refuse, and we will be forced to concede that the Dark has taken you, and the civil authorities will then no doubt do their duty.'

Translation: *Do my will, or burn.* I shaped my face into a schoolgirl expression of eagerness to please. 'Try me, Your Highness.'

He nodded. 'There is a goblin city hereabouts.' *Bet your life there is, Prince. Probably about twenty paces away from where you sit.* I nodded in my turn, brisk, sincere. The Prince looked princely. 'We understand that you can, among your other powers, secure the cooperation of the goblins. You can even ensure the submission of their lord to us as rightful ruler of this realm, and enrol them as our faithful vassals.'

I blinked. It was on the tip of my tongue to end the farce, and tell Nathan to find a long stick to ram it home with. But I thought about it, and there was a real problem I could use.

I tried to look apologetic. 'I … wish I could do that, Your Highness, I really do; but you have been, um, misinformed.'

'Oh?' Nathan's voice would have frozen the birds off the trees.

I would have to steer very carefully. 'I have to see the subject whose … feelings I am to … ah … correct, Your Highness. Through that one I can influence others, and they in turn others still – like ripples spreading out from a stone dropped in a pond. If I can control one, I can get control of others, more and more, faster and faster, until I use up all my mana. But I have to have one to start with, and that one must contact others. Once I am in his mind, I can stay with him, even beyond sight.'

'Indeed.' Prince Nathan was staring at me again. It felt like a week, but it was probably only a few moments. At last: 'Well. Let us check your story, Asta. Fortunately, we have the means.'

He muttered to a flunkey, who hurried out. Nathan leaned back again and reached out to a side table, where there was a goblet of wine. He waved me aside, and my watchers moved with me.

Time stretched out. Nathan was apparently used to having his every move stared at. Somebody brought him a paper. He scanned it, nodded, handed it back. 'Confirmed,' he said, and no more. He sat back again.

Eventually there was a stir behind me. I turned my head, but I could see nothing but yellow-and-black uniforms. Three of the big goons, the ones with the fanciest clothes and the faces like a set of clenched knuckles, hauled somebody through and dumped him on his knees in front of the chair.

He was dirty and ragged and in chains. He lifted his head.

Teska. It was Teska. Thinner, soiled with his own waste, unshaven, hair wild and stiff with dirt, shivering. There was a half-healed cut on his cheek. But it was him.

He stared at Prince Nathan, and his eyes were cringing and fawning, the eyes of a dog that had been kicked, and kept on being kicked. Pleading. And yet, with a dangerous light behind them. Kick a dog too often, and it'll go for your throat.

Prince Nathan stared back at him, and Teska winced. He wasn't used to the light, apparently. Nathan nodded, affably. 'Well. De Teska. It would seem that we have pulled your chestnuts out of the fire for you.'

He nodded at me. Teska squinted. Then he recognised me, and his eyes widened. He tried to rise, but a hard hand on his shoulder forced him back on his knees. And his stare flared into a wild hatred. Suddenly I understood. He couldn't blame Nathan for anything that had happened to him. Nathan was a god, and the gods are blameless. No. He blamed me.

'Excellent,' said Prince Nathan, as if he was presiding over a Guild reunion dinner. 'And now to business, if you please. We have called you in to consult your special knowledge of the talent, Squire de Teska. We are told that Mistress Harrower, here, needs to have a goblin actually present to … um … prevail upon him. That the subject must be in sight of her, but that she can then proceed through him to others. Say now, is that the case?'

Teska swallowed. He had not looked back

at Nathan. His eyes were blazing into mine. He didn't reply.

Nathan nodded at the guard, who grabbed Teska's hair and forced his head around until he was facing the Prince.

'I really dislike having to repeat myself, de Teska,' remarked Nathan, evenly. 'You may have noticed that I am still using your title. Your failures and deficiencies may yet all be retrieved, and my favour restored to you. But I want an answer to my question: is what she tells us correct?'

Teska blinked. The mad light left his eyes. For a while, at least. But I knew him now. He'd kill me if he could. He had been frightening before. Now he terrified me.

He passed a hand across his brow, his chains clinking. He swallowed. His voice came in a croak. Apparently one of the privileges denied to those outside the princely favour was drinking water. 'Yes,' he husked. 'It's true.'

'Good. She hasn't lied in that part at least. Give him a drink, one of you.'

Teska slobbered around the cup they held to his mouth. Water dribbled down his chin. Nathan waited, as if politely ignoring the weaknesses of the afflicted.

'Good. Finished?' he asked. Teska nodded. Nathan laced his hands together on his chest. 'So, to sum up. Asta needs to have a goblin to start with, rather as one requires a single splinter to start a fire. Correct?' Both of us nodded, but he was only looking at Teska. 'Hum. I see now why they went under the earth, and come out as little as possible. But nevertheless.'

He looked around at the courtiers and the servants and the flunkeys. Nodded to himself. 'All are excused,' he announced, 'except for Mistress Harrower, Squire de Teska and the Gentlemen of the Presence. Ser Robert, attend me.'

The tent cleared. Some of the servants seemed to think he hadn't meant them, and had to be glared at to go. But finally there was nobody but me, Teska, two of the trolls apiece, and the head troll, who was getting his orders. A few moments, and the latter rolled out. I heard his voice in the outer chamber.

'Guardsman de Hill; Guardsman de Corder. Perimeter of ten paces from the tent. Nobody allowed in but me and a prisoner, on the direct orders …' The rumble of his voice died away.

Prince Nathan didn't want us to be overheard, it would seem. But he had nothing to say just yet. He lolled in his chair, staring at the flap of the entrance. I wasn't talking, myself. Teska had managed to turn his head and was staring at me again, which was enough to give me the horrors. Then he looked at Nathan again.

'Sire,' he croaked, 'I beg you, don't listen to her. She's treacherous as a snake. Give her to me …'

'Silence, Teska.' Prince Nathan's voice was soothing. *Heel, Teska. Easy, boy.* He gave me a smile. 'If you are trying to trick me, Asta, it may come to that.' I shuddered.

So there we were, a happy little group. Nathan seemed to be thinking about something, a faint frown on his face, as if sorting through memories. Teska stared at me. The goons stood like lumps of rock. The lamps hissed and shed yellow light. It was getting late.

A step in the outer room. The head goon reappeared. Behind him was a small figure swathed in a cape and hood. Nathan sat up straighter. His girlfriend? Couldn't be. Whoever it was, was in chains. I could hear the jingle as the guard pulled him along.

The goon stood aside, and Nathan motioned the last arrival before him. The hood fell back. I saw with a horrid thrill that the face was masked in leather, and the mask was buckled and locked in place.

The head goon linked the chain into his belt, took a firmer grip on his club, and dug in a pouch with his other hand. He brought out a small key. At a nod from Nathan, he unlocked the mask.

It fell away. It uncovered the face of an underperson.

Of course. I had known him since he came in the room. I could see into his mind, poor helpless wight, because he had no defence against such as me. And in that mind I could find nothing but sorrow and regret and the most appalling despair. Self-hatred, too. And a memory that he churned in his mind, over and over. A battle, where he was fighting – fighting women in mail. Fighting and winning, for though these women wielded great poleaxes with skill and unflagging devotion, they were few and his people were many. It was hard and the cost was great, but they were succeeding. Then, without warning, the order to desist, to break off, that the plan had worked. Next, utter consternation, shock and bewilderment. After that …

Nothing. The need to fight, the rage, the certainty of right, was suddenly gone, as the mage who was driving him was gone from his mind. And now riders with banners of yellow and black were all around him, riding his people down, slaughtering them in swathes. I saw it in his mind, and I was sick and horrified, feeling his sickness and his horror added to mine. He had been caught and clubbed down and found himself before this yellow-and-black grub. And then an eternity of waiting in chains, being watched, in stone rooms and pits. Many seasons of warm and cold, cut off from all peace and his people.

It had all been for nothing. It had all been an illusion, a nightmare. And it started again in his memory. I wondered how it was that he had not run mad, with the knowledge of it.

'Ahem.' That was Nathan. I shook myself, and blanked my face to meet his eye. He must not see my rage.

He eyed me carefully, though. 'You needed a goblin. This is one.'

I breathed in, careful to keep it slow and even. 'Yes, Your Highness. A moment, if you please.'

Another careful inspection. Arienne, guide me now. Or your Lady, whoever and wherever She is. Somebody.

There was the knowledge of the key to the warren. There was an entry to it just above, a few hundred paces up the mountain. The need to go home, to the quiet and the dark, to seek forgiveness there … that I did not have to supply.

He turned and looked at me, and I could feel his disgust and his hatred of all the termites. Well could I understand it. I would not touch it. To take it away, merely for my own comfort, that was the Dark. Yet he knew me, knew my talent, knew me for what I was.

He must go home. I planted that as an overwhelming desire, and I forbade him to kill himself. That far I interfered, and may I find forgiveness for it.

'There!' I said brightly. 'Now. He'll get us into the warren, and I …'

Nathan smiled. 'You, Asta Harrower, you will be with us, within sight, but not too close to your friends. You might have a trick or two yet; I fancy you have a few.' He gestured. 'Bind her. Bring the goblin, and Teska as well. A plain cloak for me, and for yourselves. We will go incognito. Make sure we're not followed.'

They hustled us out into the night. My leg made walking slow and difficult, but I was forced to keep the pace up, hopping and scrambling.

'Follow the goblin,' said Nathan. 'And watch her. One of you by each elbow, swordpoints at her ribs. At the first sign of an ambush, kill her. The goblins will stop if she's dead.'

We laboured through the camp, which was mostly asleep. Guards were given passwords, and nobody interfered. At the edge we passed a sentry watching the ditch and wall; he challenged, was answered, and then wanted to know why we wanted to go out.

The chief goon opened his cloak to show his yellow-and-black livery with the braid and the frogging. 'Gentlemen of the Presence. Ser Robert de Jost, Watch officer, with a detail on special security business. Let us pass.'

The sentry went back to leaning on his spear. 'Pass, friend.' He sounded like he wasn't happy with the last word. Maybe there were a few too many special security details to suit him, in this army. We climbed the wall and passed the ditch – not nearly as deep as the one around the castle that the Order had dug – and started up the mountainside.

My leg hurt badly. I was limping and hopping, but I knew how much use it would be to complain. On and on we went, passing clumps of brush and then bare stony slopes, steeper and steeper. We found a goat path, and it wandered towards the heights far above us.

A few hundred paces farther on Nathan paused. He wasn't breathing hard. 'How far now?' he asked.

I consulted the underperson. He was watching the mountainside ahead with yearning eyes. The knowledge wasn't hard to find.

'About fifty paces, round the turn of the trail. There's a sign and a portal there.'

'All right. Let the goblin go ahead. I assume they won't open at all if they see us with him?' I nodded. 'Very well. Keep him on the long leash. We'll move up to the turn, take cover, and let him knock, or whatever it is they do.'

We sneaked up carefully to a place behind a convenient rock. The captive moved off the trail and looked back.

'They'll be able to see that leash. They can see in the dark,' I whispered to Nathan.

'It would be fitting that they should.' He reflected for a moment. He'd be thinking: *We've got her, and the goblin's only a puppet.* 'All right. Release him.'

The rope came back, and the freed captive walked on a few paces. He caressed a stone as if it were a well-loved piece of furniture, and then he stepped away from it, carefully measuring his paces. At ten steps he was seen as a vague shadow on the mountainside, and then suddenly not, as he stooped. There was a moment's pause, and then the mountain itself changed its outline. A hatch opened up, only a small one, and then closed again. There was no sound. He had gone.

I closed my eyes, and I could still feel his joy. I savoured it for a while.

Nathan nudged me. 'He's inside?'

I turned to him with a smile. 'Yes, so please Your Highness. And his friends have come to meet him and welcome him home.'

'Good. How soon can you reach their lords and have them come out to offer me submission and fealty?'

I let the smile broaden into a grin. If there was not going to be much more left in my life to enjoy, I was at least going to enjoy this. 'Well, of course, you will be the first to know, Your Highness.'

He frowned. 'I?'

'Of course. You're certain to be personally present when hell freezes over.'

CHAPTER

WILL

'There's a lot of activity down there.' Sister Informer shaded her eyes from the morning sun and gazed down on the camp from the castle battlements. 'They're building something. A platform of some sort.'

Arienne looked up. She was sitting on the guard walk because I was standing my watch, her back to the wall, her knees drawn up, writing doggedly in her journal. Observations about the underpeople, new knowledge of their language, sketches, references to books she found in the Order's library. It kept her mind from wandering, she said.

One of the subjects it might be wandering over was the Conclave meeting that morning. In another army it would have been called a council of war. The senior sisters and their Prioress sat together, grimly considering how this latest and worst threat might be countered. Nobody had said anything to Arienne, and the Prioress had only remarked, coolly and at large, that the attempt to bring this mage back to the Order had only failed because of bad luck – the sheer mischance that Nathan had pulled his stunt at the same time. True, but not cheering.

The meeting closed in a mood of gloomy determination. They worked out countermining measures, and started training a squad for the horrid business of actually doing it. Fire syphons. Short weapons – there would be no space to swing an axe. Bowls of water, to detect the vibrations made by digging. Test shafts were being sunk in the bailey even now. Silent signals had been devised and noise discipline instituted, to hear and not be heard.

Oh, they knew what to do, all right, and they'd do a good job of it, and sell their lives dearly. The castle would be held so long as one sister could wield steel. They'd fight it out to the last. The trouble was, they thought they might have to, now.

So Arienne came to the guard walk while I stood my watch, and we watched together. We might not be able to be together for much longer.

Now she recorked her ink bottle, laid her pen aside, and came to the wall itself. Leaning her elbows on it, a merlon to each side, she could peer over the battlement down into the vale.

There had been a clearing made in the camp, tents folded up and set aside. In that clearing a building or something was being erected. It was way over near the stream, though, too far to see anything.

'Hmm,' said Sister Informer. She turned to a runner, a novice, a lass of seventeen or so. 'Ask Sister Berengia if she would try a cast with one of her pets. Out as far as the river at least.' And, as the girl left at a run, 'Arienne, would you oblige?'

Arienne nodded. A few minutes later a sister came out into the bailey with a peregrine falcon on her fist, jessed and hooded. On Sister Informer's nod, she unhooded the bird and flew it. It whirred over the battlements, and headed straight towards its usual hunting ground – the meadow that was now under Nathan's tents. Up and up it spiralled in the clear mountain air, seeking prey.

Arienne watched it and her eyes became distant. She wasn't using them any more. She was seeing the world through the powerful eyes of the hawk.

'I can see everything, no problem. It's a lovely clear day. The trouble is, I don't know what to make of it. The bird doesn't understand human constructions at all. There's a mast or a pole or something like that stuck into the ground like a post, and it must be six paces high. Next to it, touching it, is a square of decking, apparently made of boards, and itself off the ground by a man's height or more, held up by uprights.'

A horrid feeling came over me. What Arienne was describing sounded very much like …

'A gallows,' said Sister Informer. 'Nathan must be having a few discipline problems. That's a useful bit of ...' She stopped.

Arienne wasn't listening. She was frowning at the sky, where her host was wheeling in the clean blue.

'Now there's people bringing out bundles of grass and furze.' A pause, and the horror grew. Arienne's attention was on trying to sort details out of the impressions in the bird's mind, and the bird wasn't interested in this. 'They're disappearing under the platform, trying to hide ... no, sorry, that was the falcon, not me ... and coming out again without the bundles.'

I exchanged glances with Sister Informer. She leaned over the inner guard walk, and called to the novice. 'My respects to Sister Prioress, and there is something she needs to see. Urgently.' The girl put her head down and ran for the keep.

Arienne was no longer staring blankly. She was reviewing what she had seen, putting it through her own mind, and suddenly her face contracted in horror, the colour draining from it.

'No,' she whispered, 'Dear Lady of Mercies, no.'

Rapid steps on the stairs to the bailey. Prioress Winterridge appeared like a conjuring trick and shot a rapid glance at Arienne. 'Should we sound stand to, sister?' she asked Sister Informer, and the latter shook her head.

'It's no threat to us, Sister Prioress. Not directly. But Nathan is getting ready to burn Asta Harrower at the stake.'

ASTA

They had slapped me around. They weren't very good at it. The Watch in Tenabra could have taught them a thing or two. Like, if you belt somebody in the head too hard and too often, all that happens is they pass out, and you can't do anything useful then.

I remember laughing at them, to make them do it harder, on the off-chance that they'd go berserk, and I'd be out of it permanently. Didn't work.

I came around face-down on the dirt floor of a tent, tied like a hog. I hurt, but it helped to reflect that at least I'd made them carry me all the way back down the mountain. They'd given me a pretty fair kicking all the same. I thought my leg had hurt, before. Hah!

When I rolled to one shoulder, there was one of the goons with the fancy yellow uniforms watching me. I watched him back, for a while, out of one eye. The other didn't seem to want to open. I can't say I blamed it. He acted as if I was a tub of that fire liquid the Order uses. Apt to burst into flames any moment. Just watched me, never took his eyes off, and there was something in his face. Not fear. He wasn't frightened of me. But careful, maybe, and even a little confused. Great big rough lug. One of the sort that hasn't worked out yet that you can't make anyone do anything. Not if they won't. He'd always been able to make folk do what he wanted by hitting them.

'Does it talk?' I wondered aloud, after a while. Not too much aloud. The words came out in a mumble.

'Shut it,' he said, without heat. 'Or I have orders to cut out your tongue.'

I nodded. That hurt, too. It didn't matter if I talked to this moron or not. He could do it any time, and there clearly was a reason why he hadn't. Nathan wasn't the sort to leave unturned stones about. I began to wonder what was stopping him. Maybe because he'd figured that there was no more point. But in that case, why not just take me out in the woods a way and finish it without more fuss?

I got my answer some time later. Breathing was getting difficult, because my face was so swollen and my chest hurt. The shadows were gathering around me, and I was getting to hope that I'd be allowed to slip away into them soon. No such luck.

There was a tramp of feet outside. Many feet, all stepping together. Soldiers. What fun.

The tent flap was flipped aside. Two of them came in, walking as if they weighed twice as much, and they looked down on me.

'Get up,' one of them grunted. The bigger one.

I just looked at him. So they had to bend over and haul me to my feet – no, to my foot – and drag me out. I sagged in their grip. Why should I give them a free ride?

The sun outside was bright enough to dazzle me for a moment. My two tucked themselves in

between two files of their fellows, and we all went for a stroll together. A slow stroll.

The goons on both sides were in a line, single file, five or so to a side. They were marching slow, all in perfect step, about a full pace apart, so I could see between them, for all their fancy halberds and polished gear and stuff. We were walking between two barriers of rope strung between rough pickets, about waist-high. Outside the rope on both sides stood ordered ranks of less gorgeous soldiers, crowded in, looking blank. Some moron up in front was hitting a drum, once to every step the goons took. I took care to hop out of time with it, when I did hop.

And there were women, too. Soldiers have wives and families, too. They stood in little groups behind, their hands under their aprons. I made sure I turned my face this way and that. Few would meet my eye – but I must've looked pretty rough. Some looked shocked. There were even a few shaken heads and quick angry glances at the goons, and that was something to treasure.

Yes, people. Your beloved Prince beats up little girls. How about that for chivalry, huh?

It wasn't a long walk. They dragged me into a cleared space among the tents. The two files separated and took up position, becoming a line around the space. In the centre of it was a gallows, a big one.

I knew what a gallows was. There was one in Tenabra, in the Old Market, and it was used often, especially during the holidays. That one was a

platform with a ladder leading up to it, and a crossbar to hang people from. I squinted up, and could only see a pole on this. Oh dear.

My faithful bearers got me to the bottom of the ladder, but there was a hitch at that point. On one leg and no hands – mine were tied behind my back – I couldn't climb it, and it did no good kicking me. In fact, there was a murmur from the ranks when they used their boots. They looked at each other, and there was a faint shadow of uncertainty there. Their world had always been so certain before; this sort of thing confused them.

In the end one of them climbed to the platform and the other one boosted me up so the first could grab me. He hauled me upright, and this time I got my good leg under me, and shrugged his hand off my arm. I nearly fell over doing it. I straightened my back with an effort.

I was high enough to look over the heads of the crowd. A big crowd. Most of Nathan's army was here, packed close, and outside them the hangers-on, sutlers and camp followers, varlets and what have you. All standing around waiting.

What they were waiting for became clear a moment later. There was a stir at the back, a medley of shouts to make way, and Nathan and his guards and flunkeys came riding into the circle, walking their horses. Nathan, I noticed, kept to the centre, surrounded by his bodyguard. Nobody cheered.

Once they were in, the goons dismounted and faced outwards. Nathan stayed in the saddle. He made a princely gesture. A little man in a yellow-and-black cape – like a blanket with a hole in the middle that his head stuck through – walked out into the clear space in front of the gallows. He pulled a breath in, and began to read from a scroll in an enormous voice that echoed off the mountainside.

I looked up beyond him, beyond Nathan and the ranked troops, to the mountains behind, and then farther still, high into the blue sky. There was a hawk circling there. I could watch it and try to ignore what the herald was shouting. Couldn't stop hearing it though.

The mage Asta Harrower, having defected to the Dark and being now found guilty of the horrible crime of necromancy, is condemned to death by fire, the sentence passed by a court-martial according to the law of the Riverland. Sentence has been confirmed by His Highness the Prince of the Riverland, and will now be carried out.

A heavy silence greeted this. I felt I had to add something, so I blew the loudest raspberry I could manage, with an upward inflection at the end. A few of them were in earshot, anyway. There was the faintest ripple of laughter. Officers looked around for offenders, and it died away.

A heavy hand fell on my shoulder. 'Play it for laughs all you want, Asta. You won't be laughing soon.'

Gods. That shock was the worst and nastiest part of all. I knew that voice. Teska. I turned my head.

He was wearing the usual black hood and mask, but it was him all right. My gorge rose, and I nearly had an accident. But the free hawk in the free sky had helped, somehow. I was able to answer him, steadily enough.

'Couldn't they find a real hangman, then? From what I hear, Nathan has a glut of 'em.'

He grabbed me by the hair and hauled me hopping to the stake. There was a set of irons, shackles and wrist-pieces, hung on short chains stapled deep into the wood. That wood was wet, sopping. So was the platform. They didn't want it to burn too quick.

'Of course. Of course.' He was jovial, almost chuckling, and as mad as Fred the mastiff. 'But I asked a special boon, and he was pleased to grant it. I am returned to favour. The next mage we find will be different. Not like you, you treacherous bitch.' He started locking my feet in the shackles, making sure I couldn't kick him.

'You won't have time to denature the steel, Asta,' he said. 'It's too thick. Soon now, you will be in too much pain to concentrate, anyway.'

'Whatever did happen to Widow Pila?' I asked, to change the subject.

I couldn't see his face. His voice was a shrug. 'She failed in her charge. She was dismissed, with prejudice.'

'Nathan killed her.'

'Not at all. She found other employment, in fact. Entertaining soldiers, I understand.' He'd be smirking under that hood.

I shook my head. 'Enjoy it while you can, Teska. Sooner or later you'll be up here, the main act in the show. You're working for a monster.'

He locked the last piece in place and walked away to the top of the ladder. Turned around and started down it, facing me. I could see the mad glitter of his eyes. 'Good-bye, Asta. This is going to hurt.'

I couldn't spit far enough. A shame. He lowered himself down the ladder.

WILL

There was silence on the wall. The Prioress looked down into the vale with sorrow and pain etched on her face. Twice she opened her mouth to speak and twice she closed it again.

Then she turned and faced Arienne, and Arienne read that face and wept.

'We can do nothing for her ourselves,' said Prioress Winterridge, softly and clearly. 'There are five thousand of them, and another five within call. There are two hundred of us, and a few hundred more in the hills. It's broad daylight, so he would see us coming and have ample time to order himself to meet us. He would be hoping that we'd try. I'm sorry. Sorrier still because it is clear that Asta Harrower has met the Dark and defeated it, and I cannot uphold her.' She looked away, down the valley, and then into the bright sky. 'Now she is in the Lady's hands. The only

thing we can do is bring Her attention to that fact. Sister Informer?'

'Sister Prioress?'

'Call the sisters to prayer, for the soul of one victorious over the Dark. For one of our own.'

ASTA

Teska didn't quite go out of sight, worse luck. The platform sloped a little. I could see his head as he walked out to one of the soldiers. That one was carrying a flaming torch. Teska took it and raised it high in the heavy silence, waiting for Prince Nathan's word.

As if that was a signal, a trumpet call rang out. High, tootling, not like the honking of the trumpets I'd heard before. Heads turned. Another call sounded. It was coming from the edge of the camp. It was coming closer.

People in the crowd were turning now, and there was a murmur, rising to a low confused hubbub. Something was happening, behind them, in the direction I was facing. There was movement now, glimpses of something ... and I had the best seat in the house. Better even than Nathan, who had wheeled his horse to see. His guards closed up around him. Clearly, he hadn't ordered this.

A commotion. A spill of soldiers into the square, then a rough lane formed. People were getting out of the way. A rising roar of excited talk. Teska with his upraised torch was left alone in the

middle of the space, looking silly. Nobody was watching him, now.

Around the line of tents in front of me marched a group of underpeople – five of them. One was carrying a trumpet, which he blew calls on. Another bore a flag – a white one. The three in the middle were the elders.

And I could hear them, more and more clearly as they came closer. I sent them my confusion and my warning. *No, no. You must not. Please. He'll enslave you.* Pictures of underpeople working their mines under the lash, of armies sent to fight Nathan's enemies far from home ...

But in return, I heard them. They were directing their thought at me. I could hear the elders, and through them others, more and more and more of them. I could have filled all of them with any feeling I wanted, could have made them do anything then. All of them, chains and skeins and nets of minds, all deliberately opened to me, all ready to be used. The need and the desire to use the Dark, to strike Nathan down, was very strong in me then.

No. I would not waste their lives. It was the Dark. Arienne had said it, and she was to be trusted. It was the Dark, the open bottle, the need the same as Sart's need and the pain the same as his pain. I would not use the Dark. I would not.

But there was something else. More minds opened to me, giving themselves in total trust, chains of them in the dim lights of the warren, flickering in my head like a landscape seen by

lightning. The warren, open to me, seen like a ball of wool, tunnels and galleries and shafts and caves without number, all secrets told, freely. Chains of minds leading through the blackness of the secret tunnels, to the most secret places of all, and all to one place. To this place. To a mind that was closing the circle, just below me in the darkness.

The elders marched on, to the space in front of Nathan, where he sat his white horse. I wondered briefly what he'd done with my unicorn. And Nathan must have thought of me, because he shot me a look that was hard and approving at the same time. *Now you're seeing sense. Good move, and just in time.*

I smiled at him and listened to the mind below me. A final thrust, and the underperson was through. He picked up the heavy cutters, pushed a faggot of wood aside, and began to lift himself up. Among the stacked furze-wood and in the shadows beneath the platform he was hard to see, and nobody was looking.

The elders went down on their knees before Nathan. He smiled in a regal fashion and walked his horse towards them. A single row of guards stayed before him, but the elders removed their daggers from their sheaths and laid them on the dusty ground, points towards themselves.

Nathan waved them up. They in turn stared at him, and then turned pointedly and stared at me. He followed their gaze and nodded. He bent his head and spoke to a guard. The herald scuttled to his side. The Prince leaned over in the saddle and spoke down to him.

A moment while the herald composed. Then he moved out into the open, and faced the crowd. The same deep breath. The same enormous voice. I saw the underpeople flinch from it.

In recognition of the submission of the goblin lords to the Light and to their rightful Prince, His Highness declares an amnesty and mercy to the mage Asta Harrower, on condition that she abjure the Dark …

Someone was yelling, but the voice was tiny, lost in that vast shout.

… and declare submission …

There was a flurry in front of me. Teska. Jumping, waving his torch. Pointing to the movement under the platform. He'd seen it, and he'd lost his mind altogether.

… to her rightful Prince, Nathan of the Riverland …

The torch came whirling towards me. A shriek, one that cut even through the voice of the herald: 'She's gulling you, you fool!'

The fire landed in the furze, which was tarred to light quickly. It blazed up at once. Flames shot up like a curtain, crackling, roaring, gushing up the supports.

Below me, the party that had dug up below the platform tumbled out of the earth – two, three of them. The wood was smoking already. Below, in the crowd, there was confusion. The ranks were disordered, soldiers nattering with their neighbours, pointing, arguing. They'd just heard the reprieve, and were buzzing with it, approving. But

now there were underfolk jumping up on the platform itself, two of them with a pair of heavy cutters.

Another of them came leaping up. And now some moron saw it as well as the capering Teska, and started shouting, 'Treachery!'

That was it. The guards ran in two different directions. Some at Teska. Some towards me, though I don't think they knew what they were going to do when they arrived.

Most of the crowd were soldiers, and armed. The underpeople were the enemy an hour ago. In the tumult, some fool was sure to lose his head. Some fool did.

There was a flurry of shouts. Steel was out everywhere, and everywhere there was confusion. Some were for Nathan, some for Teska, some against the underpeople, some against the Guard. A company of crossbowmen were spanning their weapons, and in the close-packed ranks, with contradicting orders being shouted, somebody's elbow got joggled just as he was putting the bolt on the slide. Someone else screamed that he'd been shot. There was a confused volley. The standard-bearer, the one with the white flag of truce, fell with a bolt in him. I felt him die, and I could do nothing. The flag fell into the dirt.

Well, if I could do nothing else, I could at least inspire Nathan's horse to buck. That didn't take much, but it took up his attention.

Chains snapped in the jaws of the cutters. The steel of the underpeople is harder than any forged

above ground. They were working furiously, and the platform was starting to blaze. Steam was coming from the wet wood.

The last chain fell, and my feet were getting hot. They grabbed me and passed me down like a sack, kicking blazing faggots aside.

And as they did, the earth opened, a dozen rents, two dozen, and the underpeople came boiling out, steel in their hands, and burst into the midst of the soldiers.

WILL

'Sister Prioress!'

'... Lady of Mercies, Lady of Victories.' The Prioress looked up at the wall, where Arienne was hopping from foot to foot. She coiled her braid on top of her head and slammed her helmet on, as she took the stairs three at a time. It was the fastest termination to formal prayers in the history of the Order.

A moment to look, and a sudden inhalation, 'Lady be praised!' and then a sudden spasm of doubt. She glanced at Arienne. 'The underpeople are attacking Nathan. Asta has called them and forced them to her service.'

Arienne stared at her. She seemed to agonise. Then, 'No. This is not the Dark. I know it. I know her. She would not.'

The Prioress switched to Silvus. 'Can you tell me, Ser de Castro? The Order will not fight on

the side of the Dark, not even against Nathan. Are they being forced?'

Silvus seemed to breathe deeply of the small air coming up the valley. He, too, hesitated. Then his face firmed. 'There is no Dark I can feel, and I believe I would detect it from that far. I think Arienne is right.'

The Prioress nodded. Her decision came instantly, and her call. 'Sister Gabrielle; Sister Celestin; Sister Informer.' Her company commanders leapt to their feet in the bailey below. They had been on their knees. 'Stand to. Throw open the gates. We attack!'

The gate was wide enough for six abreast. It took ten minutes to marshal the columns, and another ten to pick our way down the slope. Pieces of Nathan's army met us. They thought they were running away from trouble. We persuaded them that they were wrong.

Here was the ditch, and we went into line, three deep. We scrambled up the rampart, first rank lifted by second, then turning to help. Impossible in the face of organised opposition, but there was no resistance. Forward in line, shaking out into fighting formation, each sister close enough to support those on either side, loose enough to swing that dreadful poleaxe. I unlimbered my sword, the gift of the underpeople.

I have to give Nathan his due. He had been taken utterly by surprise. Not a few of his companies had simply dropped into holes. The underpeople had torn into many others that had been standing around at parade rest, packed together and already confused. He had no control, no way to pass orders. More than half his army was down in the first fifteen minutes, and most of the rest was fleeing towards the pass, every man for himself, but still he had managed to pull a few hundred out of the melee that had burst on them and had begun to construct some sort of a retreat.

There it was, a ring of pikes – and it was pulling back, step by step. Crossbow bolts whistled and thudded, and it was losing, but it tightened its ranks and went on. A knot of yellow-and-black guardsmen was within it, and somewhere in that knot, the man himself. The underpeople, lightly armed, assaulted those closed ranks without success. A trail of broken red bodies showed where the porcupine had passed, retreating, heading step by step for the pass and safety. Already it had crossed the camp wall and was on the green; already the cavalry commanders on the road would be blowing 'Boot and saddle'. They could rescue him yet. It must be finished now.

The sisters dressed their ranks. The underfolk saw it and scrambled out of the way, their minds able to hear each other. They would follow us in, once we breached the wall of pikes. Out of the front rank strode the Prioress, her banner-bearer beside her. Her voice rang out, a soprano bell that cut through the battle tumult like a knife.

'For the Lady!' The banner, the Rose in Glory, floated above her, and that terrible line of axe-heads lifted to the warcry of the Order.

'For the Lady!' we answered, and the ranks began to move, a walk at first, and then a jog.

The pikes halted. You could see officers trying to thicken it up. The crossbows of the underpeople were still taking a toll. A hundred paces, and the pikeheads shifted and wavered. Fifty, and yellow-and-black figures were running for the rear, and others were dropping pikes and burrowing into the ranks. And suddenly, the whole mass just melted like jelly on a stove.

Anyone who could, ran. Most just threw their weapons down and cried for quarter. The guardsmen in the centre fought to the death, probably out of lack of intelligence to do anything else. And Nathan.

He could have surrendered. We hacked our way through the last defenders, and there he was. I was passing busy at the time, but I know Sister Informer cried him quarter. He ignored her.

I didn't know why, not then. But he slashed at her, and the rest was like a rehearsed dance passage. She caught the cut on her haft, and her next-in-line did what she was drilled to do.

She took his head clean off.

ASTA

They carried me down to the ground, but they hesitated as they faced the flames, and as they did there was a mighty shout behind, wordless, agonised.

Teska. He was raving and moaning with hate and despair. His god had failed him and he had lost his soul. All he knew was that he hated me. He came after us, careless of the flames, whirling a maul around his head like a baton. A demon of battle, and we fled before him. He came on, gibbering.

The underpeople dragged burning bundles out of the way with their bare hands, ran over the glowing coals, and thrust me into the tunnel. It was rough and hasty and dirty. The shaft went straight down at first, and the scraping fall jarred me again. The darkness I saw wasn't only that of the underground. Darkness was creeping into my head again. I was carried, and that was a burden to them, but the underpeople move faster and more surely in their tunnels than any sunperson can. We ran into the cool, comforting darkness. Still I heard Teska groping and panting behind, glad to spend his life if only he could drag me with him.

Darkness, black solid darkness. Surely and gently, they carried me along, and the noises faded. He was still back there, though, still in the darkness behind me. I'd never be rid of him. He would follow me in the darkness forever and ever …

But there came the clang of an iron door, and the sounds cut off, and then resumed, faintly. A light scraped into being, and I was in a passage, and the iron door was closed behind me. They laid me gently on the floor, cool rough earth. Through the door came the sound of fingers

scrabbling for a hold, and then a pounding. Wordless howls and curses. I shuddered.

There was a lever, a long metal bar, in the wall by the door. The underpeople flicked a glance all around, and then one of them padded to the lever and pulled it. Over the inhuman sounds beyond the door came the faint noise of the shattering of glass.

By the time we reached the next bend, the door was glowing a dull smoky red. The noises had stopped.

CHAPTER

WILL

The ballroom of the Palace at Tenabra was an odd place for the Order to be holding a Conclave, but the Prioress didn't seem much put out by it, nor did the quorum of her senior sisters who had made the journey across the moors. A unique setting for a unique Conclave meeting. Only Conclave, sitting as a body, could make treaties binding the Order with another power. Including treaties of peace.

Nathan's army had dissolved, in the long retreat across the moors. Most of it deserted and fled; without him, its surviving commanders took to squabbling among themselves. Its remnants shambled into the Riverland by various routes, spreading tales about the triumph of the Dark. Yet, soon after that, the wounded and the released prisoners began to arrive, and they told a different story.

The wounded had been efficiently cared for. The prisoners, meaning anyone who threw down their weapons and called for quarter, had been decently treated, given food and supplies, and sent home. Women and children had been especially looked after. The dead had been interred with the proper rites, and not violated. Even Nathan had received decent burial. If this was the Dark, it was acting strangely out of character.

After such a disaster, there weren't enough soldiers who were willing to fight, and no Nathan to organise them anyway. So the remaining nobles got together a council and sent to the Order, to learn its terms.

They were pleasantly surprised. Apart from its own sovereignty, on only two things was the Order inflexible: one, that peace, law and freedom were to be accorded the underpeople, known heretofore as goblins. Their councils were to have sovereign power over their own places, the warrens, which were to be inviolate. Their elders were to rank as nobles. Their envoys were to be received as embassies.

And two: the nobles of the Riverland, the notables and gentry, and anyone else who could be assembled within earshot, were to hear the testimony of the underperson Lessersmith. It would be given under oath before the Conclave of the Order.

The biggest building in Tenabra is the Palace, and its largest room is its ballroom, occupying a whole wing. Oddly, I'd seen it before, though I don't go in for ballrooms, generally. It was a vast space, marble-floored, with glass windows that reached to the vaulted ceiling. These were flung open so that people on the lawn outside might hear.

On the dais at one end, chairs faced the body of the hall, and there the Conclave of the Order sat in full formal habit, cream-white robes over silver mail, their Prioress at their head. At the other end, a healthy walk away, was a short flight of marble steps leading up to a tall pair of double doors.

The people had been coming in for hours. First the commons, picnicking on the grass outside in the warm summer sunshine. Then the magistrates and merchants and burghers, to be seated in the rear of the great room. Then gentry, a selection from all the old families, and the nobles: the Counts of Conflans and of Nessa; the Barons of Wend, of Penire, of Wunish, of Golpi, all in court dress in the colours of their arms. Then the arch-priests. They all filed in, a gorgeous, many-hued throng. Ushers saw them to their seats, in careful order of formal precedence, and they sat.

Silvus and I rated a place on the dais: we were pretending to be guards. He had been studying the underpeople's language furiously for three months now, tutored by Arienne. Asta, too. The sooner we had a corps of interpreters, the better. But that meant finding more people with the talent.

Both of us stood in fancy dress, our own colours. Over them we wore the subdued cloaks of green and brown of the Order's auxilia. Arienne stood behind the chair of the Prioress, in a sea-green silk gown and jewels. I had promised that sight to myself, and a knight keeps his promises. In spite of her awful responsibilities, she had a smile for me.

The last dignitary arrived and was ushered to a seat. The Prioress gave the tiniest of nods to the chamberlain.

A pause, while a silence established itself and grew. Then the herald beside the great double doors stamped his staff on the marble floor, three ringing strokes. The doors swung open.

He filled his lungs with air, and the great room with his voice: 'Lady Prioress, sisters of the Conclave, my lords and ladies, gentles. Their Excellencies the Elders of the Place of Youngest Stones.'

Two of the elders only. One lay dead, killed on the field of Waycastle, and not yet replaced, for the underpeople mourn an elder long. After them came one more, walking behind, head bowed. They passed through the door, down the steps, and up the aisle that had been left for them. Necks craned and heads swivelled to see them.

The Prioress rose in her place, and her sisters behind her. After a moment, so did the rest.

Prioress Winterridge came three steps forward to greet them. There were no empty seats for them, nor any needed. The underfolk stand or

squat on their heels; here they would stand. Each was greeted as equal to equal, and then the Prioress backed to her seat and stood before it. The Conclave sat, and then the people, and the Conclave was in session.

Prioress Winterridge spoke. 'I call on the under-person Lessersmith and on Arienne Brook, who will translate his words.'

Arienne came forward. Her voice was cool and calm, penetrating to the furthest corner of the hall. 'I swear by the Lady and my hope of Her garden that I shall give the words of the under-person Lessersmith truly, adding nothing, concealing nothing, changing nothing.'

Silence. She stared at him. With an effort, he raised his eyes to watch her.

After a pause, she spoke: 'He says he will say only the truth and all the truth, and he asks that the stones crush him if he lies.'

The Prioress nodded. 'Ask his name.'

'He has not taken one. In his work he is the smallest of several makers of steel springs. The nearest words are "lesser smith".'

'How has he spent the last eight years?'

'He reckons it by cold time and hot, Sister Prioress: summer and winter. Eight winters, seven summers. He spent the time in pits and in stone rooms, locked and shackled to walls. He wore a leather mask locked on his face, and a hood over his head, as a prisoner of Prince Nathan.'

A mutter around the hall, quickly stilled.

'How did he come to this?'

'He was taken after the Battle of Hoppelin Moor ...'

Another mutter, rising. This goblin had been an enemy. The Battle of Hoppelin Moor had been fought against an army of the Dark that had arisen just after Nathan's father's death, at a time when the cities had risen in revolt, seizing the chance to throw off the shackles. But the Dark had to be fought first; that was an axiom. The battle had been long and bloody and nearly a defeat. Nathan and his contingent had arrived just in time. I knew. I had been there. So had Silvus. So had many in that room.

The Prioress lifted her eyes and surveyed the audience, coolly, calmly, and the mutter died away.

'... in which he fought willingly, because a Dark mage had taken his mind away and replaced it with his own. He remembers it with the bitterest shame. He was filled with love for the mage and hatred for the enemy. Only when the mage was killed did he recover his will and his mind. Then he fled, but was taken.'

'Who killed the mage?'

'Nathan himself, he says.'

'How does he know this?'

'The mage filled him with his own mind, for that is what a Dark mage does. But the same is true in reverse, to an extent. He could feel and see as the mage felt and saw, just as there is always a back-eddy in a stream. It is part of how the underpeople talk.'

'And Nathan killed the mage?'

'Yes. In the press of the battle. The last thing the mage felt was surprise at Nathan's treachery.'

'Treachery?' The audience was still, now, hanging on every word. The Prioress's voice was inexorable. 'What was treacherous about this?'

'The mage was in partnership with Nathan.'

Consternation. The hall was stunned. Then the muttering started, rising. The Prioress rose to her feet, unhurried, and walked forward. She stared them down. They were quiet again by the time she raised her hand.

'Some here may not like the words nor trust the honesty of a goblin.' She used the name with full knowledge. 'Yet I tell you all, there is no Dark in him. I have fought the underpeople all my life, to my shame. Who shall know more of them than I? I tell you, he is telling the truth as he knows it, and I can bring further witnesses to support him.'

It was Silvus's cue. He drew off his gauntlet. 'I am one. I say of my own knowledge and from what I saw with my own eyes that Nathan attempted to court the Dark, and I bear witness to it, and that I swear by my word and gage.' A slap of leather on stone as he threw it down.

I piped up, in my turn. 'And as much say I, by my word and gage.' I threw down my own gauntlet.

Few knew me, but most of them knew Silvus, and knew him for what he was: the soul of honour. Nobody picked anything up. They were calculating. There were nodding heads.

Silence. The Prioress seated herself again. 'What were the terms of their partnership?'

Arienne stared at the goblin, and this time her translation came word for word:

'The mage knew that Nathan had not the power to defeat the League of Cities alone. He was not his father. Many who were loyal to the old man merely feared Nathan, or dismissed him; some of his father's commanders were selling their services to the highest bidder, and the cities were wealthy.' A rumble of agreement greeted that. I remembered it, too.

'For his part, the mage knew he could never rule in his own right, not over sunpeople. Most of them hate the Dark as much as we, and unlike us, they can resist it. Therefore they combined, Nathan and the mage. They would rule together, Nathan as Prince, the mage as the power behind him. But Nathan delayed and delayed, and the mage fought the battle alone. He might have won, but at the moment of crisis, just as he was expecting Nathan's charge to complete his triumph, Nathan wheeled and struck him down.'

Silence. And suddenly it all made sense. Everyone who had been there remembered how the underfolk had fought like demons, and how Hoppelin Moor hung bloodily in the balance. How we had been winnowed down; how the troops Nathan brought had swung the tide.

When it was over, guess who was in charge? And why not? What would Nathan not have done to rule, and to rule alone?

Why else had we ever risen against him in the first place?

The rest of the ceremonial was small beer after that. Everyone wanted to get home, so they could start working out the way things would be without Nathan.

The new council of nobles, for a start. It wouldn't be like Nathan ruling alone, but a lot of the things he had set up were too useful to let go. The new post-roads and the couriers. The river and harbour works, the locks and canals, the efficient administration that crossed all the old borders, the even taxes that spread commerce. The nobles had worked together under a master. Now they would work for themselves, but they had become used to working together, and found it was profitable. Even though they had to use more commoners for advice on technical matters.

And was it true that the goblins were willing to trade? Their metalwork was a legend. Merchants started to prick up their ears and rub their hands.

The small beer of the ceremonial was, however, quite important to me. It included the induction of a novice into the Order – rather a special novice. And something else of importance.

ASTA

Well, it was the best way. I had to learn more about the talent. I had to have access to the library. Sister Prioress explained that I needn't take final vows at all, and wouldn't be allowed to until I turned twenty, anyway. The novitiate was a way into an

Order school. So I took it. I needed to thank the Lady, anyway, and to ask if She'd take care of Sart for me. He'd died three weeks after I last saw him. Teska's men had been too rough on him. I wasn't going to ask if She'd take care of Teska.

And there was one more piece of ceremonial. A wedding.

Sister Prioress gave the bride away. Arienne had never looked lovelier. Will, as is traditional, just looked stunned.

And his best man Silvus – sorry, Ser Silvus de Castro, Ambassador Plenipotentiary to the Underpeople and Envoy to the Council of Elders of the Place of Youngest Stones – could make informal contacts with merchants and with underpeople at the feast afterwards.

There he stood, stroking his beautifully groomed goatee. I passed by in the ruck, handing out wedding cake. Apparently that was a bridesmaid's job. That, and keeping an eye on the silverware. Never could tell when there might be a thief about.

'Ah, yes, Your Excellency,' he was saying to the Ambassador of the Underpeople, his opposite number. 'An excellent idea. A treaty of trade.'

Glossary

accolade	ceremony in which a person is knighted
annulet	(in heraldry) a device (a plain circle) added to the arms of a second son
bailey	outer court of a castle, between the keep and the outer wall
ballista	siege machine; giant-sized crossbow, but powered by torsion
bast	flexible bark used for basket-making
bivouac	temporary soldiers' camp, without tents
boot	holster attached to a saddle to hold a lance
cantle	curving back piece of a saddle, designed to hold a lancer in place
cassock	priest's robe, with a hood
castellan	governor of a castle
charnel pit	place to throw bones or dead bodies
cob	workaday riding horse of no particular breed
cog	short, broad-built merchant ship, square-rigged
debouch	emerge from (as of a tunnel or gate)
destrier	warhorse, charger (a special breed)
doxy	thief's moll; prostitute
fealty	an obligation to serve a lord
fence	person who disposes of stolen goods to his own profit and that of the person who stole them
flambeau	flaming torch
flannel	tell someone a 'story'; lie
flux	dysentery
frieze	heavy woollen cloth used for coats
frisk	leap or skip
gage	something thrown down as a challenge to combat; pledge or security

gage of battle	confirmation of a ruling by combat
gibbet	gallows on which a body is displayed
glommed	caught sight of
hock	horse's 'ankle'; the joint above the pastern; to hock a horse is to hit it on this joint, thereby crippling the horse
jess	short strap of leather or silk put around a hawk's leg in falconry
jink	hard turn, pushing off on the opposite foot
lance	cavalry weapon – a long couched spear; unit of cavalry – a knight, his squire(s), and mounted retainers
league	unit of distance, varying at different periods – around five kilometres
longshoreman	docker; wharf worker
mage	one who uses magic
mana	potent force from deep in the earth that mages use to fuel magic
maul	heavy club used for driving tent pegs
merlon	the part of a battlement that projects upwards
mews	artificial nest and roost for falcons used in falconry
mill race	fast stream of water that turns a millwheel, fed by a mill pond
millway	tramway powered by a waterwheel
motte	mound
mudlark	child who salvages flotsam from the river
pennon	flag borne on the lance of a knight
pommel	knob at the end of a sword hilt – a counterweight
rhamfia	a specialised poleaxe, used two-handed
recurve	bending backwards
rube	country bumpkin
rumblies	thugs

saddlebow	arched front part of a saddle
sandast	an addictive substance associated with criminals for hire
screen	body of troops detached from the main party, to warn of the presence of an enemy force
scullion	kitchen servant who does menial work
shambles	slaughterhouse
solar	upper chamber in a medieval house; a lady's private chamber
straw boss	subordinate boss; second in charge
sutler	person who follows an army selling provisions
swales	low place in a tract of land, often boggy
trebuchet	siege machine; a counterweighted catapult with a long throwing arm
vassal	person holding land in return for military service
whins	furze or gorse bushes
wheeler	(of cavalry) the horse on the wing of the line; the one that has furthest to travel when moving from column into line and vice versa and hence chosen for speed.

The author

Dave Luckett was born in New South Wales but moved with his family to Western Australia when he was thirteen, and has lived there ever since. Shortly after he arrived, he discovered a stack of old science-fiction magazines in the garage – left by a previous owner of the house – and was promptly hooked.

Dave was educated at Scotch College, Perth, and the University of Western Australia. He taught for a year before joining the Commonwealth Public Service. He is now concentrating on a full-time writing career.

Although Dave writes in many genres, and for different age groups, his first loves are fantasy and science fiction. He is immersed in these genres, both as a participant in, and organiser of, science fiction conventions, and as an avid reader. As he says, 'Reality, after all, is for those who can't handle science fiction'. He has won several Australian National Science Fiction Convention competitions for his short stories. 'The Patternmaker' was runner-up in the short fiction category at the 1995 Science Fiction Awards, and *The Wizard and Me* won the Western Australian Science Fiction Foundation prize for short fiction in 1996 and was runner-up to Isobelle Carmody's *Green Monkey Dreams* in the Aphelion awards for 1997.

Dave has written two cricket stories for younger readers, *The Best Batsman in the World* and *The Last Eleven,* and two fantasy novels, *Night Hunters* and *The Wizard and Me,* as well as the Tenabran Trilogy. All are published by Omnibus Books.

Dave is married, with one son, and lives in Perth.

The Tenabran Trilogy Book One

A Dark Winter

Dave Luckett

Shortlisted for the 1998 Western Australian Premier's Book Awards – Young Adult Division
Joint Winner, Fantasy Division, 1998 Aurealis Awards

… We – the Tenabrans – we stood before the Dark. We were among the first. Tell your children that.

And picture this: the pile of Ys, a great black brooding octopus on its rock, the outer faces of its walls washed with golden fire. Flame gushed out of the sluices to light and to burn the Dark, and the night was wicked with flying steel and thick with magic …

A sword maiden of the Order of the Lady of Victories, a small knightly force from the City of Tenabra, and a young man called Will Parkin: together they must defeat the unnatural armies of the Dark and save the castle of Ys. On their side is a knight, Silvus de Castro, who will not use his talent for magic, and a powerful Prince with plans of his own.

An epic and darkly allegorical tale of magic, goblins and knights in armour, where honour itself seems powerless against the forces of greed and worldly ambition.

The Tenabran Trilogy   Book Two

A Dark Journey

Dave Luckett

Back in Tenabra after the siege of Ys, Ensign Silvus de Castro and his squire Will de Parkin are soon the unwilling guests of Prince Nathan and his chief enforcer Georghe de Barras. They share their prison with the mysterious Master Grames – alias the Great Wandini – and his lovely assistant Arienne. Prince Nathan's interest in Silvus and Grames? Magic, the Dark magic he needs to extend his empire over all the lands to the west, including those of the Sisters of the Order. Will and Silvus have only one ally – Hrudis Winterridge, the swordswoman, now Prioress of the Order of the Lady of Victories.

This gripping sequel to *A Dark Winter* explores the theme of magic, and the good and bad purposes it can serve.

The Tenabran Trilogy is among the handful of truly exciting fantasy series ... Dave Luckett's world is as vivid as his characters, written with such loving attention to detail it's hard to believe it isn't real ...

Sean Williams